The Journey Prize Stories

Winners of the $10,000 Journey Prize

1989
Holley Rubinsky for "Rapid Transits"

1990
Cynthia Flood for "My Father Took a Cake to France"

1991
Yann Martel for "The Facts Behind the Helsinki Roccamatios"

1992
Rozena Maart for "No Rosa, No District Six"

1993
Gayla Reid for "Sister Doyle's Men"

1994
Melissa Hardy for "Long Man the River"

1995
Kathryn Woodward for "Of Marranos and Gilded Angels"

1996
Elyse Gasco for "Can You Wave Bye Bye, Baby?"

1997 (shared)
Gabriella Goliger for "Maladies of the Inner Ear"
Anne Simpson for "Dreaming Snow"

1998
John Brooke for "The Finer Points of Apples"

1999
Alissa York for "The Back of the Bear's Mouth"

2000
Timothy Taylor for "Doves of Townsend"

2001
Kevin Armstrong for "The Cane Field"

2002
Jocelyn Brown for "Miss Canada"

2003
Jessica Grant for "My Husband's Jump"

2004
Devin Krukoff for "The Last Spark"

The Journey Prize Stories

From the Best of
Canada's New Writers

Selected by
James Grainger and Nancy Lee

M&S

Library and Archives Canada has catalogued this publication as follows:

The Journey Prize anthology : the best short fiction from Canada's literary journals.

Annual.
1-
Subtitle varies.
Volume 17 edited by James Grainger, Nancy Lee.
ISSN 1197-0693
ISBN 0-7710-4378-3 (volume 17)

1. Short stories, Canadian (English). 2. Canadian fiction (English) – 20th century. 3. Canadian fiction (English) – 21st century.

PS8329.J68 1990-   C813'.0108054   C93-039053-9

We acknowledge the financial support of the Government of Canada through the Book Publishing Industry Development Program and that of the Government of Ontario through the Ontario Media Development Corporation's Ontario Book Initiative. We further acknowledge the support of the Canada Council for the Arts and the Ontario Arts Council for our publishing program.

"Rice and Curry Yacht Club" © Randy Boyagoda; "A Matter of Firsts" © Krista Bridge; "Rats, Homosex, Saunas, and Simon" © Josh Byer; "Failure to Thrive" © Craig Davidson; "Brighter Thread" © McKinley M. Hellenes; "Green-Eyed Beans" © Catherine Kidd; "The Past Composed" © Pasha Malla; "Heard Melodies Are Sweet" © Edward O'Connor; "Seven Ways into Chandigarh" © Barbara Romanik; "The Dolphins at Sainte-Marie" © Sandra Sabatini; "Matchbook for a Mother's Hair" © Matt Shaw; "Anthropologies" © Richard Simas; "Scrapbook" © Neil Smith; "Various Metals" © Emily White. These stories are reprinted with permission of the authors.

The epigraph to "Anthropologies" is taken from the poem "Here I Love You," from *Twenty Love Poems and a Song of Despair* by Pablo Neruda, translated by W.S. Merwin, and published by Penguin Books.

The lines quoted by The Buke in "Failure to Thrive" are taken from *Love Is a Dog from Hell* by Charles Bukowski, published by Black Sparrow Books.

The letter from Le Corbusier in "Seven Ways into Chandigarh" is taken from *The Radiant City* by Le Corbusier, translated from the French by Pamela Knight, Eleanor Levieux, and Derek Coltman, and published by Faber and Faber.

Typeset in Trump Mediaeval by M&S, Toronto
Printed and bound in Canada

This book is printed on acid-free paper that is 100% recycled, ancient-forest friendly (100% post-consumer recycled).

McClelland & Stewart Ltd.
The Canadian Publishers
75 Sherbourne Street
Toronto, Ontario
M5A 2P9
www.mcclelland.com/jps

1 2 3 4 5   09 08 07 06 05

About The Journey Prize Stories

The $10,000 Journey Prize is awarded annually to a new and developing writer of distinction. This award, now in its seventeenth year, and given for the fifth time in association with the Writers' Trust of Canada as the Writers' Trust of Canada/ McClelland & Stewart Journey Prize, is made possible by James A. Michener's generous donation of his Canadian royalty earnings from his novel *Journey*, published by McClelland & Stewart in 1988. The winner of this year's Journey Prize will be selected from among the fourteen stories in this book.

The Journey Prize Stories comprises a selection from submissions made by literary journals across Canada, and, in recognition of the vital role journals play in discovering new writers, McClelland & Stewart makes its own award of $2,000 to the journal that has submitted the winning entry.

This year the selection jury comprises two acclaimed writers: James Grainger is the review editor of *Quill & Quire* and the author of the short story collection *The Long Slide*, winner of the ReLit Award for Short Fiction. His memoir "The Last Hippie" appeared in the anthology AWOL: *Tales for Travel-Inspired Minds*. He is also a books columnist for the *Toronto Star* and *Leafs Nation* magazine, and has been a books commentator on CBC Radio One, CBC Newsworld, TVO, and Book Television. He lives in Toronto with his daughter, Petra. Nancy Lee's first book of fiction, *Dead Girls*, was named Book of the Year by *NOW* magazine, won the Vancity Book Prize, and was a finalist for the Ethel Wilson Fiction Prize and the Danuta Gleed Literary Award. Her work has appeared in numerous literary journals and anthologies, as well as in the 2001 *Toronto Life* Summer Fiction issue. She lives in Vancouver, where she teaches at the Simon Fraser University Writing and Publishing Program.

The Journey Prize Stories has established itself as one of the most prestigious anthologies in the country. It has become a who's who of up-and-coming writers, and many of the authors whose early work has appeared in the anthology's pages have gone on to single themselves out with collections of short stories, novels, and literary awards. The Journey Prize itself is the most significant monetary award given in Canada to a writer at the beginning of his or her career for a short story or excerpt from a fiction work in progress.

McClelland & Stewart would like to acknowledge the continuing enthusiastic support of writers, literary journal editors, and the public in the common celebration of the emergence of new voices in Canadian fiction.

For more information about *The Journey Prize Stories*, please consult our website: www.mcclelland.com/jps

Contents

INTRODUCTION

We are pleased to report that fiction writing is alive and well in Canada, and that all of the stories contributed to the 2005 Journey Prize contest possessed elements – scene, characters, a series of observations, or an interesting narrative voice – to recommend them. Every story was worth reading.

During the selection process, as we discussed what we liked and disliked about the stories, we found that certain narrative strategies and techniques seemed more effective and evocative than others. It is always a dicey task to try to define what makes a good story or poem or novel, but this is what the jury of any literary prize is forced to do in the end. A winner must be chosen, and that choice has to be justified through a broad set of aesthetic criteria that the judges can agree upon, at least for the duration of the selection process. Of the over eighty submissions, we chose the fourteen stories that, in our opinion, exemplify the strongest instincts and best narrative choices. The following points will hopefully give the reader – and the contributors – an idea of our guiding principles for selecting the stories for inclusion in this anthology.

1. A story is a story is a story.
Story is more than anecdote, or character sketch, or a very long joke with a punchline, and it is certainly more than a thinly veiled journal entry publicizing your difficult relationship with

your parents or spouse. A story is a sequence of events related through cause and effect, preferably driven forward by characters' desires and actions. Story seeks to illuminate the plight of human existence and give an accurate and honest portrayal of a specific dilemma and its outcome.

The stories in this anthology offer insight into the human condition through keenly observed detail and the telling actions of characters. In "A Matter of Firsts," we come to understand the complex relationship between a girl and her father's mistress; "Matchbook for a Mother's Hair" details the sometimes violent, sometimes tender sexual misuse of a developmentally disabled teenage boy; "Seven Ways into Chandigarh" weaves history, marriage, and architecture into a complex, beguiling narrative. These narratives couldn't be more different, and yet, because they deliver compelling story, we read them with the same zeal and excitement.

2. The writer must honour emotional and psychological realism. We would have liked to have read more stories that showed greater sophistication in their understanding of how real people think and feel. For example, there were narratives about men in unhappy relationships whose problems instantly disappeared when they chatted with a beautiful woman (yes, there was more than one example). If only life were that simple, we could fire our therapists, return our antidepressants, and focus on cloning Pamela Anderson and Brad Pitt. But life isn't simple. Relationships aren't simple. Anyone who has been in a relationship knows that. But sometimes that knowledge doesn't make it onto the page.

"Heard Melodies Are Sweet" and "Failure to Thrive" present two very distinct worlds, peopled by off-kilter, almost sociopathic characters, yet both stories remain grounded in emotional and psychological realism. We may not like all of these characters, but we cannot deny that how they think and behave is made plausible and authentic. The writers have given each character dimension and objectives, and as a result, these characters are complex, frustrating, unpredictable, and surprising because real people are so.

3. "Writing is thinking on paper."

This definition by William Zinsser should be tattooed onto every fiction writer's dominant hand. Narrative is a type of consciousness, and to that end it must possess some measure of sequentiality and logic, maturity and insight – basically, it has to make sense. Does it make sense that in the millisecond it takes for a man to get stung by a bee, he would veer off into a ten-page memory about his childhood? No, it doesn't. Could a similar flashback occur in the middle of a heated argument? No, it could not.

Along with paying attention to how they write – solidifying sentence structure, word choice, prose styling – fiction writers should also hone the way they perceive the world and human relationships. Life is complex; relationships, whether with family, lovers, or friends, are tangled with individual needs and desires; human interaction is fraught with control issues, miscommunication, hidden agendas. Stories by adult fiction writers should reveal awareness of the nuances and complexities of these experiences, as well as offer mature insight and interpretation. It is this artful intelligence that resonates with readers and lends fiction its relevance.

The effort of thinking about a story – considering its aspects, consequences, communications – should be every bit as rigorous as the process of getting the story onto paper. Even a story told through the consciousness and prejudices of an immature or repellent character must present a more sophisticated worldview to the careful reader. Good fiction often explores the moral and intellectual limitations of character; it is up to the author to illuminate the causes and consequences of those limitations without resorting to sermonizing.

"The Dolphins at Sainte-Marie" and "Scrapbook" offer two young protagonists, one an elementary school girl, the other a university student. Both writers have chosen inventive narrative structures: the history of Brébeuf and the Hurons juxtaposed with a young girl's lost dreams, and a school shooting recounted through a scrapbook inventory. Though the thoughts and observations of these young characters remain true to their respective ages, the writers' choices of focus and detail, of what to include and exclude, what to highlight and downplay, demonstrate maturity and sophistication.

4. If there's nothing at stake for characters, there's nothing at stake for readers.

We've all had first-hand experience with the perpetrators of boring stories. Their mantra, "I prefer to read stories/novels in which nothing really happens," admonishes anyone who dares utter that four-letter word *plot*. What they don't realize is that masterful, subtle stories (that is, ones without car chases, kidnappings, or murders) still have tension and, yes, believe it or not, conflict. In fact, the rule of drama is that nothing moves forward in a story except through conflict. Can one write slice-of-life stories about everyday characters? Of course. But even the most mundane person possesses extraordinary quirks and idiosyncrasies. To deny that, to create a character whose plainness and lack of desire reduces her to two dimensions, is to settle for a stereotype.

"Green-Eyed Beans," "Brighter Thread," "The Past Composed," and "Various Metals" all deal with what might be considered everyday or slice-of-life situations: marriage and pregnancy, domestic scenes, family interactions. Yet the characters are multi-faceted, intricate, and never boring or predictable. Each story is written with vivid and engaging sensory detail, and a shadow of underlying conflict that infuses the piece with tension from beginning to end.

5. Let no two people speak the same.

Henry Green, one of the greatest writers of dialogue in English literature, once claimed that he could find 138 different ways of having a wife ask her husband as he leaves for the pub, "Will you be long?" Green rightly claimed that each variation – "Back soon?" "Are you going to be gone long?" "How long will you be?" – would tell the reader more about the couple's relationship at that moment than pages of expository prose would.

The best fiction writers explore the rich possibilities of dialogue to reveal character and story, avoiding a reliance on expository internal monologue or dialogue whose obvious purpose is to fill in backstory and move the narrative forward. They are also careful to distinguish the voices of their characters from one another in the story.

Canadian English is laced with irony, droll understatement, misdirection, and revealing cultural reference points, as well as a multitude of regional, generational, socio-economic, and ethnic variations. "Rats, Homosex, Saunas, and Simon," "Rice and Curry Yacht Club," and "Anthropologies" stand out as stories that seamlessly weave lively and idiosyncratic dialogue into a narrative, with voices that are distinct and rooted in the characters' unique time and place. In "Anthropologies," dialogue serves to dramatize an unpredictable relationship, while the narrator's diction and vernacular drives the story forward in "Rats, Homosex, Saunas, and Simon." The dialogue in "Rice and Curry Yacht Club" offers an exceptional example of how comic dialogue can both suppress and reveal cultural and familial tensions and expectations.

6. Let children be children.

Children are a fiction writer's dream. Intensely curious, narcissistic, and experimental, children present the writer with raw, dramatic examples of human psychology in action. It is troubling, then, that so many fiction writers – and filmmakers and television writers for that matter – persist in portraying children as all-seeing, all-knowing, immensely wise beings, deftly superior to their adult counterparts. This view amounts to an adult's sentimental dream of innocence in which the Garden of Eden is recast as a playground, Adam and Eve as wise seven-year-olds, and the Serpent as the impending corruption of adulthood.

The child protagonists of "The Dolphins at Sainte-Marie" and "A Matter of Firsts" are rendered with subtlety, accuracy, and compassion. Neither wiser nor more naive than their years, they offer a vivid and resonant experience of the confusion, playfulness, and pain of life at an early age.

7. Show, don't tell.

This virtue is extolled in so many books on writing that it seems shocking to have to mention here. And yet . . .

In the simplest terms: don't tell the reader that a character is sad or angry, or that a situation is highly emotional or fraught with danger – show the scene, dramatize the dilemma, reveal the interaction between characters using just enough specific and concrete detail, and allow the reader to come to his or her own conclusion.

It bears mentioning that we were impressed not only by the calibre of this year's submissions, but also by their diversity. Our hope is that Canadian fiction writers will continue to embrace the short story, challenge it, experiment with it, explore it with vivacity, ingenuity, and fearlessness, and keep opening the form to new varieties of experience.

We would like to thank the good people at McClelland & Stewart for their continuing support of new and developing writers through the publication of *The Journey Prize Stories*, and all the hard-working editors and staff of the contributing literary journals who make the anthology possible.

James Grainger
Nancy Lee
June 2005

The Journey Prize Stories

RICHARD SIMAS

Anthropologies

*. . . the pines in the wind / want to sing your name with
their leaves of wire.*

— Neruda

She calls me Fritz.

"How are you, Fritz? Fritz, I haven't left the house in days. . . .
I haven't seen anyone. . . . Fritz, I feel dark. . . . Thanks for the
book you sent. Sufi poems are exactly what I need right now."

She signs her meticulously calligraphed letters "Gert." After
a month, "Your Gert." She's Helen, though. I'm John. John
David Michaels – one first name would have been enough. She's
simply Helen. But not simple at all. Smart and screwed up and
Kentucky. Painfully beautiful, she is. So, Gert, Helen.

We walk down Massachusetts Avenue toward Harvard Square.
November 1979, Cambridge, Massachusetts. She's a leaf, the
exquisite one torn from the pile, blown any which way, landing
in my cap, stuck to my sweater. Under my heel, in my hand,
ready to crumble. Almost lifeless.

"I'm so goddamned helpless," she says. "I don't care what we
do or where we go. You could leave me downtown with a credit
card, and I'd probably starve to death." I guide her to my room.
Cook an omelette. Undress her. This is the third time together,
and we're already keepers of a sort.

She likes jokes. She likes me. She's so greatly etched and
shaped, it's hard to consider and harder to look at. A temptation

I

to touch. I have a childhood photo of her and her mother standing in front of the crumbling Southern mansion. Belle and babe. I take only small square-inch peeks at a time.

It happened this way: she called me first.

"You don't know me," she said. "I'm a friend of your friends Tom and Jennifer. They said you're funny. Can you say something funny?"

"You must be Helen," I answered. They had warned me. "So . . ."

"Not very funny. No prize."

"So . . . what's the prize?"

"I want to come to Boston to visit. I don't know anybody. Can I visit you?"

"Umm."

"Friday."

"How will I know you?"

"The 3:30 bus from Northampton. I'll be last. As usual. I'll know you, because you'll be the funny one."

"But you said I didn't win the prize . . ."

A month later she's crying into the phone. "Fritz, my brother blew the head off his best friend with a shotgun in my parents' basement." It's nearly midnight. Freezing rain, bare trees. I was deep asleep in dreary North Allston. I live with Peggy and Eddy. I'm the boarder in the spare room in their unhappy but funny third-floor apartment. No kids. Sienna's the dog, a monumentally stupid but beautiful red-brown collage of retriever, setter, and German shepherd. A pinch of dachshund would have helped with brains. Eddy smokes a lot of dope and is supposed to be looking for a job. Peggy thinks I'm great because I work in a restaurant and bring home bones for Sienna. As if I feed the kids. I also pay the rent in advance. Basics help. She's impressed that I know about ten French words. She knows forty and arranges them in her own creative fashion.

"*Et alors,*" she says to me in the morning. "*Café? Ça va?*"

It's the goddamn Champs Élysées in our dumpy North Allston neighbourhood, and we are speaking French like Louis Quatorze.

"Get your ass a job," she says to Eddy when he crawls out of bed, not at all regal. When he wakes up early and when he's stoned, Eddy looks like he's wandering from a seniors' home. He doesn't even look like he owns an ass to find a job for. Skinny, wobbly legs, thin chest, short of breath, stooped, and not all with you. That's Eddy, and I like him a lot. He's thirty-three going on eighty-five. I'm twenty-six and newly arrived.

"*C'est la vie,*" I say. "*Voilà!*"

"I'm in publishing," Peggy tells me when I call to rent the room. I'm answering her ad in the free alternative weekly. It's the only one with no stipulations about who I should or should not be. I fit.

"Noble," she answers.

"Huh? Noble what?" Had I dialed the militant Christians?

"No, Peggy Noble, who do you think? *Qui voulez-vous?*"

"Publishing! Wow," I say, hoping to pull her back into English. "Really?"

"*C'est pas mal,*" she snips.

Truth is, in publishing, she answers the phone, licks envelopes, runs errands, and steals books that are about to be thrown away. Sometimes she smokes a joint on the way to work. Steering with one hand, yanking curlers out with the other, her butt sways on the vw Bug seat with rasta music blaring. At exactly 8:37 in the morning, her ass has a job. Eddy goes back to bed as soon as she leaves, and counts on me not to say a word. He loves the Celtics and anything else Boston sports. For Eddy the Boston Gardens, where his teams play, is like a divine combination of Paradise and his mother's lap. When he's asleep, and that's often, I think he's always in the Gardens. The rest of the time he watches television or hangs out with Sienna. I take the room at $125 a month, all included.

After Helen's news, I hear her bang against something where she lives, 108 miles away. There we are, a duo, semi-connected by the phone. I pull it into my room on its forty-foot cord, which from the middle of the apartment reaches its extremities. People always trip over it. I prop the receiver on the pillow, tilt it into the right position, and place a shoe between it and my ear to keep it steady to listen to my belle.

"Hello, Gert," I murmur. "Are you still there?" I'd fallen asleep, phone near my ear. Her redialing wakes me with a ratchety sound like someone tightening a locknut in my brain. She has no idea I'm still on the line. If she only knew the depth of my fidelity. It's been five weeks, and I am falling, falling.

"Hello," she barks, "Is this the Hopkins's residence? Who am I speaking with? Is this Chicago? Where's my father?" The pounding rain out my window, to the right and toward my feet, has ceased. Blusters snap the frailer and smaller leafless branches from the diseased elms and pitch the bits toward the porch roof below my window.

"It's me," I say. "Not Chicago. Not your father. Are you okay?"

"Fritz. What are you doing there? What's going on? I want to talk to my father."

"So. Wrong number. You called me first, then you flipped out in the middle of the conversation. I've been waiting." I have numerous faults. Impatience is not one of them. "What about your brother, his friend? I was worried. You feel better now?"

"Oh, I'm fine," she says, pert and with it. "That happened a few years ago. I have nightmares. That's why I called you. Oh, Fritz. When are you coming? Tell me when."

"Wait. I have to know. What did they do with your brother?"

"He went off to a camp. We had a good lawyer. He was thirteen at the time. He's a sweet kid. I still don't know what those boys were up to."

"What about you? Are you going to classes? Do you go outside?"

"I opened the blinds for an hour yesterday. The grocer delivers. I'm making dinosaurs and setting them up all over the house. The stegosaurus is a bitch to glue. Wait till you see. I love them."

"I want to see you."

I work as a professional clown. No kidding. It's competitive and pays shit, so I also work at a restaurant where I can eat meals. The restaurant is real life, the clown stuff a dream I haven't let go of yet. One keeps me fed, the other keeps me sane. Since I work late in the day, Eddy and I have time to talk. He's impressed with clowning, with performing in general, and his questions about my gigs usually lead him to comments on his favourite topic in the world – the Rolling Stones. The whole vista of the perform-ing arts, aesthetics in general, is summed up for Eddy in the Rolling Stones. Sometimes he looks like he's going to cry when he talks about their albums, their star-powered lives, and how they've stuck it out so long, the ultimate family.

"They're bettah' than the Beatles and the Who nailed tagetha'." He loves them so much he ends up speechless, shaking his head as though Jesus just walked through the wall to hold his hand. Eddy can watch anything on television with a set of headphones and the Stones on the turntable: *The Dating Game*, *The Price Is Right* reruns, the news, pro golf, it can all happen for him if Mick's singing. A hooter helps too.

Eddy takes Sienna for walks after he wakes up a second time. When that happens, he's a new Eddy Curly as he wanders around the apartment looking for Sienna's leash, a free man scratching his hairy parts under a clean and ironed T-shirt. Thank you, Peggy.

"So wheah's ya leash, Sienna?"

The she-hound jumps and whines and bumps herself against the door, and off they go, thumping down the stairs without a leash, even though they're not supposed to. A happy, leashless couple.

Today I put on one of Eddy's Stones albums, all he's got except for Ike and Tina Turner lost in the batch along with Peggy's Bob Marley, and I start a letter to Gert, Helen. How do you write to someone like that? She's beautiful, brilliant, drunk on irony, aloof, and people she's never met before are paying her to get a graduate degree in anthropology from a prestigious university that costs a fortune. Sinking in quicksand, she couldn't give a shit. Fear and hopelessness envelop her, and she can't begin to say how she got there or how she'll get out. She rarely answers her phone. She doesn't buy the books she's supposed to be reading. She doesn't write papers or teach her classes, and time is confusing and weird like a foreign language. On her way to the library she buys dinosaur models. In contrast, I am blind hope and naive courage incarnate. I march to the beat of my various ambitious themes. We match like plug and socket, the plus and minus of alternating current. We see each other once every couple of weeks. For now, I thread the needle, but I'm glad she's 155 minutes away and that I have sworn off women, or I would never be able to keep it together. Had sworn off women. I need to talk about that.

Back up five weeks. Friday afternoon, October 14. Cloudy, sixty-two degrees Fahrenheit. It's thirteen days after the Pope said Mass in the Boston Commons. I use that as a reference because I landed in Boston exactly one month before his famous visit. As if we'd consulted schedules. Adrift in questions and uncertainty, I'm a nobody boarding a plane in Los Angeles with a one-way ticket, no plan, no connections, chasing a clean start at the other edge of the continent. The Pope, a Polish superstar in his white robes, jets across hemispheres blessing millions, uttering sanctity. His motorcade ran from Logan airport through the North End and on to the Commons, past crowds crying and praying, the elderly jostling on the sidewalks and calling out in foreign tongues. Then he entered into the vast sea of the faithful, waiting in the park as if they had rained down on him, their torrent filling the basin of the Boston Commons and spilling up Tremont Street and down Charles. On television I watched the helicopters hover over a city delirious on the first-ever papal visit to North America. Eddy, in lotus position in front of the television, kept saying, "Fucking amazing!" and pulling on his joint. Two weeks previous I'd seen the stage and security preparations when I was looking for a room and getting my bearings on my new city. One of the first things Eddy ever said to me when I told him about the big stage in the park was that the Stones should play for "John Paul."

"Why not?" he asked, insisting on a first-name basis with the Holy Father. "The Stones-Pope Tour, the red tongue and white tiara. 'Sympathy for the Devil.' Mick and John Paul struttin' their stuff. Ya get it?" Eddy could see it. Thirteen days later, Helen was also on her way to Boston. That was the papal autumn.

She calls on a Sunday night. Between then and the Friday we

are supposed to meet, I have a stomach ache. I'm grumpy in the restaurant. Tips are shit. I screw up orders and go home depressed. I have two clown gigs that week. One at a children's hospital, the other for some old Austrian lady's ninetieth birthday at her daughter's house in the Back Bay. Very expensive spot. I'm supposed to be there for the grandkids, but the old ladies are pretty excited and wolfing down pizza canapés when I arrive. Chinese hired help lets me in a side door, and I put on my makeup and costume in a spare bedroom that smells like lavender-scented talcum powder. In white-face, I stumble with the easiest routines, the hidden cards and coins, my hat that won't stay on that turns into a juggling act with a champagne glass. Later, at the hospital, one of the sick kids gets a hold of my clown nose and cocks it back on its elastic, four inches from my head, a taut slingshot aimed point-blank. Another one, with no arms, howls with laughter, torso shaking like a wobbly top. The nurse laughs too. I can just see the headlines: "Happy Sick Child Maims Clown." Upbeat news with an edge. For diversion I puff up my cheeks like it's all part of a number for which the kid is my assistant. The laughs diminish a little, I'm almost in control, but he releases before I can cover my nose with my fingers. Plastic and flesh meet with a thwack. Tears fill my eyes, the whole front of my face stings, and pain spreads and intensifies like a brush fire during the rest of my act. My public is in stitches. I juggle for a while, half-hearted. No five-ball-behind-the-back, deadball-hidden-in-the-collar routine. All because of Gert. Helen is coming. On her way like a spectre on the horizon. Next morning dark smudges circle my eyes, my nose is an untouchable swollen red crown.

The bus station, 3:27. I try to be late, loitering at the newsstand near the subway, but I'm unable. Our family motto: "If we're not early, people worry." The bus from Northampton empties like a postmodern Noah's ark: one of each species, all of them weird and unmated. No one even glances at me as they disembark. Definitely non-breeders. Who do I match, I wonder, rejecting implausible partner after implausible partner.

A no-show, so I'm off the hook. Then up from the rear she saunters, Miss Kentucky, eyes and mouth that draw your flesh right away. Right away. She sports a high-collared beige fisherman's sweater, a gentleman's black homburg, and cordovan *bottines*. Black, pleated wool slacks. Her lips part, and I wait to hear my name emerge from the sweet abyss, only to hope she'll swallow it back. My father accused me of having phenomenal luck. His voice, an omen, echoes as I advance, in the moment's sarabande. I edge forward, and she hands me her bag, deadpan, then takes me in. A wrinkle appears in the right corner of her mouth, and the orbits of her nut-brown eyes brighten like warming embers, street lamps illuminating a wondrous new park.

"You look like you need some sleep," she says by way of introduction. "Will you show me Boston?" She deposits a hand on my arm, a gesture so wildly formal and elegant I'm enthralled. I guide her out of Eden and through the old city as if I've lived there all my life. Here's Copley Square. Here's the Back Bay, Charles Street. Paul Revere's Old North Church. The Haymarket, Beacon Hill. From the top of the Prudential Tower, there's the sea.

"Where do you live?" she asks.

"Over there with Peggy and Eddy." I gesture off into the light-flecked dark.

"Fun," she says. "Is my bag heavy? I brought almost nothing." I nearly leave the "nothing" bag in the observation deck. We eat steamed clams and oyster chowder near Faneuil Hall. A waitress in a serving-maid's dress curtsies and pours the second bottle of Sauvignon, breasts bulging. Very colonial. I wave her back to the kitchen, master in his public house. Dinner easily costs one clown show and a half. Though I eye the numbers at the bottom of the bill, I do not talk about work or anything else concrete. I go easy because this is only five hours old and so much is still unsaid. Like my single bed, for example. So we row to a safe island: Tom and Jennifer, our mutual friends. Yes, right. Nice, very funny, especially Jennifer. A good match. Twin peaks, both headed for teaching jobs, graduate research, success. Great, great, great. The original, perfect, beautiful modern couple. Noah's jewels, after the Fall, before the Flood. Hope of humanity. That all takes three minutes.

Wine makes her serious, which means a listener and quiet is not yet on the okay list. I am an entertainer. I tell her all about starting over in Boston and using my newcomer's curiosity to stay upbeat. To me the East Coast seems a world away from the West. By living on its two edges, maybe someday I will understand our screwball country. I've visited Plymouth Rock and Salem, the public house where the Declaration of Independence was read. I've found a sweet town on the sea, a fifty-minute bus ride from Boston, named Marblehead, where I walk. Would she like to go there? Some of the hours are a little long, but it's not every day that you get a fresh start, unbound.

She listens to me unravel. Unlike the short- and long-terms, I don't have a plan for the middle. A big question mark is stuck in the sand between survival and fame, stoically standing alone, tilted by a howling wind. At the bottom of the second bottle of Sauvignon, she reaches toward that question mark, the undetermined parts of me, with a simple glance, as I talk up Boston and Cambridge and avoid clown business. I try to work over to a few questions about her, but I get no answers. She is watching, a captive audience. A detail about my restaurant job is tossed into the ring. I can't possibly believe she'll stick to me, but I have come to count on unpredictability and the long shot to give me an edge. I suggest going to see the Turkish whirling dervishes perform the next day, a fluke idea sparked by a poster I noted as I wandered to our meeting. She smiles, a flaw and a flash in her perfect serious listener's moment. And she nods yes.

Rocking on the subway after dinner, I feel her weight lean into me. Muscle groups let go. I squeeze her "nothing" bag between my legs like a Pinkerton security man would while the train clicks through the Red Line over the Charles River and to its terminal in Harvard Square.

"Why are we crossing the river?" she asks, looking back at the Esplanade.

"We have to cross it to get home, and we can't go around it." I said the word *home*. How can she possibly not be suspicious of me? For some reason she thinks "we can't go around it" is very funny and bites her lower lip to control the giggles.

We exit at Harvard Square, the tip or the tail of Massachusetts Avenue, and the heart of the heart of student town. My work restaurant is close by, so I know this territory. I lead her down

Boylston and back toward the river. North Allston is a fifteen-minute walk, and I always walk. The red brick buildings of Harvard, their white steeples and gold crowns, are what I leave behind when I cross the bridge into downscale, clapboard, aluminum-sided, unfamous North Allston on the other side.

I turn the lock on the third-floor door near midnight. Peggy and Eddy know about this, and Peggy is very excited and probably hiding in her room. It's like Mom and Dad with their fifteen-year-old.

"Nice job," Eddy said when I told him about the upcoming blind-date visit, as if I just got a good deal on a used car. He's crashed on the couch when we enter, television lit and empty beer bottle pinned in his arms. I make no attempt to modify the scene or explain. I show her the bathroom, my very narrow room with the single bed where she returns a few minutes later dressed in flannel, ankle to neck. We tuck in like a pair of preachers, stiff, hands to ourselves.

Four months later, dead, frozen mid-February, radiators hiss and pipes rattle in the walls, but the house is Hades with too much central heat and no thermostat to control it. I open the single window of my room, below and to the right, let the sharp chill grab and hold me, breathe it in, try to wake myself. Snow and ice add a surprising elegance to our neighbourhood, and I hope it lasts.

"I can't call," she said the night before when I asked why we're not seeing each other. She said I shouldn't call her either and that she can't control how horrible she feels. It's got nothing to do with me. She said that when her mother is off medication, she wanders out of her house and the police in Chicago have to go looking for her. She said that when she was eighteen, she was married to the son of a rich man, and on her wedding night she tried to melt down the silver gifts while her mother ate the camellias in the guest-table centrepiece. She said she aborted and divorced on the same day, one year later. I wouldn't be able to understand, she said. She's right, but I try.

More than a month has gone by since I've seen her, and I have fallen, fallen. I read over my boxful of carefully calligraphed letters, look out the window. How long will she be lost in her storm? Is there a clue or a map in her notes to me? To my single bed, I wear the colourful knitted Tibetan cap with the yellow tassel she gave me. I write letters, serve tables, read books. My father also said to me once, "Son, there is no end to the end." What's love, I wonder, without a blind leap into the void? My legs kick at the empty space, searching for the bottom of my fall.

"Maybe I'll go into teaching," I tell Charles, who is a flamboyant black queen and opera student. He is also an overly zealous seducer between customers at the restaurant where we wait tables.

"It all just depends on what you really want," he answers. "You just have to find what you want, then take it." All toss and shimmy is our Charlie. He flutters magnificently long eyelashes, purses full lips, does his tenor opera laugh, gathers his dishes, and sashays back out to the tables.

At night I hear Peggy and Eddy, on the other side of my closed door, fight about the kids they don't have.

"I dunno," says Eddy. "It'd be interesting, that's for sure."

"Interesting! A kid's not a friggin' bird in a cage, Eddy."

"Who's talking birds? I mean a kid. A little human. Geez, Peg! How da ya think we all got here, anyway?"

"Yeah, but what about work? What about a house? You know, real stuff. A kid won't eat the sports section of the *Globe*."

"Why ya so complicated all the time? I say where there's a will, there's –"

"Oh, bullshit, Eddy! *Merde!* Where there's a will, there's somebody working like a slave. *Connard!*"

"There ya go with the French again –"

Peggy stamps off and takes a forty-five-minute shower, and I hear Eddy thumbing through his albums, trying not to bother anyone. The next day he'll straighten the house a little and toss out the stack of old newspapers. Me, I'm a celibate monk, except at night, in my dreams.

That first night together in October we fall asleep quickly: a grown man scrunched into his side of a single-bed space with an exquisite woman he met earlier in the day. My place in the unbelievable seems justified, payoff in relation to some other equally incredible imbalance. On the other hand, where we have landed at a given moment may be nothing more than the quirky hand of cards we've been dealt just then. Fuck the scales and their little lead weights.

"Are you warm enough?" I ask when we are settled in.

"I think so." Silence. "Can we really go see the whirling dervishes tomorrow?"

"Sure. We can do whatever we want." Then we are quiet and looking into that small darkness trapped inside my boarder's room. The single window covered by a piece of printed cloth blocks all but the smallest fragment of nightlight. We are both tired and waiting to see what will surface in that obscurity, what beyond our will. In chorus we ask that question together, but the words have no sound, and then we're gone.

Later, when the house and street are noiseless, no water in pipes or building creaks or animal-shuffling in the next room, our bodies are naked and venturing deep inside each other, sharing flesh, matching movement, and wandering out on limbs that reach up into dark, holding clouds. How did it start and when did we awake to what we were doing? We toll like bells through the rest of the night, hour after hour. To the top of a tower we climb, looking for the highest window, a final step on the stairwell until we are caught and flung. The moment we finally drift off to sleep, I see morning brightening the window frame, below and to the right.

The next afternoon when I wake, she is dressed and reading one of my books, sitting next to me on the bed. From the pile she chose my ninety-cent sidewalk special of Pablo Neruda's *Twenty Love Poems and a Song of Despair*. She looks up when I stir.

"We'll miss the dervishes if we don't get moving," she says, setting the book carefully back on the pile. As if what she's just said has more to do with the night before than the show we will see, she flushes dark crimson from neck to temples. I find her skin under the rough fisherman's sweater and pull her to me. Steal back my rib, confirm her flesh.

Later we are seated in Saunders Hall, a historic building used for concerts, performances, and lectures at Harvard. The walls, benches, balconies, floors, and ceiling are carved wood redolent with varnish and wax, and it is like we are human cargo deep in the hull of a fabulously ornamented boat. Onstage thirty dervishes circle to an insistent beat and weaving reed and flute melody, provided by Turkish musicians who sit on cushions and carpets behind them. The dancing men are white tops, spinning in place, gathering speed, their quick footsteps invisibly accelerating them. They wear variously coloured scarves tied at the waist, and white hats, and it's these bands of colour on the dizzying wicks that our eyes follow. Their formations alter with the slightest foot movement and gestures added by their extended arms. Six hundred of us are locked in their trance, an ecstatic Turkish meditation.

"Why don't they fall over?" she whispers to me. "Don't they get dizzy? I can't see where they touch the ground." I shrug and rock side to side with the rhythm. The program notes say that *dervish* means "doorway" and that for the Sufis it represents an entrance from this material world into the heavenly spiritual world. So these are revolving doors from one world to the other. They dance for more than an hour, forming and re-forming to ever shifting musical accompaniment and chanting. When they finally slow their spinning, the audience waits, held trancelike by the spectacle. Then, as if we too had been cranked up, then finally set free to move, we stand and applaud. She finds my hand and holds it as we shuffle with the crowd out into the October evening.

"It was wonderful. What an idea," she says. "I loved it!" When we're far enough away from the crowd, she tries to spin on the lawn between buildings but trips after three circles. She weaves over to a bench, hand on stomach. The sight of her stumbling in the darkness floods me with tenderness and desire. Her bus leaves in fifty minutes.

"How was that?"

"Needs work," I answer.

"I'd love to visit Istanbul," she sighs.

"You have classes."

Then nothing else as we walk up Massachusetts Avenue toward the Charles River, and our shuffling feet on the sidewalk ask, "What do we do now?" What *do* we do now? Like a dervish drunk on spinning circles, I am full of her and my improbable weekend.

At the bus station, we hold on for a moment. I buy her hot chocolate and crossword puzzles for the ride home. I say I'll call. I kiss her and she kisses back. Her bag is slung over her shoulder. She disappears into the bus and the bus disappears up the street and out of the city, and I take two and a half hours to walk back to my room in North Allston. The same 155 minutes her bus needs to cover 108 miles due west. I walk Commonwealth Avenue, counting my steps, then a circuitous route threading Brookline and unknown neighbourhoods back into Allston. I want the parallel and a doorway from one world to another. I want something to compare to, and the shadow of her shadow.

April 11, six months after it all started. Against good advice, without an invitation, I decide to go visit her. We've neither seen nor barely spoken to each other for five weeks. Her whimsical calligraphed letters have long since trickled to a stop.

"I'm coming tomorrow, all right?" I instruct rather than ask. "I have to see you. Will you just say something! Do you want me to come?"

"I'm lost," she says.

"Okay, fine. I know that. Who isn't? What else? See you around one."

Near the door before I leave, Eddy says, "I dunno. Looks like a mess. Sounds like she's having a rough time. Ya know why?"

"Flood waters," I answer, adding no explanation.

Eddy looks out the window and nods. "Ya be back on Sunday?"

"Hope so." He's alone with Sienna because Peggy has decided to spend the weekend with her friend Bonnie. They're going shopping and to a party. Eddy is going to shoot baskets with some buddies.

The bus takes me 108 miles due west on Saturday morning. The woods have come to life alongside Interstate 90, running toward Springfield, then north into the Berkshires. Pale green tips the branches and matted brush. Water drains from the fields and highway embankment. I am overdressed in a leather coat and hiking boots, so I strip down to a light pullover in the bus. Out the window the view is hopeful. People turn their gardens and tractors till the fields. The season change is a marker in the survival of my first East Coast winter. My backpack contains an orange, a bottle of water, my toothbrush, clean underwear, and a book about Sufis and dervishes that I found in the library to read on the bus.

I walk the ten minutes from the bus station and knock gently on her door at the house where all the curtains are pulled. She answers in a bathrobe and lets me in before wandering off to get dressed. Her eyes barely meet mine. She is pale, gaunt, and fatigued. I know the place from previous visits, but the lack of light in the rooms, the time gone by, what I suspect is her impenetrable low mood, make it seem different.

Dinosaur models are everywhere: on top of bookshelves, the dining-room table, the floor, perched on chairs. They vary from a six-inch, glow-in-the-dark triceratops to waist-high balsawood replicas of tyrannosaurus. They hang by fishing line from the light fixture. They stand on their haunches, flap jagged wings. They twist their necks and strike with paws. They growl and scream from the depths of extinction. Empty boxes, plastic wrapping, and hobby waste are piled high in one corner of the room and overflow into a leather chair.

After a few moments alone in the living room, my eyes adjusting to the light, I am taken by the strangeness of her menagerie and see how meticulously arranged are all these ancient, lifeless creatures in her house. With her uncountable days, she has given them life. Extinct animals rather than anthropology.

"They threw me out of school," she says quietly.

"I'm not surprised. What are you going to do?"

"I can't think about it. I don't know what to do."

She lets me hold her, but it's like I'm holding a bag of wrappings and cardboard from the dinosaurs, not her. Still, there's the smell of her hair and skin. Gert. She sinks back into her sofa when I let go. I walk around and look at the animals. They are intricate and elaborate, the result of her delicate handwork joining all of the pieces.

"What do you want to do?" I ask.

"I don't want to talk. You can stay, but don't talk. You just have to leave me alone." Fifteen minutes later she's asleep and I cover her with a blanket. In the kitchen there is a plastic butcher tray with moulding ground beef. A box of crackers is open on the counter, old coffee staining a pot. I tour around, then come back into the front room to examine the dinosaurs. They now possess her and her house.

I sit in a chair and watch her sleep. I try to think. Her mouth twitches where she is covered to the neck by the blanket, corpse-like. It's Helen who has disappeared, who is now extinct and has left me surrounded by her beautiful and monstrous creatures, and I panic. Inside of me a reasonable man wants to clean the house while she sleeps, gather the models up in garbage bags and toss them out the back porch, go buy some food, fix a meal, take her on a vacation to Istanbul. I want to prop her lifeless figure on a stand and worship her. Dance prayer circles.

I see myself in the motions and know how easily I can do that: where to shop, check on flights, do the laundry, change money, hail a taxi. I know how to start over, close the door behind me, take charge, look forward, try again. I know how to ignore the obvious. All of that. The clown showed me how.

I stand up and undress, dropping my clothes in a pile on the floor. Will she wake up and see me and begin to change? Can we open a door to another world and leave this house of dinosaurs? When I penetrate her, I hope her past will disappear and another reality will take root and heal her. I walk over to the sofa where she lies, catching the pterodactyl with my foot and tipping it over against the stegosaurus. They clatter when they topple. She stirs, and I lie down next to her and pull the blanket over us, a cover of thickly woven cotton with a frayed purple silk border.

I wake up later in the dark to her crying, a high, unearthly whine, as from a distant flying animal. "I was afraid you would hurt me," she says. "That's why I can't love you or anyone else. I knew it the first time I saw you that you could."

"Could what? Love or hurt you?"

"Both."

"I won't hurt you," I say.

"You can't help what happens," she says. "And you can't know ahead of time. Don't make promises you won't know how to keep."

I want to tell her that I love her, but before I can, she says, "It's the idea of love that you love, not me." I close my mouth in the dark house. I can barely distinguish forms, but I know there are many around us. I feel her body heave as she breathes. For the first time since I've known her, I prefer not to see her. Crammed next to me on the sofa, she trembles. I hear rain begin to tap the windows and the cement outside, and the wind move against us.

Sunlight bounds into the living room the next morning. I am alone on the sofa. She has been up before me, pulled back the curtains, and the light flowing in carries April warmth. She is dressed and has coffee. We drink it quietly in the front room, and then I get dressed.

"I guess I should go home now," I say to her. She nods, because she knows it's one of the answers we've found. For once something not a "maybe." She walks with me halfway to the bus station, arching her neck from time to time to catch the heat. All of a sudden she stops, pulls herself up to me, holds on for a long moment, then lets go, and she is gone.

The bus ride east is 155 minutes of motor groans and gear shifts. From downtown Boston I take the Red Line across the river and into Harvard Square. I walk over the bridge to North Allston. On the river below, the rowing teams stroke between the weedy banks. The birches hold delicate curled leaves.

I turn the key in my lock and smell Eddy's cigarette smoke. He is sitting on the batik-covered mattress in the dining room, looking worn and nervous. Sienna, chin on forepaws, is at his feet.

"So, ya survived?"

"I think so."

Sienna gets up and limps into the next room, a splint taped on the inside of her left hind leg. Eddy shakes his head and draws on his cigarette.

"She got clipped by a car. Some reckless kid. She saw a bird, ran after it. No leash. Pow! We're lucky she's just limping. Peg's gonna kill me."

Peggy comes home that night, and I hear her crying because Sienna got hit. Then she yells at Eddy about the leash, about beer bottles, about unemployment. While she was shopping at Filene's with Bonnie, she bought him a suit, white shirt, tie, and black shoes. She says tomorrow he's going to have to go into the city and look for a job. After they have calmed down, I hear Eddy try on the suit.

"You look good in it, Ed," she says.

"Ah, I dunno. Ya think so? It won't make any difference."

"We'll see about that. Don't get it wrinkled." During the night, Sienna can't get comfortable and limps from room to room.

May. Marblehead. I lie on my back in a grassy patch exposed to the sun. The ground beneath is warm, the branches in the trees directly over my head are in full leaf, the air rife with sea smells. I have found the bottom. The sky beyond is distant, infinite, a background for swift-moving wisps of clouds. Someone coming along the path I've just left might believe I have fallen from one of the branches. I'm just catching my breath, waiting for the next move. Chessman resting, pawn, knight, rook in his square.

McKINLEY M. HELLENES

Brighter Thread

They live here, in this city. Sometimes it feels more like they're lurking than living here, a spurious gas in the intestinal tract that is their home.

She marries him beneath the trees in Stanley Park. They don't believe in marriage, which is why they have decided to do it – to challenge their beliefs. It's easy to slide into a set of values, he tells her. He doesn't want to become complacent. He's wonderfully earnest when he says things like this. She just nods. She got what she wanted, what she has secretly coveted since the day she laid eyes on him: tall, gangling, and crooked, his body worn apologetically like a suit several sizes too small.

He doesn't love her. She doesn't expect him to. They walk home the long way, stop for noodles and deep-fried tofu, a cheap wedding feast eaten furtively, eyes darting, wrist bones exposed and pale like the eggs of nervous birds.

It's spring. She's pregnant. He hasn't noticed. She is so thin. She imagines giving birth on a pile of laundry in the corner of their room, licking herself clean, and burying the evidence somewhere. Only she will notice its scent like raw liver, the placenta a strange and bloody flower. Her offering. She could feed it to him. He might not notice. She could disguise it with spices, with coriander and thyme, a bed of grape leaves. Her blood purpling the edges of his mouth, leaving its mark. Staining him forever. He would not be able to remove what he doesn't know is there.

Her wedding ring glints as she brings chopsticks up to her mouth, sunlight glancing off a dingy windowpane, a glass of water, the corner of his eye. He bought the ring in a pawnshop, a gift for her birthday, which is also today. They didn't want to have to celebrate too many days. He doesn't have a birthday that she knows of. He has rejected the decadence of having an entire day that belongs only to him. She suggests they share hers, and puts extra candles on the cakes she buys, which are invariably lopsided or lumpy and have somebody else's name on them. Rejects or display models several days old. They don't light the candles. There are too many between them, too many years accounted for and recorded in cheap blue wax. She pulls the candles from the half that never gets eaten, cleans stale crumbs carefully from the ends, and stores them away for next year. Saving things is supposed to make her feel resourceful rather than wasteful – though she doesn't really see why. Everything saved must first be wasted somewhere along the line.

They eat without speaking, though one or the other smiles nervously at intervals over the expanse of dingy Formica. Noodles scatter and are retrieved, soggy and spent like worms drowned in a summer rainstorm. They pay and leave a tip they can't afford. They walk home slowly, fingers mostly linked between them. Her dress is yellow. She mended the torn seams after finding it in the dollar bin at the Sally Ann. He doesn't notice the neat stitches, the thread slightly brighter beneath her arms as he unbuttons her dress and pulls it up over her upraised elbows. He drapes it neatly over the back of a chair, as though her dress is a petal shed from a buttercup. Vivid, easily trampled. His body above her is kind and thin. She can barely feel him against her. She shivers and squirms, her toes curling in on themselves.

The story they tell is that they met at a rally. It's almost true. She doesn't want him to know that the first time she saw him, he didn't notice her, did not pluck her face from the crowd that swelled and swooned before him as he played his songs on a cheap guitar too small for his hands and wildly out of tune. When he plays them again she has to pretend that she's never heard them before. When he forgets some of them before he plays them for her, she cannot display her grief. He would think

it odd to mourn for songs she had never heard. That night, he
sang a song about a boy and a girl who fell in love, lived together
in squalor, and bought a lot of books instead of food. She envi-
sioned their lives together as she listened to the words she
would only hear once. He doesn't play it anymore. He doesn't
think of it when he's with her. She's not the girl he was singing
about. There is no girl for him, there is only her, and she doesn't
count – not really. He has never said this. He doesn't need to.

He didn't recognize her at the rally. He looked at her as if he'd
never seen her before. They were protesting the Free Trade
Agreement of the Americas. She went to the rally hoping to see
him. He was one of the organizers – agitators, they would have
been called back in Russia during the revolution. She knows
these things; she has read a lot. He has a Russian name. How
easily she sees him there, provoking the masses, inciting the
hearts of the workers to action. She listens to the speakers, helps
carry the banners. She doesn't say anything, doesn't chant along
with the crowd. She doesn't like the sensation of a bunch of
people all screaming the same thing at once. He can get anyone
to scream anything. She is proud of him, her face flushed with the
love she feels too soon. He could never catch up, even if he tried.
She doesn't need him to love her. She doesn't want him caught
up, the way she is, in the impossible weight of this love.

She becomes very good at writing pamphlets, designing
posters on CPUs past their prime. She renders herself indispens-
able. She walks incredible distances, satchel slung over her
shoulder, a pail of wheat paste cutting a permanent tattoo into
her hand. There is a beautiful futility in their motions that
touches her; the heft of a ream of paper becomes the most satisfying burden she knows. She grows thinner, more beautiful.
She cuts her hair shorter, like the other women, and throws her
makeup away. Her shoes become ragged, her clothes threadbare.
She doesn't buy new ones. He has worn the same two sets of
clothing since she met him. It all looks the same – his heavy
workpants, the tatty sneakers and plaid jacket. He grows a beard
one winter and forgets to shave it off when the weather turns.
She cuts his hair once a month, hers every six. She knits him a

toque for Christmas. He steals her a new printer cartridge. They live that way. A shy kindness permeates.

The first time he gives her an orgasm, she cries. She wants to keep it, this small gift. It flutters in her like a heartbeat, the flap and release of a minute set of wings.

The other women don't like her. It is as though they can detect the residue of mascara on her eyelashes, the crisp texture of her hair betraying a vanity they cannot abide. She will have to be more careful. She will have to cut some pieces shorter than the others, forget to wash her face so thoroughly before she leaves the house. She doesn't wear deodorant anymore, but she still smells fresh and clean, like sweating fruit. She can't help this. Sometimes she wears his T-shirts, hoping the sharp, human scent of him will somehow rub off on her, disguise her among them. He smells warm and musky, like horseflesh in summer. She buries her nose in his neck when he is sleeping. Sometimes he pulls her arm around him, tucks her hand beneath his armpit. She is only ever warm where she touches him.

"I'm Jewish," she tells him one night. They are in bed. He is smoking. She has a book propped up against her chest, but the light is off.

"So am I," he says. His cigarette flashes in the dark and then subsides into something dimmer. Guilt swoops in and descends. They swallow it whole. A rabid hunger greets it.

The baby is the size of a pea. There is still time, until suddenly there isn't. Suddenly, the baby is a grapefruit with fewer segments. Split them up, and they will not grow again. Not everything is an earthworm, she reminds herself. Not everything is multichambered, like a heart.

He doesn't ask any questions when she makes appointments at the clinic and then cancels them. Instead, she starts making appointments with a midwife she knows. Her vision of bloody rags drying in the corner of their bedroom hasn't gone away. She no longer envisions what will occupy the shoebox beneath their bed, but she knows it won't be this baby. This baby will sleep between them. Or with her, if he chooses not to stay. She hasn't yet managed to pin him in place like one of her posters. This is no world, people will say, no world to have a child in. She knows what they will mean: he is another man down. Another comrade martyred by an outsider's famished cunt.

"I'm pregnant," she tells the dishwater.

"I'm pregnant," she whispers to the cat, who knows what it's like.

"I'm pregnant," she says to his back, emphasizing her words with gentle strokings. He stiffens, relaxes, stiffens again. Turns toward her. Lights a cigarette and then puts it out again.

"What are you going to do?" he asks.

She doesn't say anything for a minute. "What are you?"

"Whatever you want," he says. "It's your decision, your body."

"I know." They both know this isn't what she asked. The next day, she makes an appointment with the midwife, whose name is Charlotte, who has never had a child. He walks with her. They have both made their decisions. She isn't sure what his is.

Charlotte's hands on her belly are cool and smooth, like any other doctor's. She can feel this woman's breath dusting her thighs, like the wings of night insects, as she probes her vagina gently with practised fingers. The hands inside her are long and brown. Resting against her belly, she can see that they are made up of a series of lines. She stares at them intently, seeking out the one line that could cause them to unravel. She would tug on that line. She would hold it between her teeth and pull.

SANDRA SABATINI

The Dolphins at Sainte-Marie

She waited all day for the dolphins. She walked in the sun across packed grit that worked itself between her feet and her sandals, her new ones, whose straps blistered the edges of her toes. She walked around the stupid settlement, through the longhouses, the chapel, the dreary yards between the buildings where Father Jean de Brébeuf and Father Gabriel Lalemant had baptized babies and talked to the Hurons, whose real name was Wendat, but nobody knows that now, about God. The blonde tour guide loved saying Gitchi Manitou. Had them all say it out loud together. Corrected their pronunciation. Her top two buttons were undone, and all the guys beside her were saying how they wanted to gitchi some of that manitou. It was disgusting.

Penny had all day been certain that this dreadful place was the appetizer to the splashing cool of a dolphin and killer whale and sea lion extravaganza. She waited and moved when told and tried to be respectful, but it was making her dizzy.

She had sold chocolate bars and awful Florida oranges, cookie dough and frozen chicken parts to all her mother's weary neighbours so she could go on the final trip of her Sir John A. Macdonald Elementary School career. She told them all she was going to Marineland. In Niagara Falls. There would be porpoises and dolphins, and she could tell the difference. Seals and sea lions, and she could and did explain which was which while she took the money and made change and said she hoped they all had a good day or a nice evening. It was a place her mother's

24

widow's pension would never allow them to go, even if her mother could drive and they had, by some miracle, bought a car. Her school was taking her. All she had to do was raise a few bucks, so she had worked hard, getting perfect on her math homework. She had carefully sliced poster board, measured and made folded tabs to glue into a white dodecahedron. She had coloured her title pages, all the pencil crayon strokes smooth and parallel, seamless pale reds and blues announcing the true history of the coureurs de bois, whom she loathed.

Pemmican. Her teacher had dug up a recipe and prepared it for the class. Six pemmican patties, formed out of dried ground beef instead of buffalo, held together with dried cranberries and suet. Mrs. Maddocks had made them all try some, and Penny had gagged and vomited on the floor beside her desk. After she had washed her face and dried her eyes and nose, she was told that she would not have made a very good explorer. She thought she would have been a great explorer; she just would have chosen her territory with a little more care, a place where the food was all over the place and not dried out, and wrapped in leaves for quick access. She would have chosen Marineland, which she knew had ice cream stands and burger places and candy floss retailers right on the paths between attractions.

Now she was poleaxed, gang-pressed into attendance at the Shrine of the Jesuit Martyrs. She had no idea how far she was from Marineland. Assumed maybe a twenty-minute bus ride. But time was ticking.

Here is the chalice, tall, heavy, and worn, that the Jesuit fathers used for Holy Communion. Here is the crooked wooden cross on the wooden wall. Here is the historic altar, covered in rich red cloth, six tall candlesticks with long, leaning candles, genuine historic beeswax, crafted, never manufactured, in the traditional manner. The backs of Penny's knees were aching; when she stood in one place for too long, the walls moved around her and her breath came short and shallow. She told her mother once about this, and her mother said don't worry about it. But Penny would not be surprised if she died young.

The Jesuits had an office, a hospital, windows that locked with a peg through a hole. In sight of the Wendat longhouse, they hung their vestments precisely on a rail, leaned historic Jesuit rakes against the wooden walls. They were tidy, those Jesuits.

She looked down at the pamphlet, creased into her damp palm. "The spell of Sainte-Marie among the Hurons lies in the very land upon which it stands."

Champlain was here.

The Wendat were here first, matriarchs, traders, shamans, and farmers. The Jesuits came with Champlain to educate them.

Educate them for what? In the heat and closeness of the room, Penny thought it seemed like they were already pretty well educated. Probably a Wendat kid her age would know the distance between his own village and Marineland, which was more than she knew. She stood still while the guide showed them samples of what would have been the many useful things that Huron children their age would have known how to make out of clay. The guide held up the lacrosse stick and swung it around a bit, talking about how important lacrosse was to the Huron people. She had them try striking a flint, had them slip their feet into snowshoes.

Everything was dreary and grey. The sun petrified the weathered wood and the fences and upturned canoes, all their imperfections and age in sharp relief, death everywhere; even the water in the canoe canal looked like it had given up, still and stagnant while the blood pulsed into Penny's lips and through the artery in her hot neck. Penny thought she was being herded toward a gravestone. That might be interesting. But she leaned across smelly Martha, whose parents thought she was too young for earrings and deodorant, and read, not about dazzling, brutal death, but about the careful restoration of the Huron's primary heat source, which represented the earliest surviving masonry in Ontario. Somewhere between 1630 and 1649, at least three stone fireplaces were skilfully built in the north court area. Well.

At Christmas, Mrs. Maddocks made the class put gingerbread houses together to sell at the assembly. She brought bags of Smarties and licorice and tubes of coloured icing for mortar, squares of stale gingerbread that bent when you pushed too hard, trying to get one wall to stick to another. On their way into the gym, the parents had to run a gauntlet of twenty-six earnest small houses, garish and tilting, before they could sit down on plywood chairs to listen to the Christmas choir sing "O Holy Night" and "Kum Ba Ya." The parents belonging to the other children in different grades breezed through, but the grade six parents, to a man, stopped and cheerfully, or not, handed over their five dollars to Mrs. Maddocks, with her smiling Paris red lips and cracking blood on the cold sore at the corner of her mouth.

Penny's house had collapsed, so her little brother stuck a Lego fireman in the blobbed white icing beside the broken front door. The cheerful licorice wreath lay unravelling beside the mushroom snowman. Then her mother, breathing hard from the walk down the hall and the minutes that had passed without a cigarette, had to say, "Only five dollars? What a steal."

The gingerbread houses and the concert had raised over a hundred bucks for the trip to Marineland. They spent the whole year fundraising for this trip. Penny had seen the Marineland ads on TV. Everybody loves this place. Blue water and sky. Everyone clean and smiling. Water splashing everywhere and nobody minding. This must be a stop on the way, this grey place, all hot and dry. Penny was hot, her feet burning. Her mother had put tuna with mayonnaise in her lunch. She'd die if she ate it. And where were the dolphins?

Enough about Father Brébeuf. And he was the lucky one.

After the mashed potatoes with cream-corn gravy, after the hamburger hash and the vinegar salad, after cookies and milk, Penny's mother moved slowly back to the couch, legs splayed by enormous white thighs that spread and lapped over her calf at the knee. Sitting, she was almost as tall as when she stood. Her backside hit the noisy couch springs so much sooner than the rest of her. Sometimes, once the blanket covered her stomach and legs, she would let Penny fold herself behind her knees and against her hip. Penny would rest there, still and quiet, listening to the lullaby of her mother's labouring chest as it moved air in and out.

Brébeuf was warmly welcomed by the Hurons. He couldn't really persuade the adults to give up their notions of heaven, which they believed was a good place for Frenchmen, but would be uncomfortable for a Huron looking to spend eternity hunting and fishing with his ancestors. The Christian heaven sounded too lazy, though Brébeuf himself, robust, handsome, and winning, was a good argument in its favour. Lalemant, on the other hand, was skinny, almost starving in his mission field, and weak. Whether the Hurons accepted the Christian heaven or not was soon moot. When the Iroquois, sick and tired of the meek Hurons and the disease-spreading Black Robes carrying death and anguish everywhere, attacked the mission at Sainte-Marie, they killed or captured many of the Hurons and tortured the Jesuit fathers.

All the boys on the trip turned to face the guide.

At Marineland there is a deer park. You walk through the gates and right up to live deer that come close to you to be patted and have their backs and antlers scratched. There are dozens of them, mild and friendly. Penny had never seen a live deer, not in a field, not dead on the road, not even at a zoo. There are bison and elk. There are belugas and rare grey seals. There are tuneful California sea lions and leaping dolphins all jumping through hoops, rolling in the air, playing horns, and twirling red and blue balls in the air. She had seen them advertised with laughing blond children and pleased men and women looking on. Her mother could never go. She couldn't walk through the turnstile. Even if she had that much cash, she wouldn't fit. She couldn't wear her slippers to Marineland. Penny never asked to be taken. Instead, in the freezing winter, she had knocked on Mrs. Moore's door and listened to her hundred-year-old talk about her nieces and nephews, about her grandnieces and grandnephews, about the first time anyone in town ever saw a television, about flying in an airplane and listening to the radio when the bombs were dropped in Japan. Penny didn't know what bombs, nor why anyone would attack Japan. She could have told Mrs. Moore that Hitler was a bad guy, but she could not have named either Churchill or F.D.R. Not Stalin or Hirohito. Certainly not William Lyon Mackenzie King. Finally, finally, Mrs. Moore had handed over two dollars for a chocolate bar, fifty cents of which would go directly to supporting Penny's drive to see dolphins, if not in their natural habitat, at least as close to it as she could ever hope to get.

Penny had missed two choir practices and was no longer allowed to sing, not even with the flat and quiet altos. She had lied to Miss Hepburn the second time. Her mother needed her to go to the bank at lunchtime. She had to cash the Workers' Comp cheque, the one they lived on because her father was killed at work, though not before he had called her a monkey because she loved bananas, not before he hid her face from the terrible flying monkeys in *The Wizard of Oz*. Her mother needed her to go. These were the things Penny said, using her dead father, her fat mother, and their poverty against the fragrant, glossy, and groomed teacher to get out of being expelled from the Christmas choir, which every kid in grade six got to be in, only because they were in grade six and had to raise money for the June trip. She didn't say that she had forgotten, that she had, as always, gone home for lunch for her two peanut butter sandwiches. That once she got home through the glass front door and into the haze of blue smoke around her mother's head and the burnt coffee smell of the kitchen, school was gone, the cruelty of Jennifer's nice clothes and good manners and the horror of boys who ran up behind her and kicked her feet out from under her so she slammed hard on the ice, of the terrible certainty of other peoples' skipping games, turned to vapour.

The Iroquois stormed the mission at Sainte-Marie and captured Brébeuf and Lalemant, among others whose names the guide did not mention. They dragged them to St. Ignace, which they had already captured. When they got there, the waiting Iroquois were ready with stones and clubs to beat the fathers before Brébeuf was tied to the stake, which he is said to have kissed. They lit a fire under his feet and slashed his body with knives, poured scalding water over his head in a mockery of baptism and decorated his neck with a collar of red-hot tomahawk heads. They thrust a flaming iron down his throat and sliced the skin from his head. Brébeuf was stalwart, and while he could still speak, is reported to have said that God is the witness of his sufferings and will soon be his exceeding great reward. His torture would end with his life, but theirs would go on for eternity. Lalemant was forced to watch for four hours while his brother was beaten and burned and cut. Brébeuf himself neither flinched nor cried out. Because of his bravery, he was killed in a relatively short period of time and his heart was cut out. The Iroquois are said to have passed the heart around to their warriors so that they could drink the blood of so valiant a man.

Lalemant, weak and thin, did not fare so well, and his torture was extended to nearly seventeen hours. There is no record of the Iroquois warriors drinking his blood.

At home Penny ate white-bread sandwiches held together with thick peanut butter. She scratched the dog's back and ate her sandwiches and watched cartoons until she looked at the clock, too late, and ran with her coat open and flapping in the wind, to the stinking gym where Miss Hepburn taught the choir the harmonies of the "Huron Carol."

The second time she was late, she lied about the cheque and the bank and her mother's need. Miss Hepburn told her to stay after practice.

"Penny, dear, you've missed two practices."

There was no answering that. She knew she was not dear.

"I have a special job just for you to do."

And Penny believed her. There was a job only she could do. She imagined singing a solo. The angel choirs. The stars dimming. Penny could do it. She could nail it.

"I'd like you to sit beside me on the piano bench and turn the pages of my music. Would you do that for me?"

Miss Hepburn, all accordion neck and bug eyes. Bending and sincere. "Would you?"

Penny still had to wear the white blouse and black skirt. She was still a member of the choir. She was turning the pages of the music. Not a solo but very important. A fatherless child with important work to do, work that would keep the music coming. Her mother had horned her wide feet into men's shoes and cabbed them all the five-minute walk to the school on the Thursday night of the concert. She had slapped down five bucks for the gingerbread tenement and taken up two seats in the gym. And Penny had sat right under the shining piano light watching for Miss Hepburn's nod. She turned the pages flawlessly.

On the way to Midland, Penny emptied her lunch from the grocery bag she had put it in that morning. She held the bag crumpled in her hot hand, ready to bring to her mouth. She could throw up. She was good at it. Discreet, quiet. No retching or moaning. If you wait long enough, with your lips closed, and breathe through your nose, if you wait long enough, enough force gathers. In a smooth motion you can bring the open mouth of the bag to your face, part your lips, and let whatever needs to propel itself out. She was good at it, and the bus was bumping over calm roads and the ride was long and the wretched blue sky was merciless in the square window.

How do they keep the dolphins happy? How to take them from leagues of open ocean, salt streaming and breeze blowing, and shut them in blue plaster pools, a circle of space, table salt in the water carefully maintained at 3 per cent? Do the dolphins care if the herring are dead or alive when they eat them? Listening to the sea lions as they honk horns and juggle balls in the air, balancing on one shining fin, do the dolphins slaver? Do they imagine crunching bone and sinew? Marineland looks so happy in all the pictures, all marine lions and lambs, all concord and play. The dolphins swim in pairs. They lift and thrust, they are airborne, they fly through hoops, they grin and kiss the cheeks of lucky children, and all the while they smile and the people smile too.

Penny felt the rough wood of the fence longhouse and the chapel. The dust beneath her now coated her skin. She could feel it on her tongue. The guide was going on, talking through the minutes of her life, talking them right away so they were gone. She was thinking of the words *Midland*, *Marineland*, all the *m*'s and *l*'s and *d*'s mixing up in her anxious ears, so longing to escape the one and get to the other, when she sat down, sick. No one had said Marineland. No one but she had ever said that word. She had raised money for an *m-l-d* place, but it was the wrong place. She was not going to Marineland. Midland. Midland. Sainte-Marie among the Hurons. This was it. It was breathtaking. Her throat closing around the hard pit of stupidity. Of an unfortunate slippage among letters and the awful result. She saw everything. Her own round eyes through bevelled glass and her neighbours looking down at their kitchen floors before they walked down the hall to their own front doors to listen to her pitch her grade six class trip. No one had said anything. No one noticed the incongruity between her zeal, her babbling impatience to raise the money and get on the bus. Her mother had signed the form without reading it.

After the concert Penny scooted to the back of the gym, pink and warm, to ask how her mother had liked the show.

"I thought you were in the choir. I couldn't see you."

"I was at the piano beside the teacher. She needed me to turn music pages."

"Oh, for God's sake."

How Penny had dragged her from the hollow at the end of the couch, the springs long unsprung, from the space that contained her spreading girth. How she had dressed in clothes and shoes and lipstick and presented herself, for once, to be proud of the damned kid, and for this? Penny heard it all, the shades and tones, all the gradations of her mother's disappointment. She had come, bought a gingerbread house and a ticket to the concert for herself and for Penny's brother, and all the money would get Penny to the dolphins.

No dolphins though. Only poor Father Brébeuf, brave and strong, winsome and kind, and no less dead than her own father, whatever he was like.

CRAIG DAVIDSON

Failure to Thrive

Some prick taped a glossy of a cirrhosis-ridden liver to my locker door. A blacky-grey sack dimpled with milky lesions, gallbladder a rotten green bulb.

Okay, yeah, I'll cop to hoisting a few – didn't I pull the "human martini" gag last Halloween? IV bag feeding gin into my left arm, vermouth plugged into my right, mouthful of cocktail olives – but at least I'm up front about it, unlike The Buke, that filthy lush, gin blossom so massive, Mir cosmonauts could spot it from orbit. *Hello, Kettle? This is the Pot calling – you're fucking black.* Winds me so tight I've got to take a nip from the flask, Bacardi Gold cut with a splash of Cepacol Mint to mask the smell. The inmates at Shady Nook Rest Home may be two exhales from the boneyard, but their sniffers are tip-*top*.

Tak Morita, Squeak, and The Buke ring the break-room table. Dark pouches under Tak's eyes and The Buke's kisser two inches from face planting into a bowl of microwave oatmeal. Squeak's yipping about some girl who's got his drawers in a twist.

"We've been dating a month." Squeak's got a high voice, as if there's a pea whistle lodged in his throat. This, added to the fact he's a generation younger than the rest of us, compounded by the fact he doesn't drink on the job and otherwise favours pineapple-and-parasol fairy cocktails, opens him to a great deal of ridicule. "And yesterday she tells me she's a lesbian!"

"She's no lez," I say, pulling up a chair beside Tak Morita.

"How do you know, Katz?" says Squeak.

"'At twenty-three she likes young neat unscratched girls with faces like the bottoms of new saucers,'" The Buke says into his oatmeal. He's a full-blown tier-five souse: that gigantic schnozz webbed with so many shattered capillaries it looks like someone's flattened a jellyfish across it. His existence functions as a cautionary reminder of the dangers of mixing alcohol and literature: as a college sophomore he embarked on a week-long bender with the Killer Bs – Jim Beam and Charles Bukowski – riding shotgun. Upshot: every sentence exiting his mouth is cribbed from *Love Is a Dog from Hell*.

"Shut up," I tell him. To Squeak: "How old's this chick?"

"Twenty-one."

"Twenty-one!" I slap Tak Morita's back. "Oh, man, Squeak, she's shitting you!"

"Shitting you," Tak Morita agrees, pan-Asiatic accent skimming the *t*'s – *Shi-ii-ing ooo*. He sips from a mug of coffee. I note the oily sheen of Comrade Popov's vodka on its surface.

"'She's wild but kind my six-foot goddess makes me laugh, the laughter of the mutilated who still need love . . .'"

"Do not speak unless spoken to," I warn The Buke. To Squeak: "At that age nobody knows what they are. Christ, at twenty-one Tak here could've been the percussionist in a goth-rock band –"

"I waa *no*," Tak states for the record.

"– and The Buke could've been formulating theorems on the effects of –"

"'I was living with a fat woman, Marie, in the French Quarter and got very sick . . .'"

I level a finger at The Buke. "I'm not telling you again. My point, Squeak, is this: anyone saying they know who or what they are at that age is a liar."

"Riar," Tak Morita echoes.

"So why'd she say it?" says Squeak.

"My guess? She's giving you the slippery palm."

"Srippery paam."

"Giving you the ol' heave-ho, Squeaker m'man."

"Heev–a *ho*," Tak Morita says. Tak emigrated from Vietnam a decade back. Tells me his father runs a forgotten POW camp somewhere in the jungle. Says they've got MIAs imprisoned thirty years, ex-paratroopers so brainwashed and beaten they're docile as lambs.

"'Imagine him in a rocking chair with his false teeth and a glass of buttermilk . . .'"

I slam my fist on the table. "Too early, Buke, too *damn* early for your bullshit!"

The Buke stands. Shaped like an Erlenmeyer flask, bubble-butted and pigeon-toed and dressed in diaper-white orderly scrubs, arms bent at robotic angles. He passes through a set of swinging double doors into the ward, the shuffling of his crepe-soled shoes merging with the somnambulant zzzzz of electric wheelchair motors and the TV noise of a cookie-cutter game show.

"I know it was you!" I holler after him. "The picture of the goddamn liver! People in glass houses! People . . . in . . . glass . . . *houses*!"

After work I walk to Blue's Taproom.

The custom of Blue's are hunched over the bar as if stationed on an assembly line. A clock with moose turds for numerals hangs above the cash register. On a raised TV, Ron Popeil mutely hawks a product called the Pocket Fisherman. Order a shot of gin with a tonic sidecar but, after a moment's consideration, make it a double shot and axe the sidecar.

A woman sits two stools away. Long and lean with scabby elbows and a mess of claret-coloured curls piled atop her head. Her pointed nose accords her face the rough aspect of a lawn dart, which, though in no way appealing, is mitigated by my stern adherence to the equation:

$$\frac{\text{RELATIVE UNATTRACTIVENESS}}{\text{RELATIVE INTOXICATION}} = \text{TOLERABLE MEDIAN}$$

"Hello, sailor," she says.

I smile. I'm smiling at most everything nowadays. The trees. The sky. Any old thing.

She closes the distance between us, pulling a short glass of Jack Daniel's along the bar. I am forced to confront her spectacular ugliness: face furrowed with hairline cracks like the veins in granite and poorly concealed by overabundant makeup, the smell coming off her a peculiar amalgam of Cover Girl and farts. I imagine tossing her into the air on the lawn of some lakeside cottage, legs squeezed tightly together, arms spread at her sides in an inverted V for balance, body revolving until her nose buries in the dead centre of a plastic ring for a ten-point score – bull's eye!

"Don't ask me why I come to this dump," she says.

"Slumming, are we?"

"Oh, you," she says, as if I'd said something rakish. She grabs me by the collar. Her corneas are yellowed like old newsprint and the angle of her nose is sharp enough to carve roast beef, but when she pulls me toward her I allow myself to be pulled. Her name is Jackie, with a *qu*. She tells me I'm amusing, breathing the words into the crook of my neck, although I don't recall saying anything remotely funny. After several resolve-bolstering rounds – two for me, three for her – we walk out together.

The route taken to my apartment is deliberately disorienting in hopes Jaquie won't be able to find her way back with a compass and a bloodhound. My gut tells me her level of intoxication facilitates no more than basic locomotion, but she looks at me slyly, out the tops of her heavily mascaraed eyes. I check her wake for breadcrumbs.

"Haven't we been here before?" she says as we pass an adult video store.

"No." In fact we've passed it twice.

"Mel's Discount Video Emporium." She reads words fanned across the frosted-glass window. "Go inside?"

"We're not dressed for emporium shopping."

"In here, then." She pulls me into a magazine shop.

It's blindingly bright inside, doing Jaquie no favours: hers is a face for mood lighting. Magazines organized in neat strata: Sports, Entertainment, Travel, Automotive, Business, Arts and Crafts, the most daunting array of pornography – *Ass Masters Monthly*? – I've heretofore encountered. Scan through titles with mounting mystification: *Modern Barn Building*, *Rodentia Digest*, *Atlantic Shrubbery*, *Amateur Crochet*. I grab a copy of *Weekly World News*. "Woman Talked out of Suicide by French

Fry!" the headline blares, above a picture of a crinkle-cut french
fry upon which the rudiments of a human face have been poorly
superimposed. Apparently the french fry was a compassionate
and convincing orator: the woman was beautiful; she had a
stable job, owned an economical, rust-free car. Everything to
live for.

"Getting something?" Jaquie's clutching a glossy fashion rag;
"Ten Foolproof Ways to Make Your Man Squeal!" reads a teaser.
I reach into the racks with a boozy sense of purpose. The maga-
zine is called *Asian Cult Cinema*. "This."

"Kin-*ky*."

Back at the apartment, lights out, clothes off, she mashes her
tits into my mouth. They taste of Javex. Kissing her is like licking
an ashtray smeared with Revlon's Love That Red. She insists on
switching on the bedside lamp to assault me with a body covered
in animal tattoos. She orders me to tongue the panther beneath
her left breast, grab at the wolverine on her inner thigh. "Pinch
it," she says. I'm skulking through a whitewashed jungle,
defenceless and alone, surrounded by bloodhungry beasts. "Bite
the crocodile," she commands, but I can't find it, and this failure
displeases my scarecrow-goddess. I bite at a mole on the swell of
her hip instead, revolted to find it hard as calcified bone. "Bite
the croc. *Now*." Shards of memory flicker before my eyes in
nickelodeon-style stop motion but I can't truly identify them,
they're not mine at all, unrecognizable photos taped in a
stranger's scrapbook.

When I wake, Jaquie's gone, along with the quart of gin I keep
under the bathroom sink and a novelty switchblade-comb. I
retrieve the emergency stash – a bottle of Ten High bourbon –
from the toilet tank and fix breakfast. A couple Kentucky
Colonels have me feeling like a human being again.

I nuke a bag of popcorn and thumb through *Asian Cult
Cinema*. Skim an article about a remake of *Tetsuo*, the hard-core
horror masterpiece, documented with several stills of decapitated heads on pikes. The heads all share a similar expression of
surprise, with their wide eyes and tongues protruding at crooked
angles. More time is devoted to an exposé of Yumi Amoto,

Tokyo's reigning scream queen: her discovery in the fishing village of Ikebara and her daily regimen of diaphragm exercises for improved screeching capabilities.

In the magazine's final pages, amidst adverts for ancient Asian hair tonics and powdered rhinoceros penises and ninja throwing stars, a capsule ad draws my attention:

GENUINE SNUFF FILM
THE *REAL* THING

A mailing address follows. I fix another Kentucky Colonel and root through drawers in a fugged-out haze, ferreting out chequebook and pen, cutting a cheque for $50.95 plus $7.95 s&h, licking and sealing the envelope.

Hand already in the mailbox, I try to stop myself – *crumple the letter, goddamn it, tear it up* – but it slips from my fingertips. The red drawer hinges shut.

At work The Buke watches, muddy-eyed, as Squeak and I administer therapeutic massage to inmate #044. The Buke's raided the janitor's closet again; he clutches a Lysol-soaked rag, occasionally raising it to his nose.

"Put that away," I tell him. "Stuff'll strip your nostril lining."

"'I know a woman who keeps buying puzzles,'" he says. "Chinese puzzles," he clarifies, snuffling his rag.

Inmate #044, female, mid-eighties, moans incoherently. She's lying face down on the bed, naked to the waist. We're kneading the muscles of her arms and upper back to prevent atrophy. Her skin is yellow and unnaturally smooth, as if she'd lathered with soap and forgotten to rinse. As I rub, it becomes smoother and smoother, and I wonder how long it will be before I arrive at the ultimate smoothness of bone.

A water bottle filled with Smirnoff and Tang hangs in a mesh pouch at my hip. I take a healthy pull. "Gatorade," I say, solely for #044's benefit. "Gotta replenish those electrolytes."

"She dumped me," Squeak says. "My lesbian girlfriend."

"Saw it coming, Squeak. Saw it coming *miles* away. Hell, even The Buke could've told you."

The Buke, who's twisted the rag ends into plugs poked up each nostril, sniffles morosely and looks away.

"I should've known," Squeak says, flexing #044's elbow joint. "Our first date, she tells me she's big into women's tennis – she's never set foot on a tennis court!"

"Blinded by love," I say.

"She wid her Cleopadra moobie-star bogs . . ." The Buke's pronunciation screwy with that rag-stuffed nose.

I lower #044's arms to her side and ease her onto her back. The gown is bunched around her waist, flat, yellow breasts exposed. A burnt-clove smell comes off her body.

"Her colon's compacted," Squeak whispers. "Needs to be dug out."

I wince. "Flip a coin."

We're rummaging in our pockets when The Buke yanks the rag from his nose, snaps on a pair of latex gloves, rolls #044 onto her side, and says, "Her kisses taste like shit soup."

"Thanks, Buke," says Squeak.

"You're a peach," I say.

Walking down the dim hallway with its water-stained walls and cracked tiling, I hear #044's shit dropping into a stainless-steel tureen. The sound is hard and metallic: excised buckshot.

The videotape arrives two weeks later, wrapped in butcher paper and smelling of unknown spices, affixed with portrait stamps of beetle-browed Asian politicos. The tape itself is less exotic: a standard Fuji T-120 with the word *Movie* scribbled on its label in a hand unaccustomed to cursive.

Tak Morita and I call in sick and convene at my apartment for Margarita Monday. By four o'clock the empty bottle of José Cuervo has rolled beneath the sofa, and salt is mounded on the coffee table in coarse drifts. Tak's socks are AWOL, toes glazed with Triple Sec. He's found a child-sized cowboy hat in the closet, blue foil star on its peak and a whistle fastened to the chinstrap. He looks asinine: the bastard love child of Tom Mix and Tom Vu.

"Kat-*zu*," he hails as I return from the mailbox. "How-dee, par-dunaa!"

"Howdy, you godawful drunk."

Tak places the whistle between his lips and blows anemically. "Wa thaa?"

I slot the videocassette into the VCR. "Something from your neck of the woods."

Static dissolves into a shot of a low-ceilinged room. Exposed pipes run overhead. Walls draped with milky plastic tarpaulin and floor covered in gaudy Asian newsprint. Centred in the frame is a man in a wooden chair, wrists and ankles lashed with wire. Poverty is clearly expressed in his shabby clothes and dirty feet. His eyes dart about with a look of predetermined desperation, as if to acknowledge that every choice he'd ever made, every path he'd elected to follow, had led, circuitously but inexorably, to this end. Or maybe he's just piss-scared.

Two men enter the frame. One is bowlegged. The other sports red cowboy boots and is missing the lion's share of his right arm. Both wear balaclavas and carry black-bladed cane machetes. They jabber at their captive in scattergun dialect. Bowlegs spits on him.

"What are they saying?"

Tak shrugs. "They Thai."

Bowlegs slaps the captive man's face. The sound of flesh on flesh is tinny, as if coming from the end of a long corridor. Then he punches downward and breaks the man's nose. The man does not scream or cry out. A light bubbling noise, but I don't know where it comes from.

One-Armed Cowboy chops down with his machete, severing the pinkie, ring, and middle fingers of the man's right hand. Dark arterial blood pulses from the stumps. The man's mouth opens. Nobody speaks. It is all very controlled. Disciplined.

Tak Morita blows the whistle again. I slap it out of his mouth. His skull reels to the left, jaw snapping shut, cowboy hat sailing off his head.

Bowlegs pulls a T-handled leather punch from his back pocket and stabs into the man's chest and abdomen. Stabbing with no particular vigour, not too hard or too deep, penetrating the first layer of muscle. Something sickeningly playful about the way he does it. No blood at first, no sound either except for the newspapers under the man's feet. Then blood blooms on the front of his dirty white T-shirt, pinprick petals. The camera angle doesn't change: the same impersonal, sharply focused, middle-distance shot. A digital counter in the bottom left-hand corner ticks off the minutes, the seconds.

The man is crying now, the sound somewhere between a sob and a scream, eyes wide and black and vacant. This lack of dignity in the face of death angers One-Armed Cowboy, who hacks the toes off the man's left foot.

Outside, the sky's last light burns away. The downtown skyline glimmers distantly beyond the room's bay window. The door slams as Tak Morita takes his leave.

It happens quickly. Bowlegs, either tiring of the game or dissatisfied with the reaction, stabs the leather punch into the man's throat, a half-inch above the clavicle bone, puncturing the carotid artery. The man gasps as if he's been doused with ice water. Bright blood wells around the tool's silver shaft. When the leather punch is withdrawn, a red stream spurts from the wound to plaster the far wall, and the man's eyes roll back as though in a terrible daydream.

The television screen dissolves into static. I am acutely aware of my smell, a powerful stench of sweat and endorphins, wet moss burning.

I crave fresh air. Hit the street. November wind scours my face but I'm so bombed the chill fails to register. On the sidewalk, bloated pigeons fight over crusts outside a Pizza Pizza while trolling hookers look on disinterestedly, and a speeding ambulance fishtails the wrong way down a one-way street. The sky is a swath of jeweller's velvet, utterly starless, the dazzling lights of peep-show marquees and all-night sex shops and low-rent titty bars bleeding along the peripheries of my vision, their colours deeper than anything I've ever known, or can put a name to.

I find myself back at the magazine shop.

The Film Magazine section.

Squeak and The Buke bathe inmate #017, male, late eighties, deaf as an earthworm. A bracket-mounted television is tuned to MuchMusic, a rap video playing in hearing-impaired mode: a black bar across the bottom of the screen, the words OOH, BABY, BABY, PUT YO' THANG ON ME, tiny white clef notes denoting a certain lyrical quality. I slam a slender red book on the floor – *Drinking and Damage: Theoretical Advances and Implications for Prevention.*

"Who put this in my locker?" I'm Section-8, haven't slept for days, guzzled a mickey of peach schnapps – Jesus Christ! – for breakfast. "You, Buke? Piece of shit souse. You should be gassed."

The Buke scrubs #017's wasted arm with a sponge. "'I nap with helicopters and vultures circling over my sagging mattress . . .'"

"Fuck you. Fuck your tonsils."

"'They are whores without souls,'" scrubbing, scrubbing, "'and they are magic because they lie about nothing.'"

"Fuck your . . . *hat.*"

"When's the last time you took a bath?" Squeak asks me.

A transparent runner of saliva unravels from #017's mouth. His naked body repulses, fascinates: a lunatic pattern to his liver spots, and I am convinced, were I to connect them with a felt-tip marker, they would disclose an earth-shattering epiphany.

"Do it again," I warn The Buke, "and I'll slap the taste out of your mouth. I'll throw you such a beating your mother will get whiplash."

"She's dead," says Squeak. "Now, stop it."

I am undeterred. "I'll kick your face in. I'll smash every bone in your body and burn your house to cinders. I'll –"

"Shut up, Katz," says Squeak.

My gaze rises to a contraption mounted on the wall: an automated air freshener that, every fifteen minutes or so, releases a burst of peppermint-scented mist to mask the stink of dying people. Beneath the company name, a motto is printed in red block capitals: BECAUSE WE CARE.

"Care about what?" Squeak and The Buke aren't looking at me. "What possible causes can an air-freshener company care about? Human rights? The AIDS epidemic? You can't just throw around words like that." Blood pounds rhythmically in my skull. "*Care.* Can't just say . . . about what? Nuclear disarmament? The war on drugs? I don't . . . can't fathom . . . you make fucking *air fresheners*, for Christ's sake!"

I feel dizzy and nauseous. A sweet schnapps film coats the inside of my mouth. #017 is staring at me, or maybe just the space I occupy. His lips move but no sound comes out and I'm thinking of that scene in *The Deer Hunter* where Christopher Walken plays Russian roulette, a .38 pressed to his temple, eyes burning twin holes through the movie screen.

Videotapes trickle in over the following weeks. Some are held up at customs, who send polite letters requesting I claim them in person. I resist their overtures.

I open one box to find the corpse of a very large, hairy spider. Its egg-sized abdomen has broken open during transport and formless innards coat the box in yolk-like tendrils. A note written in a functionally illiterate hand reads: HOPE IT KILS YOU SIC FUCK.

I scrape the spider's body out of the box with some difficulty – its guts adhering to the cardboard like viscid, half-melted candy – and set it in an empty mayonnaise jar. My recent termination has curtailed any access to formaldehyde, so I fill the jar with Bombay Sapphire gin, sparing no expense on my pickled little friend.

I sit in the apartment, drinking, watching. Some are clearly fake: the woman choking back a giggle as what purports to be blood but is obviously spaghetti sauce wells between her prodigious cleavage. Some are not what they purport to be, but are nonetheless fascinating: footage of elephants butchered by Aussie poachers in Cambodia, shot in the head with high-powered rifles and crumpling to the ground with reluctant inevitability, skulls destroyed and huge black eyes focused on nothing, then chainsaws revving, chewing through the tough skin anchoring tusk to jaw, mud-caked ivory pried free and the massive animals left to bleed out, legs jittering, tails swishing, eyes glazing. Others are revelatory: pirated CNN footage, never aired, shot during the siege of Sarajevo, of carcasses – women, children, waterlogged dogs – floating down the Keva River, hanged men and boys garlanding trees like so much human tinsel, blindfolded men led onto dusty laneways, shot through each kneecap, run over by military Jeeps. Many of the tapes have been transferred, poorly, from 8mm film stock; on the dark and grainy peripheries, I see, or think I see, shadowy shapes moving, but no amount of tracking, pausing, or replaying can reveal their meaning or intent.

How long do I watch the tapes? Days, definitely . . . a week? Delivery men arrive with food, booze. The phone rings, a woman's voice asking if I'd be interested in a free trial offer on Time-Life encyclopedias. The apartment fills with empty takeout boxes, greasy cardboard mountains illuminated by the TV's cathode glow. Someone bangs on the door, complaining of a rotten smell. My beard grows in patchy, fuzzing the hollows of my cheeks, itching dreadfully.

It's a Wednesday, maybe, when I run dry. Paw through empties, wet my lips with the dregs. Rank sweat flows from my pores, stinking like mink musk, an obscene amount of sweat, hair plastered down and dripping from my cheekbones.

Resting atop the television: a mayonnaise jar.

Contents: Twenty liquid ounces of Bombay Sapphire gin. One large, dead spider.

The gin is warm after sitting on top of the TV for days. The spider's legs, dappled with fibrous hairs, prick my upper lip. Whatever contribution it makes to the gin's bouquet is lost on me. Bitterer, perhaps?

I stare into its giant eyes. Shards of me – the curve of a stubbled cheek, the lower helix of one wide eye – dimly reflected in those dark convex globes.

Hi-Fi Bonanza is open twenty-four hours, angling to corner the insomniac's market on plasma screen TVs and low-end Blaupunkt speakers. At 3 a.m. it is deserted save a single dozy sales clerk. Halogen lighting maps unbroken gridlines across the ceiling, giving the store a washed-out aspect, everything bleached.

"Need a video recorder."

The clerk stares up from a copy of *D-Cup Blondes* tented over his lap. Face so badly pockmarked it's criminal: the stump of a termite-ravaged elm. Wearing a red polyester vest with stains of nameless origin and a nametag: Drake.

"A VCR?" Drake asks, gagging, covering his mouth.

"No. A video camera. A camcorder."

Drake is disinclined to remove the magazine from his lap. "Over there." A vague flourish. "Next to the car stereos."

I select a Sony Handycam with auto zoom and picture-in-picture capability. $1079.23 after taxes. Drake throws in a spare battery pack, cautioning me not to tell his boss or he'll be shitcanned.

"Your secret's safe with me, slugger."

Early morning mist not yet settled into dew dampens the hairs on my neck. The moon hangs in its western orbit, the disembodied head of a sideshow oracle.

My keys still work. I let myself in soundlessly. Handycam slung on a strap around my neck, viewfinder bumping my breastbone.

Tak Morita is passed out in the break room. I zoom in on his face flattened against the tabletop. Liquid snores exit his mouth, and his flesh, framed in the viewfinder's box, assumes the pallor of chilled butter. "Work it, baby," I whisper. "Own that space."

Ease open the door to room seventeen, housing inmates #039–#042. Hallway light spills across scuffed tiles separating Craftmatic adjustable beds. Four germicide-sprayed pillows cradle four shrivelled heads too insubstantial to make more than token impressions in them. Eight arms laid across threadbare coverlets like driftwood splits.

I frame #039 – male, early nineties, admitted due to a clinical failure to thrive – in close-up, but, as his face is longer than it is wide, I cut off his chin and the majority of his forehead. My hand enters the frame, grazing his cheeks, his cobweb hair.

I remove my clothes, unclasping my belt, heeling off my shoes. My naked body is pitiful, paunchy and lacking definition. Turn the camera on myself, panning up from legs to stomach, arms, face. The Handycam emits a faint hum as tape spools through the feed chamber.

A hand falls on my shoulder. I do not flinch or cry out. A familiar voice says, "I've watched snails climb over ten-foot walls and vanish. You mustn't confuse this with ambition."

And for a moment everything unfolds in the way it occurs in movies, things take on the aspect and parameters of a celluloid reality. I hear the swelling of a phantom orchestra, the rising timbre of a church choir, fireworks bursting in slow motion overhead, the Technicolor image of two men touching in dim half-light, their breathing rendered in crystal-clear Dolby Surround Sound.

None of this is real, you see. None of this is actually happening.

All of this is a movie I once saw.

CATHERINE KIDD

Green-Eyed Beans

This question of answering when and where an event took place becomes more complicated, according to the theory of special relativity, because rods can change their lengths, and clocks change their rhythms, depending on the speed at which they operate when they are in motion. Therefore, we must answer the questions when and where an event took place in terms of a definitely moving system, or in terms of the relationships between two moving systems.

– from *World Book Encyclopedia*
entry for "Theory of Relativity"

The groom from the riding stable sends red roses to my mother. I never see the little gift cards but there must be some, somewhere. According to stubborn faith in things unseen, the cards are hidden in a kitchen cupboard behind all her baking ingredients, or upstairs among her mysterious jars and bottles. I don't snoop through my mother's things anymore. I began to dread someday finding the bottled tongue of the woman I used to think she'd smothered when I was a child, the woman who lived tongueless in the basement of herself. Or perhaps after a certain point with people, the case is simply closed, and sealed with wax. You stop trying to figure them out. You just let them be there in the room, like a lamp that's turned on, or one that is turned off.

Just now I see her. She is a cool queen sitting out there on the lawn, a chess piece near the bleached yellow circle where the plastic turtle pool used to be. Not a pool for turtles, but a pool of moulded plastic in the *shape* of a turtle, with a small slide extending down the turtle's neck and into its shell. The shell of the turtle was concave, inverted and green like a coloured contact lens. Then the other day, one of the daughters of the cedar-haired woman slid down the slide and broke the turtle's neck. A bit of her leg flesh got caught in the snapping crevice, bruising her badly. How she screamed and screamed. The pool was taken away the same day, by the groom from the campus riding stable, who was always cheerful about doing things in the yard next to my mother's.

Just now she is snapping string beans. When I watch her through the kitchen curtains, the flowers on the table blur and bleed. Roses and baby's breath, corpuscles inside her house. If I focus instead on the dozen red roses right here on the table, then it is my mother, and the lawn, and the pile of beans she's snapping, which mesh together like cells, sunlit yellow-green. The cellulose fibres of a plant.

Baby's breath. The smell of it recalling nausea. Two lobes hang heavy on either side of Rose's face; those are her cheeks, with such tiny red lips between. A cyclopean nipple. A cupid's bow, eructing.

Rose is my little girl. I love her best when four fingers and her thumb are curled boneless about a strand of my hair, or held fast to one of my own fingers, which, unlike hers, are bony and yellow. Rose is less than one. I have loved her best when her pastry cheeks, her tiny, restless lips are fastened sucking to my breast, suspending for a moment the crisis of being, or provoking it.

You're hungry. My mother says this. I step over the threshold of sliding glass doors onto the concrete patio, hot to my feet, then cool onto the lawn, and this is the first thing she says to me. She seems to say it every time she sees me looking at the baby, whose crib has been set out here on the patio, like a cake, with a gauzy yellow cake-cover to keep mosquitoes away from her blood. Sweetly, it seduces them.

I am both sulky and hungry today, apparently, yet I step out and turn a cartwheel on the grass, not gracefully. But for an instant, my hands are feathered green, and my legs are spread wide open to the sky. I feel the oily sun-heat slide between them, and think of mermaids in green bathing caps with sequins. Turning and turning, their feet turning to fins.

I'm not hungry at all, I say to my mother as I slouch down like a walrus beside the growing mound of string beans. *I ate all those oysters*, I tell her. *I ate the whole tin.*

In fact, I'd even licked out the tin, unable to shake off the image of a cat cutting its tongue on a jagged lid while licking oyster juices from a can. *God knows* where these images come from. The desire for symmetry perhaps, or resolution, the probable resolution of metal against skin. In my mind, any television army doctor hurrying toward a helicopter with supplies will always be decapitated by the spinning blades, just as my mother will always lose her fingers in the soup she purées in the blender, in my mind. It seems inevitable, aesthetically. I will always cut my legs in the shower, even if the razor sits untouched on the edge of the bathtub. The image seems to leap up at its own possibility. Or perhaps I must change my sense of possibility.

Looking at a surface of skin inevitably recalls the fluids coursing beneath it. It is incredible to me that people manage to remain discrete and self-contained at all, without somehow rupturing and flowing together, like a broken yolk or the piebald Fraser. Some people are tougher than butternuts to crack, and are in no danger of this loss of identity. My mother seems to be one of these people. Some people carry their own containers, like the one I used to carry my retainer around in. They do not open unless they are pried.

But I do clearly recall the silky rush of water down my legs in a wash, and wondering what its ingredients were. Whether silvery particles of memory could be lost in afterbirth, the bathwater with the baby. This is the only explanation that makes any sense to me right now. Sometimes when I look at Rose, I find myself believing that she must have absorbed in utero whatever it is I can't remember. As though forgetting were a liquid environment from which other things were born.

Salmon Court. This is the name of the cluster of housing units where I've been staying since just before Rose was born, with my mother and sometimes Dr. Spector when he is not home with his wife. The housing units are arranged in a big circle, with a breech for cars to drive in and park in the centre, like marbles in a chalk circle. All the front doors of the cluster open onto the parking lot and courtyard, at the centre of which is a concrete-bordered island with a single tree. It is a large oak tree. These housing units were built in 1967, but the tree must have been there before that, judging from the magnitude of it. Which is strange, to build a circular cluster of housing units around a single tree, as though it were the tree's idea. I imagine the roots of it underground, pale as larvae fingering the soil, spreading out their shadow-branches like a phreatic brain. Around the outer circumference of Salmon Court, all the patios glint their sliding glass doors like the grooves around the edge of a quarter. On the day side of the circle, where my mother sits snapping string beans, the lawn slopes down to the highway. On the night side, which seldom gets much light, there's a green ravine. I imagine that from the air, the student housing units of Salmon Court must look like a big green eyeball with a high concrete brow, that's the highway, and a deep crease beneath it, that's the ravine. The eye of a waking dragon, with a single tree growing out from its pupil. Since I've been forbidden to stimulate my brain with books, for the time being, I amuse myself with this sort of aerial nonsense.

Out here on the lawn is a metal swing set and one of those carousels you sit on while someone pulls you round and round until you're sick. The campus housing unit was built for married students with children, which theoretically would be my mother and I, respectively, though I'm not particularly a child and she's not particularly married. And neither of us are students. Dr. Spector had helped my mother get the place through some connection, and he visits her here when his wife thinks he's lecturing at the Faculty of Dentistry.

At her most sentimental, my mother occasionally reminds

me, *You know you'll always be my little girl.* But it is only in this sense I am one, and only since the birth of Rose do I ever remember her saying it. I outgrew swing sets and carousels at least ten years ago, and Rose won't be old enough to play on them for another five years at least. So my daughter and I don't really fit in here at Salmon Court. The other mothers in the housing unit have children who are two or five, or seven or ten. Some of them seem to assume that Rose is my mother's daughter, because whenever we're outdoors it's generally my mother who dotes on her. So they must wonder what I am doing here.

I see the swing set and the slide and the carousel every single day, and I think I dislike them. It is interesting to me that many playground toys are essentially vehicles that don't go anywhere. You can go up and down, or back and forth, or round and round, but you can't *get* anywhere in particular. I suppose there's a certain hopefulness in sheer motion for its own sake. There must have been a time when I just wanted to *move* and didn't really care if there was no point to it. It's probably good for children to do that, I suppose. They can worry about destinations later, as long as they don't wait too long.

My little brother, Gavin, had learned quite young how to leap from a swing in mid-air, his sneaker feet landing in the sand like paratroopers before tearing off in some other direction, toward some other destination. He'd been quite good at this, which is probably why he isn't living here now. But it had always made more sense to me to simply stop pumping, rather than leap, then wait for the swing to come to a natural halt, or at least slow down enough to jump off without risking injury. Some people would say this was sensible. But it's not very courageous, and it takes much longer than jumping in mid-air.

My brother, Gavin, is in the army now, stationed somewhere along the eastern border of Turkey. It's difficult to pick him out in the photos he sometimes sends home to my mother, it's been so long since anyone's seen him. I admire the multiple anonymity of uniforms, and admire how his voice tends to fluctuate between crackling static and the deep tones of a full-grown man neither of us really knows, when he phones home at Christmastime, maybe.

The swing set and the carousel in the yard are painted shiny stripes of red, blue, and yellow. *Primary colours.* It's eerie how they sometimes look more real than anything else here. If these days were a movie, the scene would keep cutting back to the swing set and the carousel, as though they represented the most primal objects on the landscape. The most uncomplicated or uncontaminated ones. There must be a type of purity in motion for the sheer sake of moving. Which is why so many sentimental love scenes show couples dancing, and everyone gets choked up, trying to remember the last time they did something for the sheer kinesis of it.

Take from the unsnapped pile, Kitten, not the bowl, says my mother. *That pile is the heads, see.* I keep eating all her raw string beans, heads, tails, spines, and all. My appetite keeps changing, even now. Sometimes I'm still eating for two, or three or four, or even less than one, though my mother says these things should have long stabilized by now. I think she'd used the word *cemented* or *crystallized*, rather than *stabilized*, some word associated with her work at Dr. Spector's clinic. My mother thinks that my maternal habits should have become as routine as flossing by now, but I have to wonder how she never noticed that she herself is the only person ever in the history of the family to floss routinely.

Rose stares at the sky through the yellow netting of her crib. Her face does a twist and seems to recoil into itself, scrunching her eyes and trying to swallow her lips both at once, her fingers opening and curling shut like sea anemone.

It would be nice to have a few pictures of Rosie-Posie where she isn't scowling like that, says my mother. *Honestly, the two of you are quite a pair. Like a couple of old women.*

Every time my mother catches my daughter not scowling, she runs for the camera. But I think maybe Rose scowls because she can see things the rest of us can't, like through walls or underneath skin. Babies are supposedly unable to distinguish between themselves and other objects on their landscape. When

Rose is looking at *something*, supposedly, she assumes that the thing is part of herself. But I do wish that whatever it is she sees didn't make her scowl all the time. It seems a bad reflection upon *something*.

The groom from the campus riding stable comes toward us, up the hill, with a red plastic pail. It always surprises me that he is so young. I know from the water slooshing over the side of the pail that there are pretextual goldfish inside, my mother having offered to assist a man named Troy in the design of an ornamental pond for the new Japanese pavilion across campus. My mother knows nothing about designing a pond, but she endeavours to wear outfits resembling the outfits of women who look like they might. The groom from the riding stable also knows this man Troy, who is sort of his boss, but neither one knows that they both know my mother quite minutely.

Sometimes the groom from the stable comes up the hill with miniature trees to show her, or a model bridge to straddle ornamental streams. It doesn't appear she's explained to him yet that it's actually a certain architect she's recently become interested in, and not a certain architecture. She tells the groom that his goldfish are *beautiful, beautiful,* over and over again.

Yeah, they're beauties, eh? he says, chewing his cheek, while my mother's lips make goldfish bubbles, saying *beautiful, beautiful* over and over again. There is material evidence in the pucker of my mother's lips, an emphasis on *ooh* and *oh* sounds. A goldfish-bubble, kissy-lip phenomenon that only appears when she speaks to men who are her lovers. More haphazard versions of these *ooh*s and *oh*s were extended to men in general, but with certain men became more pronounced. Suddenly she'll choose to speak of ladies' shoes, the rolling blues of noon in June, her collection of ornamental spoons, and beautiful tunes she couldn't seem to remember the lyrics to. She'll tilt her head and hum a few bars, hoping the man will join in with the words.

But the groom shakes his head and has no clue. The tune must've been before his time, he says. He lifts his trouser leg slightly at the knee, then squats down beside my mother. They talk instead about how greatly appearances are improved by the addition of flowering plants. The groom squats with his brown trousers bunched up, while my mother smooths her yellow sundress quietly over her thighs. Then she seems to remember that Rose and I are sitting close by, and that we've never formally been introduced to the groom.

That's my daughter, Agnes, and that's baby Rose, my daughter's daughter. Look at her, will you? Have you ever seen such a lovely little girl? Rose is such a good baby, such a quiet baby. She never gives us any trouble at all. My mother laughs and adjusts her sunglasses. *Agnes there was born face first, imagine.*

It surprises me greatly that she's been telling people the face-first thing since as long as I can remember. My mother's thighs spread open very wide, with my startled red face peering out from between. Sometimes she even reaches out and frames my face in her labial hands when she tells the story, pressing hard against my temples, giggling at the redness of my cheeks. I can't fathom why she'd want to conjure up this image to near-perfect strangers, let alone to her lover, who is scarcely older than I'll be next birthday.

I don't mind her telling the story so much when it's taken to mean I was born full of curiosity. That I'd wanted to take a good look at the world from the very moment I was pushed into it. But sometimes she adds the detail that I had tried to brace myself back with my elbows, as though I'd taken one peek and decided I was better off where I came from, which was why they had to resort to extracting me like a tooth.

Wasn't really my fault, I tell the crouching groom, who doesn't seem to want to know any of this.

I remember your father wanted to call you little Thel, my mother says in a voice like tinkling bells, while the groom attends awkwardly. *But it was such an old-fashioned name. Besides, you weren't all that little, as I recall. You had a good coupla pounds over your own Rosie-Posie, over there.* My mother reminds me frequently of this, crossing and uncrossing her legs and lighting a long, skinny cigarette, rubbing the place on her belly where her scar would be.

I didn't retreat back inside, I say. *I was pulled back, and out some other way. It's not like I was planning things that way.*

Well, that's sounds like you all over, says my mother, who believes I've been evasive about rites of passage since the day I was born. *Not saying a body shouldn't do things in her own time, and on her own legs, Kitten,* my mother says, *once she's located them, that is.*

Sitting out there on the lawn, my mother looks as though she has no legs at all, her yolk-yellow sundress tucked under her knees like a pedestal, a sunnier yellow than my fingers holding back the kitchen curtain. I have retreated back inside the housing unit, my mother having embarrassed both me and the groom with the story of my birth. I wait in the kitchen until the groom goes away again, taking his red bucket of goldfish with him. My mother and the groom don't kiss each other this time, as they usually might, maybe because they think I am watching.

Now she sits cool as an egg on the lawn, as though waiting for something else to happen. Some other rupture to her serenity. The sound of the telephone ringing, or Rose crying, or dusk descending like freon gas. She doesn't keep her eyes on the beans she's snapping, not always, but lets them wander like sheep over the lawn, gathering wool. Sometimes she gazes across the yard, to the communal driveway where a hanging sign says "Salmon Court," in painted orange letters on brown wood. The sign is suspended from a L-shaped wooden gallows, like in a ghost town, swaying when it's windy and soaking up rain, getting bloated, then drying out again, and weathering, weathering. The driveway leads up and around the centre of the courtyard, in a loop, then doubles back in a running knot, trailing off to the road.

Listen. Lately I've been making some plans. I've been thinking about writing a very long letter to my daughter, Rose, who will be one year old soon. Or sort of a letter, more like a zoological garden of things past. It seems the right time to do it, to pen things in writing, though it's plain that once creatures of memory are penned, their behaviour changes irrevocably. Like creatures in a zoo, the memories become aware of being watched, and have more limited options for how to respond to the watchers' eyes. But seeing as there's this ongoing concern regarding my inability to remember things properly, I must backtrack. I must follow tracks backward, and retread them. Once I catch up to myself in the present, I'll be ready to find some way of jumping off the swing. Though it remains to be seen what that might mean.

When my mother finally comes inside, she sets down her big bowl of green beans and touches a certain place on her throat with her hand, the place she always touches. She rubs it with her fingers as though invisible stitches were itching her. She comments out loud how little she notices the mountains here, despite how huge they are, looming green and purple like cabbages at dusk.

EDWARD O'CONNOR

Heard Melodies Are Sweet

They do a little blow before going over, Hoxford, the famous defence attorney, and the girl who calls herself Jessie. He's been with her once or twice already and finds her amusing, amusing enough he's asked for her specifically this time around.

She has straight blonde hair that reaches halfway down her back, which is standard issue for one of his dates, as are the regular features and flawless complexion. What kills him is her voice, low and a little squeaky like a pubescent boy's. There's a film actress has a voice like that whose name Hoxford can never remember.

The other thing he likes about this Jessie is the look she gives him (a) whenever she says something startling, or (b) whenever he says something nice to her. A steady sidelong look, as if she's summing him up. As if on the verge of trusting him but not able to convince herself that's such a great idea.

They're in his condo on Front Street, up near the top of the building. The sun is setting, and the living-room window gives them a view of the Toronto Islands and the empty expanse of Lake Ontario beyond.

Hoxford cuts two lines on a mirror in a gilded frame, one of the antiques he's managed to salvage from his divorce. In the mirror, his face looks drawn and baggy-eyed, as if gravity more than age is to blame. While he chops and arranges the powder, he tells her where they're going.

"A guy named Donald Dambois. Hadn't seen him in twenty years, then I wind up standing behind him in line at Sam's. I recognized him immediately, big bear of a guy with a messy-looking beard. But I notice the whole time we're talking, he's staring at the CDs in my hands. I had what, five or six, and I could tell he was embarrassed because he only had one. Stupid, isn't it, to get worked up about something like that? I felt sorry for him, quite frankly."

"How do you know what he was thinking?" she says. "Maybe you were imagining it."

"He was staring at my hands and blushing. I wasn't imagining that his cheeks turned red."

As soon as they do the coke, he doesn't want to go. He feels like staying in his apartment all night and getting really ripped with this girl who never agrees with anything he says. He wonders if that's part of her act, if they've worked up a profile on him at the service, and this is something they've told her to do – to contradict his every word. The truth is he doesn't care if the attitude is real or fake; he just enjoys being with her. He leans back against the cushions of the couch and drapes one arm along the top. With his fingers he can play with her hair.

"We were in residence together at university. For nine months, we slept in the same room. When we went to bed at night, we'd talk in the dark as we were drifting off to sleep."

He makes a conducting motion in the air with his hand to give her a sense of drift.

"We'd tell each other our dreams, our fears, what we really thought about the other people we knew. It was easy with the lights out, in our separate beds. Easy to be honest. I don't think I've ever unburdened myself like that to anyone since, not even my wife."

"One reason you're not married anymore."

She's giving him that look now and it makes him smile. People, especially women, tell him he has a nice smile. It makes him seem kind, they say.

Hoxford stands up, and Jessie remains seated on the couch. She won't say it, but he can tell she wants more coke. He goes into the kitchen and opens the refrigerator, which is empty except for a bottle of Tabasco sauce and a gift-wrapped bottle of Montrachet. He brings the wine back into the living room and hands it to her.

"You give them this. It will look better than for me to be the bearer of such an expensive gift. Less embarrassing for my old friend."

Hoxford has arrived at the point in his career when he can charge his clients a fee even he thinks borders on the obscene. Despite the alimony and child support, he still has lots of money, and he's learned how to hide it and make it work for him. Donald Dambois does something with books, editing or translating them. He was always good with languages but never understood a thing about money. Hoxford supposes Donald might make one-tenth, if that, of his own annual income.

Halfway down, the elevator stops and an older man and woman in evening dress step in, spicing the air with perfume and talcum powder. The woman ignores Hoxford and the girl, but the man, who has a flesh-coloured hearing aid in one ear, gives Jessie an appraising look. As he turns his back, he grimaces. Hoxford is buzzing from the coke and can't stop talking. He raises his voice a little to ensure that the old man will be able to hear.

"I knew his wife too. The most beautiful woman I ever laid eyes on, absolutely ravishing. And it wasn't just me who thought so. Every man she met fell in love with her immediately. Comical in a way, the effect she had. I watched her walk down Bay Street one day near Bloor. She literally stopped traffic and she wasn't doing anything more than strolling along, minding her own business. Twenty years old, in the full bloom of youth, and nobody could resist her."

"Could you resist her?" says Jessie.

"Oh, I didn't even try. In fact, you could say I broke her in for him."

The elderly woman blinks when Hoxford says that. The man with the hearing aid turns to confront him, and it's satisfying to see that his face has gone pale. For a moment he thinks the man will spit on him. Then the elevator doors open, and he takes Jessie by the elbow and pushes past without asking to be excused.

It's one of the first fine evenings in May and what Hoxford likes to call the magical hour of dusk. In spite of the mild weather, he prefers to keep the windows of the Lexus up and the air conditioner on low. They have to cross the viaduct to get into the east end of the city. One wing of the suicide-prevention fence has already gone up; when the other is in place, the bridge will look like some elongated angel getting ready to soar. He wonders how many people made use of the unfledged angel to send themselves soaring into the next world. Where will Toronto's terminally depressed go now that their favourite launching pad has been denied them? Jessie pushes in the lighter and takes a cigarette out of her purse.

"I just want one before we get there."

"Are you nervous? There's no need to be."

"He didn't actually invite you over, did he?"

The lighter clicks. She presses it to her cigarette, and he gets a whiff of toasted tobacco. She lets the smoke drift out her nose.

"I had to insist," he tells her. "I had to talk him into it. But when I called this afternoon to confirm, he was fine. Listen, this won't take long. Dinner, coffee – then we're out of there. Maybe hear some music afterwards."

"Why did you insist when you could tell he didn't want to?"

Hoxford shrugs.

"It's not him, actually; it's his wife I want to see."

"Did you really fuck her?"

"Let's just say we had a brief encounter."

"But good enough to bring you back after all these years."

"Look, why do you have to be so crude?"

He keeps his voice even when he says that, but the words alone are enough to shut her up. She smiles and snorts to indicate she couldn't care less whether he thinks she's crude or not, but he can tell the thrust has hit home. She presses the window button and drops her half-finished cigarette into the slipstream, then folds her arms and looks straight ahead.

Hoxford is enjoying himself. He feels certain the evening can only get better from his point of view. Now that he's cast Jessie off, in a manner of speaking, he decides to reel her back in again.

"Remember that girl from Afghanistan who was on the cover of *National Geographic*? The one with the mesmerizing eyes?"

"Of course. They just went back to try and find her again."

"Exactly. *That's* the kind of beauty this guy's wife had when I knew her – she was startling, unbelievably beautiful. The only difference was that Estella had a kind of tenderness in her face that wasn't there with the girl in the magazine. They found her, you know. Did you see what she looks like today?"

"She looks like an old woman," says Jessie.

"In her early thirties, but her face has turned hard like a piece of stone, and the beauty's completely washed out of it. This is what comes from a life of unrelieved brutality. Did you see what they had the idiocy to ask? They asked if she was happy!"

Jessie laughs. She has a softly honking kind of laugh, unforced and easy on the ear.

"She told them she'd never been happy," says Hoxford. "Maybe once, on her wedding day, but that was it. What an incredible story."

"And this is how you feel about this woman, Estella? Like we're not going there just for dinner. We're on some kind of expedition in search of lost beauty."

"That's exactly how I feel. It's uncanny, you know. Sometimes I think you're able to read my mind. Before I speak, you already know what I'm going to say."

Out of the corner of his eye, he watches her struggle to suppress a smile. To cover her happiness, she says the first thing that pops into her head.

"They have kids, this couple?"

"Oh, I don't know."

Then he allows some unbridled emotion into his voice.

"Who gives a shit whether they have kids or not?" he says savagely. "We're not going there to see their kids."

She gives him a goggle-eyed look.

"I was just wondering."

And with that, she turns her head to stare out the window the rest of the way.

They live in Riverdale, Donald Dambois and his wife, Estella. Hoxford can't remember what her maiden name was, though he'd known it well at one time. How he hates Riverdale, this depressing neighbourhood that's somehow transformed itself into one of the hottest real-estate markets in the city. It always seems dark to him there, with the same kind of darkness a forest has. And the houses, no matter how big or imposing, always have a dingy, ramshackle look. As if their roofs leak and basements flood. As if termites are boring through their foundations, and they're getting ready to collapse from the strain of it all.

The street he's looking for is lined with cars, so Hoxford has to park a couple of blocks away and they walk over. He in his immaculate leather bomber and Jessie in leather skirt, ice-blue stockings, and a possum jacket she's dug out of some rag-and-bone shop on King Street. Her spiked heels scrape the sidewalk as they stride along, and a young mother pushing a pram moves to one side to let them pass. Hoxford can see a baby crying, waving its tiny fists. Jessie begins to sing. A lullaby, but not so much to the baby, because she goes on singing when they're well past the pram. She's really singing to him, to Hoxford, her john.

Golden slumbers kiss your eyes,
Smiles awake you when you rise.

Her singing voice is flat and husky, but that she should even try, Hoxford finds amusing. No, gratifying might be a better way of putting it.

"The enduring charms of Sir Paul," he says.

"Thomas Dekker, actually. From the sixteenth century. Sir Paul's a real fucking kleptomaniac when it comes to song lyrics. For this, he just provided the musical setting."

The first time they went to bed, and once the sex was over, she made him a bet for fifty dollars. Completely coked out, she was sitting with her back against the headboard and the sheet pulled up to cover her breasts. She held one fist in the air with index finger extended and moved it back and forth, as if under-lining her words for emphasis.

"Give me the first line of any English poem, and I'll tell you the title and who wrote it."

"What kind of a game is this," he said.

"It's a game I like to play."

The moving finger underlined the sentence.

"But how do you know?"

"What?"

"That I know any poems at all?"

She stared at him without saying anything. He could tell she wasn't stumped. She was just taking her time answering.

"Well, you read. There's at least one book in every room in this apartment, including the kitchen and the shitter. So – fifty bucks says you can't stump me."

He did read, if only because it gave him an advantage in court. In training himself as a young lawyer, he'd found there was nothing like a well-timed quote from Shakespeare or Milton or Frost to turn a juror's head. But it surprised him she'd noticed the books. He had no bookshelves because he didn't like the clutter they attract. Often when he'd finished with a book, he threw it out. Or if he thought it might be useful for reference, he put it in a banker's box in his storage area.

That night, he played her game for a while and then pre-tended to grow bored with it all. Actually, he was dumbfounded. She nailed every single poem, even one of the more obscure sonnets from the *Astrophel and Stella* sequence.

"Quite the trick," he said as she was leaving, and handed her an extra fifty-dollar bill, red and crisp. She grinned and licked her lips when she took it from him.

The door opens as soon as Hoxford knocks, as if they've been waiting in the foyer. Three of them standing there with arms around each other, Donald, Estella, and a kid who looks to be six or seven years old. All three are smiling, as much, he thinks, to encourage each other as to greet their visitors. Estella's hair, which had been lush and black as midnight, has gone grey before its time, and not just in streaks but completely. It has a brittle look. So does her face, which bears all the long-term and contradictory marks of pride, resignation, courage, and depression.

"Hello, you two," says Donald.

Estella and the boy make what can only be described as signs of welcome. They're both stone deaf.

Hoxford doesn't trust himself to look at Jessie until he's shaken Donald's hand and kissed Estella on both cheeks. He introduces Jessie as a friend of his. It's amusing to see that for the first time in their acquaintance he's managed to engineer a situation in which she, usually so self-contained, feels perplexed, uncertain of what to do next. And now – the real payoff – Donald and Estella perceive Jessie's surprise and realize Hoxford hasn't prepared her. They're embarrassed for Jessie's sake, and this intensifies Jessie's own embarrassment, but it also mitigates – without eradicating completely – their dismay that Hoxford would bring a girl like her to their home, because they can see at once what she is. The waves of discomfort wash back and forth, but Hoxford himself remains unperturbed, taking from the others' difficulties the exquisite pleasure of the connoisseur. The only wrinkle to his satisfaction is the little boy, who can't take his eyes off Jessie. He stares at her so intently Hoxford wonders if a kid that young can already feel something like lust for a beautiful woman.

In the living room, while they're all still making their adjustments, Estella takes the two jackets to put away. As she's walking out, Hoxford sees her stroke the possum fur and press it to her nose. Immediately, and against his better judgment, he feels a surge of tenderness for this woman he hasn't seen in twenty years. Imbedded in the tenderness, perhaps because it strikes him so unexpectedly, is the faintest hint of fear.

Jessie is crouching on her heels in front of the child.

"What's your name, buster?" she says.

He spells out something with his fingers and makes an urgent sound in the back of his throat.

"I'm Sean," says Donald, the translator.

"Oh, that's a fine Irish name. Is your mum Irish?"

"I don't think so," says Donald as Sean signs. "She's Canadian."

Jessie laughs and pushes herself upright.

"Well, whatever. I have a sentimental attachment to that name. My first boyfriend's name was Sean."

Hoxford can hardly believe his ears. What a laugh, he thinks. Her first boyfriend was probably a gangbang.

Estella comes back into the room. She's signing to her guests, asking what they would like to drink.

"Oh, here, we brought some wine."

She takes the bottle, presses it to her breast, and points at it.

"It'll be warm by now," says Hoxford. It's probably fine, but he would like something stronger for an aperitif.

"Then what would you like?"

Jessie says Coke, and the boy signs and Donald says, "Me too."

There is laughter, then the boy points at Jessie and makes a fanning motion with his fingers. Estella laughs in a way that puts Hoxford's nerves on edge.

"You're gorgeous," says Donald to Jessie. There's something in his voice that makes it plain he agrees with Sean's assessment. "You look just like a peacock."

Jessie beams and mugs a little. She has the rare quality of knowing how to take a compliment, and it's clear she finds the kid charming.

Hoxford steals another look at Estella, whose eyes are flashing between Donald and Jessie. She's thinner than he remembered, the bloom of youth vanished for good some time ago. She looks a little used up, quite frankly, a trifle worn out. No one would describe her as ravishing now, or as a peacock for that matter. At most, they'd say she's handsome, and Hoxford has always felt that to be a truly sterile term when applied to a woman.

He still hasn't said what it is he wants to drink, and when Donald presses him, he parries with a laugh. He uses laughter as a weapon, Hoxford does: (a) offensively, to ridicule people; (b) defensively, to keep them at bay.

"Oh, anything. Whatever you're having."

Donald nods at Estella, as if answering a question she asked before their guests arrived. When she goes to make the drinks, they settle themselves, Donald on one sofa and Hoxford and

Jessie on another, with the little boy perched on a Windsor chair. As Jessie sits, her skirt does what it was designed to do, it gets out of the way of her thighs. Donald's face goes as red as that day in the record store.

Jessie and Sean get their Cokes in highball glasses with plenty of ice, and Hoxford and Donald each get two fingers of Scotch in an old-fashioned glass, neat. Estella hasn't fixed herself anything. She's sitting there with folded hands and a bored look, as if attending a concert or religious service.

"Well, I was going to make a toast," says Hoxford. "But if you're not joining us, I'll refrain."

She shrugs and makes a wiping motion in front of her face. The meaning is so obvious, Donald doesn't bother to say anything and for a moment there's just the silence.

"You don't care for Scotch?" Hoxford persists.

A little exasperated, she holds up both hands and signs.

"I like it," says Donald – he's obviously said this before – "but it doesn't like me."

Getting her into bed had been much easier than Hoxford had thought it would be, and that was the main reason why: she turned out to be something of a lush. He'd invited her over for dinner – he had his own apartment by then, the year after he'd been in residence with Donald – and as soon as he saw how quickly she drank her first glass of wine, he knew he was in, in like Flynn.

His candle days, he called that time of his life, if only because it seemed like every time he fucked a girl, it was done to candlelight. There were seventeen candles on the mantel of the false fireplace the night Estella came over. He got her to help him light them all, like it was a game they were playing. They'd already finished the first bottle of wine by then, and when he turned off the overhead light, the candles flared, shadows conquered the corners of the room, and Estella made an appreciative noise deep in her throat.

He fixed *poulet Marengo*, a dish that was hard to screw up but never failed to impress. At table, in fact all night long, he did the talking for both of them, and there was very little blank time, very little time when you couldn't hear his voice going or both of them laughing. Sometimes he would tell a story that she would follow with both hands, as if she were translating for herself. At others he would ask a question and answer it himself, and she would indicate whether she agreed with the answer or not. If not, he would answer it again until he was able to phrase in his own words what she was thinking. By the time they got up from the table to dance, they'd killed three bottles. He hoped she wouldn't be sick later and then thought, what does it matter if she is?

Estella stood on his shoes in her stockinged feet, and, as much as he could, he moved his feet in time to the music she couldn't hear – some bitter, depressing ballad by Sarah Vaughan – and she rested her head against his chest so she could feel him humming. When the song was over, he stopped humming, stopped moving his feet, and she went up on tiptoe to be kissed.

Before going into the bedroom, they put out the candles one by one. When she blew at the first, spittle coated her lips, and she giggled and gave him a sneaky, sidelong look. He could see how drunk she was. "Wait," he said, and opened a cupboard beneath the mantel. He took out two brass snuffers, handing her one and using the other himself. She enjoyed that, pressing the brass cap over the flame and holding it there for a moment. One by one, it got a little darker in the room, the grey smoke rising from each dead candle and fading. There was the heavy smell of burnt wicks, and by the time they were finished, it was completely dark. When he took her by the hand, she squeezed so hard it made him realize how frightened she was.

Donald is using the word *indulgence*. Single malts are the one indulgence he permits himself. He goes to tastings and every so often springs for a bottle. The peaty ones are his favourites, just those that nobody else likes very much. Hoxford holds his glass to his nose, and the scent of iodine digs in.

"Scotch and books," he says.

He means that his host has more than one indulgence. The walls of the living room are lined with bookcases that Donald probably made himself. They're all stuffed to overflowing and many of the books look like they're falling apart. The spines are cracked and you can see yellow pages of foolscap sticking out, no doubt covered with Donald's painstaking notes. How can anybody read like that? thinks Hoxford. Where's the enjoyment?

"There's a big difference between an indulgence and a passion," says Donald.

So, he can feel passion for a book? Paper, ink, and glue – this is all it takes? What about other people? What about women and their living flesh? Book collecting has nothing to do with passion, Hoxford's sure of that. It's nothing but an escape from everything passion signifies.

In bed with Estella, he discovered he was the first to get there. This surprised him. He'd assumed anyone so beautiful would be more experienced. There was plenty of blood. In the bathroom mirror, he stared at himself, smearing it up from his groin over his belly. Womanly blood, he thought. She wasn't a girl anymore, thanks to him. He even tasted it, the blood from her torn hymen, before washing and returning to bed priapic. They had sex again, then fell asleep facing each other, her wine-sour breath on his face. As he was drifting off, he felt her take his hand in both her hands, cupping it, the way a kid would hold a grasshopper or cricket. This is something different, he thought, and then he was off. In the morning he found his hand still imprisoned. He wondered if this had something to do with her deafness, as if she were stilling an organ of speech, the better to sleep.

Once they were up, it was painful trying to get her to leave, and he avoided her from then on. Not that he didn't like her, quite the opposite. But really – a deaf girl? And if they had kids, wouldn't they all be like her? The thought of such need and imperfection was more than he could bear. Better to end it as soon as possible, before the complications multiplied themselves.

"How many children do you have?" says Jessie. She's looking at the photographs on the mantel above the fireplace.

The question irritates Hoxford, and he takes a good shot of the medicinal-tasting Scotch.

"Four including Sean, who's by far the youngest."

Sean and Estella are both signing, and then Sean's hands keep working after his mother's stop.

"William will graduate from university this year, and his sisters, the twins, have just started. They can all hear perfectly, but Sean and Estella have taught them to sign and they've become quite good at it. Especially Marcia. In fact, she wants to work with the hearing impaired after she graduates."

"That's wonderful."

"Is it?" Hoxford mumbles.

Jessie gives him a warning look. For the first time this evening, the little boy moves his eyes from Jessie to him. For some reason, Hoxford is touched by Jessie's look, by her concern for social decorum, and he remembers how much he likes her at times.

"This is an Islay, isn't it?" he says to Donald.

Sean makes a quick questioning motion with his hands, and Hoxford knows what he is asking without being told. It's like with French – he can follow the conversation of children but with adults he's lost.

"What did you say?" says Donald.

"You heard me."

"I did, but Sean couldn't make it out. Your mouth hardly moves when you speak, and that makes it difficult to lip-read. Especially when you're using unfamiliar words."

Hoxford shrugs to indicate he couldn't care less. He assumes the kid won't have any trouble understanding that.

Dinner is lasagna, Caesar salad, and a ready-bake loaf of Italian bread, the sort you find in a supermarket's freezer. They didn't go to any trouble, thinks Hoxford. Then as he begins to eat, he's transported. Not in the sense of having a fine culinary experience, but back in time to the days when he was avoiding Estella, the days when he could have had her for the asking. Whenever people got together back then, lasagna was the meal of choice, the easiest thing to make for a crowd and always the best.

There's a decent Chianti to go with the food, and even Estella allows herself a glass. The wine puts colour in her cheeks, but she still looks old, he thinks, older than she should. Hoxford finds himself wishing she'd let herself get a little drunk. Maybe then he could recognize something in her face that's survived from her youth. Maybe then she would look him in the eye, which she's avoided doing all night.

How enduring shame can be, he thinks. From a lush she'd gone to being an out-and-out slut. He kept track in a notebook he filled with reflections on the different women he'd bedded. From what he was able to determine, in the year after him, she'd been with at least eight different men. That was a lot for anybody. Anybody but a pro like Jessie.

Then, the next year, she stopped drinking, stopped fucking around, and her life stabilized. She was shacking up with Donald, and it was obvious to Hoxford – to everyone, really – that the two of them were made for each other. For one thing, Donald was the first of her men to learn sign language. Hoxford knew it was stupid, but as soon as he realized she was happy with someone else, he began to want her again. For years he dreamed about her, and in his dreams she could speak perfectly and for some reason that in itself – that she could talk in his dreams – made him understand what a fool he'd been to turn his back on her.

Hoxford's plate is empty. He realizes that the dinner talk, which surrounded and included him when they first sat down, has adjusted to his distraction and moved on. The other four are having a high old time without him. Donald has stationed himself at the head of the table, with Estella on his right and Jessie on his left. Sean is beside his mother and Hoxford beside Jessie. Sean's concentration on Jessie is so intense it's as if he's chainsawed a line across the table, cutting Hoxford out of the conversational round. This doesn't bother Hoxford in the least. In fact, it amuses him that this dull, underachieving, middle-class family has allowed itself to be enchanted by a young prostitute.

Sean collects the dinner plates, while Donald makes coffee. Estella has done everything else, and now she's relaxing. Sean brings her an ashtray and a leather cigarette purse that he opens by pressing a snap. He hands his mother a cigarette, pinching it by the filtered end, and lights it for her, his tongue stuck between his lips in concentration. As she draws back, she smiles her thanks. Finally, Hoxford sees something familiar – or *reminiscent* might be the better word – in her face, her eyes glazing with pleasure as she inhales. She looks at Jessie and points with her cigarette at the ashtray.

"Yes, I would," says the younger woman, and the two of them laugh, the one so pleasant sounding, the other hampered and abrupt. When Jessie takes a cigarette from her purse, Sean springs up to light it for her. Donald brings in coffee on a tray.

"Lovely," says Jessie each time he puts a cup on the table. "Lovely" four times, and when Sean gets a glass of milk, "I bet you'd like another Coke instead."

"No more Coke for Sean. He's addicted to that dreck, and if he has one after dinner, he won't go to sleep."

"Well, I'm a caffeine addict too, Sean," says Jessie, and the boy blushes with pleasure. "Only my beverage of choice is coffee."

"The last respectable addiction," says Donald.

"It really is, isn't it? I've noticed that writers, for one, tend to be coffee addicts."

"Whoever said writers were respectable people?" Hoxford expects to get a laugh from the line, but neither Donald nor Jessie pay him any mind.

"Do you do any writing yourself?" Donald asks her. His voice has taken on the considerate, careful tone one uses on a first date. Hoxford looks at Estella, who is staring at the ashtray while she smokes but seems to sense what each person is saying.

"Oh, I guess you could say I keep a journal."

"Really." Donald can't keep from giving Hoxford a look. "Well, I'm sure it's full of interesting material. Who are your journal-keeping mentors, if you don't mind me asking. I assume Anaïs Nin, for one?"

"Well, I don't know. Do you really find her all that interesting?"

"Well," says Donald and stops. It's obvious what he means. He means to say: No, but then I'm not a woman.

"I've read Kafka's journals and John Cheever's. And the notebooks of Georges Bernanos, the guy who wrote *Diary of a Country Priest*. If I've got to have mentors, I guess those are them."

"I'd say they're some of the best. But good God, do you mean to tell me young people still read Bernanos?"

"I don't know about everybody else," says Jessie. "But I do. And talk about a coffee addict. That guy set the standard."

"Well, I salute you." Donald raises his cup and sips from it. "But when did they finally get around to translating his *Cahiers*?"

Jessie stares at him before replying. Only Hoxford can tell how much she is savouring the moment.

"As far as I know, they haven't."

Hoxford watches Estella look at her husband from beneath her brow, watches several thoughts play out across Donald's face before he resigns with a smile and says nothing. Hoxford himself finds this all highly amusing.

"You really are the eighth wonder of the world," he tells Jessie.

She gives him that special look, the steady, sidelong stare. For a moment it's as if they're the only two people in the room, and he can feel her resistance crumbling. Why would he bring me here, she's asking herself, if he didn't really like me? Then he completes his thought.

"An educated whore."

Silence envelops them all. Out of the corner of his eye, Hoxford can see the little boy make that questioning motion with his hand – What did he say? Estella puts her hand over Sean's and stills it, then brings it to her lap and holds it in both of hers. For the first time all evening, she looks Hoxford in the eye, but there's nothing to read, for him in hers, nothing but indifference and the inability to understand what he's doing there.

Outside again, Jessie refuses to go back to the condo with him. At the same time, she makes it clear she wants her money. Hoxford finds this not just amusing, but downright funny. He walks along the street to the car and she pursues, making her demands.

"I haven't had sex yet," he reminds her.

"You got your sick, twisted pleasure, though. Quite enough of that for one night."

"Not the sexual kind, and that's what you get paid for."

She grabs at his elbow and pulls him around. It's dark out now and the haloes of the streetlights are alive with moths and mosquitoes. Jessie jerks her head at a building across the street. It looks like a meeting hall for some sort of evangelical sect, and the parking lot beside is empty and unlit.

"What do you want me to do, give you a blow job in the parking lot?"

He waits just long enough to assure himself this is a genuine offer, then reaches in his pocket and holds up the pre-arranged wad of cash. Her face has gone flinty with anger and contempt. She snatches the money and only then starts to cry, and he stands there for a while, watching her wobble off down the street on those spiked heels, her shoulders hunched and arms around herself as if to hold in the sobbing. She'll age now about as quickly as that girl in Afghanistan, he thinks, the one who had never been happy, except maybe once on her wedding day. That's the part that kills Hoxford – that the girl said "maybe" even about that.

MATT SHAW

Matchbook for a Mother's Hair

Where do I start, my name is Gordon Ween.

I am seventeen and three-quarters. Three-quarters is three fingers out of four fingers, or three fingers over four fingers. Seventeen means that I have seventeen wholes – which I learned is seventeen groups of four fingers out of four fingers.

Mother played cards. There was Mrs. Baker, Mrs. Gingrinch, and Mrs. Lowell. In the afternoon, at a table in my house, they played Yuke Her. I do not know how to play Yuke Her but I watched them every afternoon. When they played they tried to yuke each other, Mother and Mrs. Baker would look at the numbers they held in their hands and add them up and sort the pairs, and Mrs. Lowell leaned over Mrs. Gingrinch and then leaned back and then someone would lay cards down and Mrs. Lowell mumbled a dirty word and Mother scolded her, not in front of Gordon, don't say those things in front of Gordon, she said. Then the cards were down and Mrs. Lowell and Mrs. Gingrinch would be happy. On the table were cards with coloured shapes and unhappy faces, the shapes of shovels and hearts.

The house? The house was my house. The table was round and pretty, there were red flowers with thick stems on it in a bowl. It was an eating bowl, not a flower bowl. It was low and wide, for soup, but Mother always cut the stems and sat the petals in the bowl so there was no stem. They were coloured little heads, especially when they were tulips, and they got darker and darker until they curled and new heads were on the table for Yuke Her. As the heads turned dark and sad their smell eroded and the bowl dried out. There were four black chairs around the big table, but my chair was by the window looking at the four big chairs. The window drapes were the colour of hedges and there were no dishes in the sink.

There were always bottles on the table, green with purple labels, and Mrs. Gingrinch always laughed when she said we almost don't need the flowers on the table, these bottles are flowers themselves and make us bloom when we drink she said, and she giggled as she looked at me sitting in my chair.

My chair, I sat on a chair beside the table. It was my chair, I always sat in it, and it was red. It fit my back and Mother liked it because it always makes you sit up straight, Gordon, you never sit straight enough. People will not like you if you don't sit straight, Gordon, what will Mrs. Lowell and Mrs. Gingrinch think of you if you slouch, Gordon.

Oh no, Mrs. Lowell said, don't listen to her. You know I like you, you know how much I like you, I've shown you how I like you, you know that. She never said that when Mother was there, when Mother was there she said nonsense, Rette, you'll hurt the poor boy's feelings. Gordon is absolutely wonderful, we all love Gordon.

Did you know the pretty parts of flowers are the reproductive organs, said Mrs. Baker.

They're certainly more used than yours, said Mrs. Gingrinch, you're ugly.

I am not, said Mrs. Baker, her best friend.

Gordon, said Mrs. Gingrinch, don't listen to your mother. She's turning red because all day she loses all she has to us. Terrible. She's terrible.

Mother glared at her.

See, said Mrs. Gingrinch, she doesn't laugh at it because it's true, Gordon. Mrs. Baker and your mother never win together.

I don't cheat, and we win sometimes, said Mrs. Baker. It's not true.

You know it is, said Mrs. Gingrinch, you take from Rette too. I never won when I played with you, either. But Rette never stops playing with you and she never understands our faces.

I understand there's nothing else to understand in your faces, said Mother.

If you understood any faces, you would understand Mrs. Baker's, said Mrs. Gingrinch. Her face is so plain she cannot lie. Even when she puts on her mascara and makeup you know she is trying to hide her thoughts. When she tries to hide her thoughts you know exactly what they are. But you can't see that, said Mrs. Gingrinch, and we can so we win.

My face is not plain, said Mrs. Baker.

It is so, said Mrs. Gingrinch.

I do not wear makeup to hide things. I wear it to look pretty, said Mrs. Baker.

Hm, said Mrs. Gingrinch.

Mrs. Gingrinch and Mrs. Baker were best friends. They fought all the time at Yuke Her, Mrs. Baker accusing Mrs. Gingrinch of cheating and Mrs. Gingrinch calling Mrs. Baker too plain, she said a face that ugly should be much better at hiding things. Mrs. Baker is ugly, she looks like a squirrel I saw a dog catch from a tree. I would never say she looked like a squirrel from my chair because I wasn't supposed to talk from the chair I was supposed to watch for cheating.

If I talked Mother always told me to stop talking. Everything was good until I talked so I didn't. That's why I never said that Mrs. Baker looked like a fly I hit with a newspaper – it crawled on its broken legs – or that Mrs. Gingrinch sometimes farted when she took me upstairs every week to show me. Even though I knew what she wanted to show me I wanted to see again and I wanted to tell everyone at the table that all of them, except Mother, showed me the same thing all the time but only Mrs. Gingrinch smelled when she showed me, and I thought that was funny. They looked funny when they climbed on me to show me what they called love. When I talked it was never bad until Mrs. Gingrinch, Mrs. Lowell, and Mrs. Baker went home. Then Mother would drink more of the bottles with the purple labels and stand up.

Wait for me in your chair, Gordon. I mean it.

So I sat and didn't say no because it would make it worse.

There are reasons I ask you not to talk, Gordon, but you

didn't listen. You remember what we do every time you do talk when I tell you not to. I would never hurt you, Gordon, but you have to understand this, Gordon, even if it is the only thing you understand. You have problems, Gordon, but you're not a completely stupid boy.

For each thing I said while she yuked her friends she plucked one hair from my head and she tickled my face. Here's another one, she'd say. Her lighter was the colour of a fire engine like my chair. She held the hair up to my nose and flicked the lighter and held the lighter to the scared hair.

I do this for your good, Gordon. Other mothers will hit their kids, I only make you sit here and ask you not to talk. If you talk I make you smell your hair burning. This will teach you that I love you and will make you a smarter boy than you are. It could be worse, Gordon. Other mothers don't love their children but I love mine. We could be poor or we could die in a fire ourselves and smell like this, this is what you will smell like if you are on fire, said Mother. It could be worse. Fire would be worse.

What did it smell like? I do not like to remember, I like Mrs. Lowell, Mrs. Gingrinch, Mrs. Baker but mostly Mrs. Lowell.

Mrs. Lowell, Mrs. Gingrinch, Mrs. Baker never burned my hair. Mother never talked about burning my hair at Yuke Her. They drank and laughed and they looked at me with eyes that made me smell smoke and matchbooks when they lit their cigarettes and drank from the bottles. They played every morning and they finished before I was supposed to eat.

Mother did this on purpose. Gordon, she said, today I want you to walk Mrs. Baker home. Then you can eat your lunch, I will make you mashed potatoes and a sandwich, a tuna sandwich, dress warm it's snowing outside, she said. I don't like tuna sandwiches but I never said that I don't like tuna sandwiches because I'm not allowed to talk in my red chair, just watch for cheating. I walked Mrs. Baker or Mrs. Gingrinch or Mrs. Lowell home every day and we walked slowly so I would not have to eat the tuna sandwich until I got home and if it took longer then it would be longer before I ate the sandwich.

Mrs. Baker went home on Monday and Wednesday and Mrs. Gingrinch went home on Tuesday. I always walked fast with

Mrs. Baker because on Wednesday Mother would make me mashed potatoes and no tuna and I like mashed potatoes. Mrs. Baker is ugly and I do not like to walk with her anyway so I walk fast. On Thursday and Friday and Saturday I walked Mrs. Lowell home and Mother and Mrs. Gingrinch and Mrs. Baker stayed at the Yuke Her table and drank from the bottles all day. I walked slow on these days because I did not want to go back to the house when they had the bottles empty.

Who was first? It was Mrs. Lowell who first showed me things. That day we walked fast because Mrs. Lowell was walking fast and looking at the watch on her wrist. It was ten after twelve, which means that we had fifty minutes until one o'clock because there are sixty minutes in one hour and twenty-four hours in one day.

Why are we walking fast, I asked Mrs. Lowell.

Because, she said, I don't have too much time and there's something I need to show you. It's cold, Gordon. It's January. Aren't you cold?

It is wrong to be cold. Show me, I said.

I can't show you here but I will show you. It's a thank you for walking me home.

We are walking too fast.

If we are not fast I will not be able to show you because someone will come home. Besides it is very very cold and you are not dressed properly. Why does Rette not dress you better?

I did not know other people lived with Mrs. Lowell. I never heard about other people when they played Yuke Her. It was twelve-thirty when we got to her white house, which means we had thirty minutes to one o'clock. Inside she sat me at the kitchen table, I sat at a chair, a chair different from mine. It is not red but tall.

Can you show me what it is, I like surprises, I said.

She bit the corner of my ear her brown hair smelled like mangoes and she wore purple rings on her fingers ice, and there isn't any time, face icicles that fell from the roof as she touched me and shattered into pieces glass prisms her rings grey purple with red amethysts she moaned I screamed she took me upstairs to the bed lie there and don't move, there isn't any time, don't move the bed shook I shook isn't any time I never felt it before it was powerful as the hairs lit in my face does my mother do this do this I screamed don't move she screamed Mother doesn't do this to me and we both moved and then the hair split and the clock on the bedside table wasn't counting anymore and then there wasn't any time and she sped up and then I didn't move and it was finished and there wasn't any more time and I didn't move.

I didn't talk because I didn't want to make Mrs. Lowell angry. She was not angry she was glowing and her mouth did not smell so dirty now, so much like the smoke when she was in Mother's house. She was on her back on the green sheet the colour of hedges. Her feet were sweating. She smelled like mangoes and cigarettes.

Do you know what that was, she said.

I did not want to answer because I did not want to be wrong. I don't know anything.

Did you like what I showed you, she said.

She put her hand on me and rubbed her palm against me and said you are very good. I just wanted you to lie still and you did and it was wonderful. You made me feel so good.

Your feet are sweaty, I said.

Next time we walk home I will show you something else, she said. You can never tell your mother that I show you things. She wouldn't understand and then I couldn't show you anymore. You have to be quiet. You have to go because Mr. Lowell will be home soon and you can't be here when Mr. Lowell gets here.

Her feet were moving and rubbing me. The smell of mangoes was flying out of the window and Mrs. Lowell made the clock move again.

We are lovely and beautiful but your mother has never understood lovely and beautiful. She understands nothing about faces.

I wanted to leave.

No, she was not the only one, the other women at the game too. Mother told me to walk Mrs. Gingrinch home. It was winter still. Mrs. Gingrinch never said she was going to show me anything and we walked slow so I did not know anything.

Mrs. Gingrinch lives in a small house with a garage. It is white with tiny windows. The curtains are the colour of toothpaste, red white green, you can see them through the window. The shutters are blue. It was so pretty I wanted to go inside.

Are we going inside, I said.

No, we are going to go in the garage.

I'm cold, I said, I'd like some hot chocolate inside.

No, sweetie, you can't go inside. Mr. Gingrinch is upstairs in bed, sick. You can't come inside, Gordon. But you can come warm up in the garage before you go home. We can sit in the car. The garage will be warm. You like cars, all boys like cars.

The garage was not pretty. There wasn't anything there I wanted to see and it was grey and the car was too small for my knees.

I said, I don't fit, my knees are too big. Why can't I have any hot chocolate and then she touched me, like Mrs. Lowell. This is different now it knows she pulled the seats back and climbed on top and it was noisy the sounds of saws and wood the sound of pain and work and effort and the vice clamps closed and it was noisy and she moaned and I screamed and it was nothing new but it was and she said move, why aren't you moving so I moved a little but the car was too small for me to move and she moved more than me it hurt like a saw might hurt like a nail like a chain like a lawnmower on my belly and "me" parts and I screamed and she screamed louder and all I wanted was a hot chocolate and it was the sound of work and effort it was all sounds and Mr. Gingrinch was in the house somewhere and then she started making farting noises and she said don't laugh don't stop and it was the sound of work and effort and a lawnmower on my me parts. When she was finished showing me she fell asleep in the back seat and I sat beside her watching the clock in the garage. It was ten after one, which meant there were fifty minutes until two o'clock.

Now when they played Yuke Her it was different to me. Mrs. Baker was still ugly, Mrs. Gingrinch still called Mrs. Baker ugly. Mother still drank and burned my hair under my nose after the women left. A horrible smell, like Mrs. Gingrinch's smells but the same the same.

Rette, that's cheating, said Mrs. Lowell. She slammed the cards on the table.

I am not cheating, said Mother. I made my own son watch to show there is no cheating. If I was cheating Gordon would've said something, wouldn't you, Gordon.

I didn't say anything. If I did Mother would burn hair under my nose.

That doesn't matter, said Mrs. Gingrinch, you're taking advantage of us, you and Mrs. Baker.

I don't know what's going on, said Mrs. Baker.

That's because nothing is going on, said Mother.

That's because you're ugly, Mrs. Gingrinch said.

I'm not ugly, said Mrs. Baker.

Mother knocked the flower heads on the floor and the low wide bowl broke into pieces. Mrs. Gingrinch shook a bottle with a purple label shouting this is ridiculous, this is ridiculous while Mrs. Lowell bent over to pick up the shards of the vase.

Don't get up, Gordon, she said, you'll hurt your feet.

Get up, Gordon, and clean your mess, said Mother.

Gordon should do the work, said Mrs. Gingrinch to Mrs. Lowell. He never does anything, he just sits there.

Why should he do anything, said Mrs. Lowell, this is not his fault he is not his fault. You leave him alone, it's not his fault who he is.

I walked Mrs. Lowell home. It was snowing it was sunny. We walked slow but when we got there we went upstairs and Mrs. Lowell told me that I was so good at lying still, she liked it best when I lay still and she moved and I liked it that she liked it. I did not want to think about Mother burning my hair there is all the time in the world she screamed and I did not I know this know there is a pattern a nice pattern and I lie still there is all the time in the world but I still don't move the smell I notice most is Mrs. Lowell's feet and my sweat much more pleasant than Mrs. Gingrinch in the car and much better to look all the time in the world at than ugly Mrs. Baker and I screamed and that made her scream louder and louder and the more I lay still the more she moved and when she finished I was sure there was all the time in the world.

I liked that she liked it, I liked her better than Mrs. Baker. I don't want to tell you about Mrs. Baker, with Mrs. Baker it felt dirty it was not fun then, not fun or warm it was almost as bad as the fire and hair. Mrs. Baker never took me home, we just went to a park. It was so cold and I wanted hot chocolate but knew I wouldn't get any here.

Why, I don't want to talk about it. It's not special.

She threw herself under a tree, take me now, she said.

I didn't understand. She grabbed me and pulled me under. The snow was soft and cold under my knees. She had a green hood and that made it better but it was so hard the sun was on my back and the wind bit my face not warm with Mrs. Lowell not work with Mrs. Gingrinch just empty like the bottles on the Yuke Her table, empty like the numbers on the cards, empty like the lighter Mother owned it was too much work and she screamed a little bit but I never said anything I knew I was doing it now and it was just doing not like Mrs. Lowell Mrs. Baker was not anything she was like Mother said ugly people are empty inside it was hard I knew what I was doing but it was empty.

I did not like when Mrs. Baker did that with me, but not because she was ugly. She was ugly, but she was empty. Mrs. Gingrinch was empty too, Mother was empty, Mrs. Lowell was not empty. And when it happened again every day it never felt better with Mrs. Gingrinch or Mrs. Baker, it felt awful and wrong, like cheating at Yuke Her.

When they played Yuke Her now it was awful. They were always fighting. I sat and did not talk while Mother and Mrs. Lowell, Mrs. Gingrinch, Mrs. Baker threw the flowers and the bottles and screamed and it was horrible and when it was all over I didn't get tuna anymore. They didn't talk about me but they looked at me when they fought and I sat with my hands on the knees of my pants in the red chair at the window. Mother kept shouting at me speak Gordon you son of a bitch tell them I am not cheating I just want to win and win. I win, everyone gets angry with me you dumb shit, you retard, speak.

Rette, not in front of Gordon, said Mrs. Lowell. It's your own fault for cheating.

Mrs. Baker said, I'm not cheating, Rette, it's you, I'm sick of losing with you.

Mother hit Mrs. Baker and she had the same look on her ugly nose she had when I finished at the park. I said that's the same look you had at the park and Mrs. Baker looked at me with scared eyes but no one else heard me. Mother threw the bowl at Mrs. Lowell and hit her in the face. The flowers fell everywhere on the floor and Mrs. Lowell screamed a different scream. Blood came through the fingers on her face and ran down her and she put it in her hair when she tried to push the hair off her face. She left with the trail of blood. Mother stopped and Mrs. Baker cried and Mrs. Gingrinch had her hair in a mess.

I walked with Mrs. Gingrinch. I did not want her, I wanted Mrs. Lowell but now Mrs. Lowell would never come back again she would never have a face again. It was not mine but it was pretty and she was better than Mrs. Gingrinch or Mrs. Baker. Mrs. Lowell.

I was angry. At the house we went to the garage. I did not want hot chocolate. She pulled me into the car and started up the engine. There was the sound of the radio. Mr. Gingrinch is upstairs, sick, asleep, she said. I told him someone was coming to fix the car today there could be as much noise as she wanted. She said she really needed it now. I was angry and I wanted to hurt her, she was so mean and empty as empty as Mother.

I touched her first. She moaned and she touched me back you are going to move she said to me that is wonderful and I moved I was so angry I was like nails a saw a car engine and she scratched my back and bit my ear and I moved I moved I moved I did not lie still and I thought about Mrs. Lowell I wanted to cry I wanted to make Mrs. Gingrinch cry and scream and scratch me harder because I was moving after she told me not to but Mrs. Gingrinch was screaming and holding me all the time in the world because Mrs. Lowell would never come back it was two-thirty which means that there is forever before Mrs. Lowell comes back and tells me to be still. Her head moves everywhere and I grab hold of her hair it is three o'clock which means we have been in the garage for thirty minutes.

You were incredible, she said, you moved so much oh my God.

She fell asleep on the back seat and I started to cry I felt so bad. I don't know what I felt it was awful worse than the burning hair or Mother throwing the vase at Mrs. Lowell. I was so cold and empty, Mrs. Gingrinch and Mrs. Baker were so awful and empty. I got out of the car and closed the door softly and closed the garage door when I left so Mrs. Gingrinch could have her nap in the garage and I went to the park. When I got home Mrs. Baker was gone. Mother made me tuna but no mashed potatoes and she burned a whole patch of my hair in front of my face and screamed.

You were so bad today, Gordon, shame on you, don't you understand what you're doing, I asked you to talk and you didn't.

Mother, I don't know what to do, I cried, you hit Mrs. Lowell I am just supposed to sit by the window and tell you if people are cheating.

You don't even understand what you're doing you're a dumb boy, Gordon. A dumb boy and you don't even do well by me and if you don't do well by me then those women don't deserve your kindness, they're mean dumb bitches and we don't need them. You are a burden, Gordon, a mule. You are good for nothing more than watching your mother play cards and being stupid. Those women don't like you, Gordon, they wanted you to say I cheat all the time at Yuke Her.

I do not know what else to tell you. I do not know what else. I don't know why you keep asking me about Mrs. Gingrinch, Mrs. Gingrinch is empty. I don't understand you, why you ask me about what happened to Mrs. Gingrinch. This story is not Mrs. Gingrinch's story, it's Mrs. Lowell's. This is about Mrs. Lowell, where is she. I told you about Mother and my chair. The car you put me in never takes me home, I want it to take me home. Where is Mrs. Lowell, I told you about my chair.

KRISTA BRIDGE

A Matter of Firsts

Y our father's New York mis-
tress was the one you met. The exotic one. She used to say,
"'Balls,' said the queen. 'If I had two, I'd be king.'" That was her
expression, whether something irritated her, like losing her keys,
or whether there was a pleasant surprise, like one last piece of
birthday cake in the refrigerator. Balls, said the queen. Your
father tried to correct her usage. The phrase had exasperation in
it, he claimed, and was appropriate only as a response to something negative. She said, "Perhaps you're right," and smiled, but
you could tell she was not the type to capitulate in action.

Of course, it was not open to you that she was your father's
mistress, although you clearly knew, and they knew it. Your
father often went to medical conferences in New York, and he
couldn't tolerate hotels, their bed sheets gave him a rash, so he
stayed with her – Ella, an old friend from medical school. This
is what he told you and your mother, although there was an
impish smirk about him when he said so, a conspiratorial wink,
as if such patent untruths, and the acceptance of them, were in
keeping with the true spirit of family. Three times when you
were thirteen he took you with him to New York because your
mother had to look after your grandfather, who was in and out
of the hospital. Around you, they acted stiff and professional, no
sly looks or illicit touches. Of course, the minute you saw her,
you knew she was no doctor. It was the body that halted your
gaze. Unexpected: its creamy fatness, so graceful, so much itself,
that it challenged thinness everywhere. A fatness impossible to

reduce with euphemisms. A soothing romantic welcome. This body rolled out of itself. Said, I am the way to be.

She lived in the Bronx, on a quiet dead-end street lined with trees, in an old brick house with high ceilings and a rickety wood porch in the back. The air smelled like freshly cut grass and homemade shepherd's pie. On the other streets in her neighbourhood, the air smelled like fried food and smoke, traces of cumin and paprika drifting by on the breeze. You could hardly see to the sky. Everywhere you looked were apartment buildings with fire escapes zigzagging down the crumbling brick. There were groups of teenagers lounging on front stoops, yelling at each other in languages you didn't understand. Your father wouldn't even let you walk off Ella's street alone. Her house was big enough for a family of eight, but she lived there alone. She had bought it with her first husband, who had left at her request two years later, gladly signing the house over to her because he hated the way it felt empty no matter how much furniture they bought, the way their voices echoed in the large square rooms. He said that people start off with a backyard vegetable garden, not an acreage of farm; a marriage needed a small, fertile space in which to grow. Ella said to you, "There is no such thing as being prepared for marriage. I was prepared. But not that prepared."

She told you that she dated her husband for seven months, and then one night during a walk through the park, he got down on one knee and proposed. (This was an essential part of the story, the getting down on one knee. It exposed their romantic folly, the traditional gestures that failed to pan out into traditional emotions.) He had no ring at the time, and insisted that a store-bought engagement ring wouldn't be good enough for her. He would fashion his own with the minimal help of a jeweller. For the next two months, he drew up sketches hour after hour in his tiny apartment. He picked up pencils in restaurants and brainstormed plans on greasy napkins. Six months later, the ring still was not made or even in the works. The sketches had been abandoned and he said to her one day, "You don't really want an engagement ring, do you? It's such an extravagant expense." And she had said no, of course not, she was not an envier of diamonds.

They got married not long after, with plain gold wedding bands, and went on a honeymoon to Key West. It was on that honeymoon that she was reluctantly, forcibly, made aware of what the engagement ring incident just dimly foreshadowed. She and her husband went out to dinner one night to a restaurant that was dusty and poorly lit. It was on a narrow downtown street, a street with no other shops or restaurants on it, and there were flies on all the tables. Her husband was always on the lookout for the cheapest restaurant, always had an eye out for a deal. They ate the same dinner, the same food, crabs and black-eyed peas, but he was violently sick later and she was fine. They were sitting in the hotel room, and he was shivering, crouching on the bed with a blanket wrapped around his shoulders. Then he took off for the bathroom.

He was there for a long time and she was on the bed reading a book; she was absorbed and couldn't divert any attention from *Sister Carrie*. After a while, she thought maybe she should check on him to see if he was okay. What she saw, across the long, narrow bathroom, was her new husband naked, on all fours, vomiting into the toilet. He had all his clothes in a neat pile at the door, and he was naked and heaving. On all fours. She had the back view. She told you it shook the foundation of her belief in what she was doing, this perspective like an aerial view of his penis hanging down, his scrotum tightening each time he heaved. An aerial view. In every word he spoke after that, every touch of his hand, she saw the aerial view and, with it, the chipped affection, the shock of revulsion, the bitterness and fatigue – the detritus of a thirty-year marriage – piling at the door of their week-old union. She even made an unsuccessful attempt to book a plane ticket home. She saw the direction they were headed in, the headiness, the glorification, the dependence, then the genital views, the aborted optimism. The triumph of the unflattering. Only twenty-two and married for three days, she already knew that one corner of her marriage was over, the corner in which she stored hopes of rescue and release, where she still believed ecstasy could be a daily event. Before she left, her mother told her, "There are things that scare women on their honeymoons. No matter how long you've known him. There are things that will scare you and make you want to come home. You can't come home." She was prepared. But not that prepared.

This story, combined with her favourite expression, caused you to see her as a woman eminently concerned with balls. In those days, vulgarity and glamour were inextricable in your mind, bound together in all things attractive. There was nothing in these early exchanges about genitalia that troubled you. Already you had separated your relationship with her from her relationship with your father. The story about her honeymoon helped you understand why she liked your father, why being with a man as remote as him was freeing to her when it was only oppressive to you. But everything else about them was separate. To you, she said, "Love is a euphemism for lying. Falling in love is lying to yourself. You think you're falling in love with someone, but really you're falling in love with someone wanting you. Bear this in mind." And you did, for years and years.

The other thing you bore in mind for years and years was the first time you saw her, standing on the front lawn of her house under the shade of a willow tree, looking exactly the opposite of what you had imagined. As you sat next to your father on the plane to New York, you pictured a woman who always wore red pumps and silk dresses. You hoped for a cool elegance, a high-heeled woman rarely affected by heat. Shiny, straight hair. A doctor's air of presumption, that New York woman's mix of candour and detachment, deserving. It was July, and in fact the mistress was sweating so profusely that she looked as if she had just stepped out of the shower. When she looked at you, you could not help but smile. Married men do not introduce their children to their mistresses. You knew this. There is a wrong-ness about it – a cheeky, bald-faced wrongness – but somehow the mistress's fatness made it right.

"The gap between your front teeth is about the width of a cracker," the mistress said. Just like that, even before her name. She extended her hand palm down, as if waiting for a kiss.

The name Ella made you think of a beachy calm, sustenance and refreshment.

You could not stop smiling.

Leaning against the willow, she stared at you with mellow

concentration, as if she were holding a ruler up to that gap, approving of these places you broke off more than the places you stayed together. A look that transformed your plainness into something less neutral. You tried to imagine how she might be seeing you, but you could not settle on something reliable. Whenever you heard a recording of your own voice, you thought it sounded juicy and plump, like the voice of an ugly person. When you saw yourself in the mirror, you looked much wider and lumpier than you realized. This always disturbed you, not because you were less attractive than you hoped, but because of the constant misleading of self, the inaccurate cataloguing of your own value, the predictable return to foolishness. While Ella looked at you, you tried to stand erect and forthcoming, like someone open-hearted, yet discriminating. You worried she might just see a sogginess, a frizzing that wouldn't be tamed.

"Lovely," she said. "Just lovely."

On that perfect hot day in the honeyed laziness of air that doesn't move, at the age of thirteen, you learned what it might feel like to be memorized.

On one of the New York visits, you heard your father and Ella in her bedroom at two o'clock in the morning. It was the only time you ever heard them together. They didn't say much, but each sound was lined with erotic urgency, a moody pulse. The tender coercions of love. The mistress was a woman who knew how to say *baby*. Like she had thought things over, and it was the only word she could come up with.

You always thought of her as the exotic one. But why? It was more than the New York accent, which made you think of chipped teeth and long, black hair. It was more than the way she looked, the skin stretched to excess and the mop of sandy curls. She rode her bicycle, with its wicker basket on the front, everywhere she went, and despite her weight looked as nimble as a child, almost as if her weight helped her achieve balance, that Southern lady's sense of unhurried pace. These things you admired. They made her watchable. But the exoticism came from somewhere else. It seemed to you that she'd had so many lives before the one you knew her in.

On your first morning in New York, as you ate breakfast, she told you about the honeymoon with her first husband, about the aerial view.

"Men can do such things to you," she said. "You have to be so careful, careful not to let yourself go too much. Sex especially, honey, watch out. You're so young; your emotions will get involved. It's a matter of firsts. That's all."

She told you about how, as a child, she would lie behind the living-room couch all day. The sun shone down just so through the front window, and she lay there. Her sisters would fight over dolls and sweaters while demanding sandwiches and forming accusations, and her mother would come up with activities to keep the fighting to a minimum, arts-and-crafts activities like painting their own stained glass. Ella stayed away. She was that contented behind the couch. Only when communication was absolutely necessary did she send out word. She delivered notes through the dog. *I vote hamburgers for dinner. Would someone be so kind as to send a glass of water? It is not true that I got my math test back last week and failed.*

"I called him my own personal Purolator courier," she said. "He would take the notes in his mouth and drop them at my mother's feet."

Her second husband had been a photographer for *National Geographic*, and he had been to Africa, he had flown his own small plane over Kenya. You thought that she probably had no use, ultimately, for your father, and you greatly respected her for this.

You asked what it was like living in the house where she had planned a future with her first husband.

"The first week after he left, my furnace went out and I couldn't get a man in to fix it for a week. It was so cold that frost flowers were forming on the windows, and none of my blankets did the trick. I discovered when I was cleaning that my husband had forgotten just one belonging, his red sleeping bag in the back of the closet. So for all that week I had no heat, I wrapped it around my shoulders day and night. And I moaned and wondered if I'd made a mistake and I cozied up under that sleeping bag as if it were the man himself. After the furnace man came,

I cranked up the heat and sweated it all out. I put the sleeping bag back where I found it and haven't looked at it since."

She filled the copper kettle with water, passed her hand under the tap, sprinkled water on the burner, and relaxed against the counter as it hissed, as if that was the only end her story needed. "I'd rather be trampled by a horse than ground up slowly by nostalgia."

In the sunny kitchen, she was naked under a lace nightgown and you could see everything. You hadn't seen your own mother naked since you were four or five, but it took you no time to adjust to Ella's failure to cover up. There was your father's mistress in the kitchen cooking, and there was her entire body. Your father had once said about her, after an argument, "She's in fine form." And this hadn't made you think of debates at all, of feisty opinions and an unwillingness to back down. It seemed to refer to her body. Such fine form. She walked around, smiling at you from time to time as if she had no idea her nightgown could be seen right through. The rolls of fat like bread dough. You wanted to squish your hands in and feel the warmth. Your father had already gone off to his conference and he was gone all day. She made you an omelette, with brie, portobello mushrooms, tomatoes, and spinach.

"We need to fatten you up," she said.

You felt she was taking responsibility for you, tending to you. Normally, you picked at your food, and your father talked about how all the women in his family had no fat on them, they were as thin as could be. He said this with a bit of mocking, as if you were all silly for being thin, but it was clear that he was proud too, proud to be affiliated with this clan of rigorous, thin women. But you stuffed your omelette in quickly and asked for more. You wanted her to see that you were not like most people: you approved of fat, curbs of skin folding, one onto the next.

Ella's face was round and lineless. Your mother was bony and gaunt. She held her past tightly, refused to distribute childhood stories as entertainment. Although you made these comparisons, sitting in Ella's kitchen as she talked in her lace nightgown, they did not mean you saw Ella as a more desirable mother. That was not how you saw her.

A man knocked on the front door, and she reached into a closet in the kitchen and pulled out a bathrobe, wrapped it tightly around her before answering. So she must have been aware then, she must have been aware of all that could be seen.

You were just a child. How can it grip you even now, after all the men, the men and the years?

Later that first day, she took you over to a local outdoor swimming pool. She wore a wide-brimmed straw hat and didn't swim, but sat on a lawn chair waving to you when you looked her way. She was wearing another lace top, but this time she had a shirt on underneath. The pool was full of people, so you couldn't swim properly, but you tried your best to look as if you were cavorting around, having a good time. The sun was hot, beating down on the water so that it felt like a bath. There were no trees around, just a parking lot on one side of the pool, an apartment building on the other. You snuck looks at Ella and hoped she wouldn't notice. You took water into your mouth and streamed it out through the gap in your teeth.

You wanted to call out, "Come swim with me," but you hadn't the courage. She looked so serene in her straw hat.

When you were ready to get out, she wrapped a fluffy pink towel around your shoulders, then followed you into the change room, which was a large cement area with no private, curtained areas. You tried to change from your bathing suit into your clothes without showing your body and without looking as if you were hiding it from her. By accident, you dropped the towel when you went to put on your bra. It was your first bra, and you were not an expert at getting it on and off. So surprised were you to find yourself standing before her, watching calmly, that you simply stood there topless, exposing breasts you were barely familiar with yourself.

Ella said nothing at first. It occurred to you that all you would ever want from love was someone to call you *baby*, to say it at the lowest pitch of longing and regret.

Finally, looking at your stomach, she said, "You have a scar."

The year before, you had had your appendix out. The scar seemed new, still pinkish-purple. She leaned in and traced an index finger over the thin raised dash, still tender in the way that scars with a history never quite stop feeling tender. You hadn't let your stomach be seen since the nurse held your hand in the recovery room as you cried with anaesthetic nausea and unanticipated soreness, the awareness that something had been removed that could never be replaced.

But you stood there with Ella as her finger skimmed over your scar. You closed your eyes and held your wet bathing suit against your leg so that the water trickled down your thigh.

The fingers have a memory far longer than the mind's.

After dinner, your father wanted you to give a recital of your grade eight Royal Conservatory pieces. In her living room, Ella had an old Steinway grand piano, barely in tune, with heavy ivory keys. Your father always organized concerts of this kind, after elaborate family dinners on Christmas and Easter, mobilizing aunts and uncles and cousins and grandparents into the living room for an impromptu piano recital. For days before, he would hound you into extra practice, then on event day would find himself at the dinner table folding his cranberry-sauce-stained napkin, the thought occurring to him just then that they might all enjoy a musical interlude. You would play your pieces from List A through to List D, then the two studies, waiting after each for your family to clap obediently like a symphony audience, waiting, after the second study's final note, overdramatized with a pedal sustained too long, for the lone "Bravo" to issue from your father, standing in the doorway.

The same you did for Ella. Only she didn't clap, and even your father seemed embarrassed by his "Bravo" in an audience of two, as you kept your foot on the pedal and the sound of the final, off-tune A-flat of Study no. 3 hummed in the air.

"I'll teach you a real piece," she said. "Something worth knowing."

She nudged you off the piano bench and pulled from inside it the yellowing pages of Debussy's *La fille aux cheveux de lin* and set them before you.

"But it's grade nine," you objected.

"It's slow. You can learn it."

The following morning, after your father left, she went through it with you, telling you where to pedal and where to create the legato with just your fingers. She corrected you at the end, when you played the reprisal of the primary melody too loudly.

"Softly," she said. "As if contemplating."

You played it every hour on the hour twice, and when you performed it for your father on the last day of the visit, you let the music fall from the stand because your fingers held the tune.

On the second visit, you got the flu. You lay in bed sweating and shivering, and Ella took your temperature and murmured in concern. She blotted your forehead with a soft flannel blanket. Your temperature went up to 102, and Ella called your father at the conference hotel and got him out of one of his seminars. Over the phone, he suggested a cool bath. She came into the guest room and put a hand on your cheek. You opened your eyes but could barely see her because the window was at her back. There was just her silhouette, the sheer white curtains rippling around her.

"You need a cool bath," she said.

You stood and allowed yourself to be led to the bathroom. So weak you felt, so glad to be weak. She held your hand as if she was initiating you into something.

The bathtub was a large, claw-footed tub and the water in it looked clear except for specks of rust, barely visible. Dust floated in the stream of sun through the window. She undressed you then. You leaned against her as she pulled your nightgown over your head, as you stepped out of your underwear. You rested against her arm as she helped lower you into the tub.

You were sweating, and she turned on a fan and set it in the doorway.

"You'll have hot and cold on your skin now," she says. "You'll like it. I know your skin."

Ella kneeled and leaned against the white porcelain, wet her hands. She held you forward gently, your chest against her forearm, while she spooned cool water up over your back. Then she reached for the soap and held it gently while it glided over your back, as if it were soaping you itself. Lifting your foot, she rubbed her thumb along its bottom, and she worked the soap between her hands and made hills of lather along your arm. She hummed.

"I could wash your parts all day," she said.

She did everything for you. Soaping you with conjugal diligence, she held a wet washcloth against your forehead and made sure each part got as clean as the others. She cupped your foot as if she was measuring its exact weight. Then she rinsed you, making waves in the tub and letting the water lap against your breasts before she scooped it into a small wooden bowl and poured it over your head, shielding your eyes with her hand.

"There you go, baby," Ella said. "Clean as clean."

That evening you spent on the couch covered in an old afghan, afraid to be alone in your room because every time you closed your eyes, you could see, through the dark inside of your eyelids, enormous black birds with long, trailing wings gliding over your head. Ella made you chicken noodle soup from scratch, and you hoped that your father wouldn't arrive and make a fuss that you were spreading germs in the communal areas of the house. On the coffee table was an old photograph of a balding man with a younger, black-haired woman looking formal and legitimate in a wedding photograph beneath an overgrown oak tree.

"Who are they?" you asked Ella when she brought you a bowl of soup.

"My parents."

"They have a grumpy look about them," you said. "Like someone's forcing them to apologize."

"I suppose they do, don't they?" she said, looking at the picture curiously, as if she had just spotted in a crowd the person she was searching for.

Her mother was Canadian and had grown up in Windsor, she told you, and her father was an American living in Detroit, and they met when he was visiting relatives in Windsor for the summer. For their first date, they arranged to go see a matinee of *Guys and Dolls* across the river in Detroit. She had suggested meeting him at the drugstore on the corner of his street. She was liberated before women were liberated, Ella said. Also, she knew that making an impressive entrance meant more than just sweeping down the stairs while your date stood at the front door under the eyes of your father. She was a woman who knew her entrance. She did not go to the trouble of hot rollers and her bangs taped to her forehead all night for the sake of one mere boy. She dressed for her larger public. An entrance meant a bevy of turned heads; it meant all eyes, male and female, compelled to take her in; it meant the odd reverential whisper passed between strangers. And so she swung open the door of the drugstore and stepped inside and, agreeably, it was as busy as she had hoped it would be. She stood expectantly at the door, wearing a trench coat buttoned to her neck, the collar up around her throat, and the belt pulled as tightly as the need to breathe would allow. She registered Ella's father registering the turned heads, the hushed comments, and was satisfied. He announced that he had to drop a book at his aunt's on the way out of town, and off they went. Up in the old aunt's apartment, the heat was stifling, and the aunt repeatedly invited Ella's mother to remove her coat, and Ella's mother repeatedly refused. The aunt had set out cookies and tea, so they were obliged to stay for a time and be entertained. For half an hour, the aunt encouraged Ella's mother to take off her coat, and for half an hour she declined, until sweat was forming on her upper lip and beginning to drip down from her carefully set hairstyle. Finally they left, and in the car, Ella's mother took off her coat, right there on their first date, revealing that she had on only her bra and underpants. Then she rolled down the window and fanned her forehead, checked her hair for signs of humidity in the rear-view mirror.

"You see, back then, all the latest fashions were in the department stores in Detroit. You couldn't get them in Windsor. My mother thought she didn't have anything grand enough to wear to the theatre in Detroit," Ella said. "So she planned to go into the department store before lunch, buy a fancy new dress, and wear that."

Your father had come home from the conference halfway through her story, and stood in the doorway still holding his briefcase.

"It was a nicer time then, don't you think?" she asked. "You could take your coat off and let a boy see your bra and underwear and it wouldn't proceed to God knows what else. He wouldn't assume. That was probably the happiest time they ever had."

Your father set down his briefcase and shook his finger. "I thought we were against nostalgia."

"It's not nostalgia. It's just remembering," she said.

And they went into the kitchen and left you staring at the Steinway grand.

Is it nostalgia or remembering when you still play, twenty years later, *La fille aux cheveux de lin* without missing a note?

You never did feel that love enriched your life. Mostly all it did was remove the finer points of happiness.

Walking alone on a tree-lined, windy lane in the country. Floating on waves in Miller Lake, looking up at the cliff face. Lying in bed at night, preparing to sleep, preparing to stay awake.

There are experiences diminished by companionship.

It was your father who said this first, but it was a long time before you realized how true it was. He was going to the botanical gardens, and Ella wanted to go along. She hadn't been in years. He said she had to stay with you, you were too young to be left alone in a strange place. "She'll be fine," Ella said. "She's not a child." She looked at you gently, but regretfully, as if you alone were keeping her from something she very much wanted. They stepped into the next room, but you could still hear them.

"I prefer to see it alone." His voice made it clear that he had long since decided. You wondered if he had already moved on to the next one. Even then you understood that there is always someone ready to step into your place.

"We could experience it together," she offered.

"There are experiences diminished by companionship."

She came back into the room, looked at you, and delivered her expression, but this time sadly, without its usual bite.

"'Balls,' said the queen. 'If I had two, I'd be king.'" She rolled her eyes jokingly, but couldn't hide the sadness in them, in the downturn of her lips.

And even though she must have resented you, even just a bit, she was good to you when he left. She made iced tea and filled the glasses too full, so that when she dropped in ice cubes the liquid overflowed. She laughed as she mopped up the counters. You didn't blame her for wanting to go with him. Already, you understood how it must be to feel you'd give almost anything for half an hour alone with someone.

She took you to a park near her house. There was a small group of older Asian men and women practising tai chi on the grass. At the far end, there was an area of thick trees, and she led you toward it.

"This part used to be all trees. Then they cut them down. Here, it used to feel like a forest in the middle of the city. They were so thick, you could stand in the middle and it would be dark. The sun didn't come through. There are trees in there great for climbing. I'll wait out here on the bench. Go have fun."

Through the darkness of the heavy shade, you could see a tree with solid branches low to the ground, moving up the trunk as close together as steps. This tree you climbed and sat on a branch with a U-shaped curve like a seat. The ground was carpeted in rust-coloured pine needles and the air was dark and cool. You leaned against the trunk and looked out at Ella sitting on the bench, gazing across the park at something you couldn't see. That morning, you had sat on the toilet while she had a bath. She soaked for half an hour, running more hot water in when the water cooled. When she was ready to get out, she pulled the plug and stayed in the tub, humming, while the water got lower and lower. From where you were sitting, it looked like she was rising up to the surface of the water, floating there.

She gave you presents when you left New York. A collection of poems by e.e. cummings, a Bessie Smith CD tied with a purple ribbon, a plastic heart pendant, a stuffed walrus. Your favourite: a tarnished silver comb, embedded with tiny coral and amber stones, a family heirloom.

When you married your husband, you wore it in your hair. Something borrowed.

PASHA MALLA

The Past Composed

In the end, all the ruckus seems to be about a boy up Judy's tree. I stand there at the bottom, his backpack in my hand, looking up through leaves just starting to bleed the reds and browns of autumn. He's right near the top, this boy – a dark silhouette against the late afternoon sunlight, perched on a branch, shaking, terrified. Inside the house Judy's dogs are still going crazy.

"Hey there," I say, squinting.

"A squirrel chased me up here. I think it had rabies."

"Was it frothing at the mouth?"

"Frothing?"

"Yeah, like with foam coming out of its mouth."

The boy says nothing. The dogs have stopped barking, and the only sound is the dull, faraway hiss and hum of the city.

"You want to come down? I don't see any squirrels around."

He considers for a moment, evaluating the situation – or me, maybe. Then he swings down effortlessly, monkey-like, and lands with a dull thump on the lawn. His clothes seem to belong to someone years older: a Lacoste golf shirt and beige safari shorts, with a pair of blue socks pulled tightly up to his knees.

"All right?" I ask, and hand him his backpack. He's a funny little man, maybe eight or nine. There's something familiar, and vaguely cunning, about his face.

The boy stands there, scanning the front lawn, nervous. I look around too, then up at Judy's house, where I notice, wedged between a pink triangle and a MIDWIVES DELIVER! sticker, the Block Parent sign in the window.

"Oh," I say. "Do you want to come in?"

The boy eyes me, then the house. Eventually he nods and replies, "Okay."

I lead him inside, where the dogs greet us with an inquisitive sniff before letting us through to the kitchen. The boy edges by them, saying, "Good dogs," a gleam of terror in his eyes. I pour him a glass of milk and we both sit down at Judy's tiny kitchen table.

"You know," I say, "next time you get a squirrel after you, best place to go probably isn't up a tree."

"I came to the door first, but there was no answer."

His glass of milk sits untouched on the chipped Formica tabletop. "You got a name?"

"Pico," he tells me, kicking at the chair with his heels. "Are you even a Block Parent?"

"No, no. That's the lady who owns the house. My sister, Judy."

"So who are you?"

"I live back there." I point out through the kitchen window at the shed in the backyard.

"What?" Pico snorts. "In that thing?"

I tap his glass with my fingernail. "Drink your milk, Pico."

By the time Judy gets home, I am making dinner and Pico has left. He thanked me for the milk, then disappeared down the street.

Judy appears in the kitchen, the dogs sniffling eagerly behind her. She slings her purse onto the table and sits down. "Fuck," she sighs. The dogs settle at her feet.

"I've got ratatouille happening here, Jude, and there's tabbouleh salad in the fridge."

"No meat? *Pas de viande!*" Judy, bless her, is trying to learn French.

"Sorry."

"Christ, Les," she huffs. "You're starting to make me feel like one of those crazy vegan dykes – living on nuts and fruits and berries like a goddamn squirrel."

I laugh and tell her about Pico.

"*Pico?* What is he, a Brazilian soccer player?"

"No," I say, stirring the ratatouille, recalling the boy's face. "He looks more like a mini Richard Nixon."

Judy smiles and points at the classified ads I've left on the table.

"Any luck?" she asks.

"Nothing yet."

"Not that I want you gone." She has a grave look about her suddenly. "I mean, you're welcome here as long as you need to stay."

"I know, Jude," I tell her, sprinkling some salt into the pot. "Thanks a lot."

After dinner I head out into the backyard and work until dusk. The table I'm redoing right now is some cheap pine thing I picked up for forty dollars at a garage sale. But with the right stain, corners rounded off, and a good number of chips whittled out of the legs, it'll go for close to a grand in one of the antique stores uptown. I can just imagine some family huddled around it for supper – Mom in her apron doling out fat slices of meat loaf, Dad asking the kids about school, and this sturdy old table anchoring it all like the centrepiece of a Norman Rockwell painting.

Soon it's too dark to see much of anything, so I head inside my little cabin. Before I moved in at the end of the summer, Judy did a nice job fixing it up for me; she put down rugs and painted the wallpaper a quiet beige colour, even brought her fish tank out and set it up in the corner. It's an A-frame, this thing. Like a tent. At first it seemed claustrophobic, but it's turned out pretty cozy.

The fish are good to watch. There are three of them, all the same species, although what that would be, I have no idea. But there's something soothing about them, these shimmering, fluttering things, all silver glitter in the light of the tank.

We always talked about getting a cat, Rachel and me. But we figured we'd try fish first, and if they didn't die right away, we'd chance it with a cat. But less than two months after we moved in together, before we'd even had a chance to go fish shopping, Rachel got pregnant.

At first having a baby seemed too big, too adult, too far removed from the safe little niche we'd carved for ourselves. But once we got talking to Judy, started considering her as our midwife, things began to take shape and make sense. At night, in bed together, Rachel and I would lie with our hands on her belly, talking about the future, how one day we'd look back on our apprehension and laugh. But I guess everyone constructs, at some point, these perfect versions of how things are going to be.

A week or so later, I'm in the backyard, down on my knees sanding the table legs, and Pico appears at the gate.

"*Hola*, Pico," I holler. "Come on in."

Pico reaches over the fence, flips the latch, and moves across the yard toward me, plucking an old seed dandelion from the grass on his way. Today is chillier; he's in a mauve turtleneck and a pair of pleated jeans. Pico leans up against the table, twirling the dandelion in his fingers. He lifts it to his mouth, sucks in a great mouthful of breath, and blows. The grey fluff catches a breeze and lifts scattering into the sky.

"Nice one," I say.

"How come dandelions aren't flowers?" Pico twirls the decapitated plant between his thumb and forefinger, then flicks it at the ground.

"Because they're weeds, Pico."

"But they look like flowers. When they're yellow."

"Well, that's their trick."

"Yeah?"

"Sure. They pretend to be flowers so you keep them around. But they're weeds."

"They look like flowers to me," says Pico, as if this settles it.

He starts walking around the table, running his fingers along the wood. Before I can warn him about splinters, he yelps and springs back like something's bitten him, his hand to his lips. Right away, I'm up beside him. "You've got to watch that, Pico."

"Ouch," he says, wincing.

I guide him into the shed, where he sits down on the bed. I find tweezers, and Pico puts his hand out, palm up, quivering.

I smile, the tweezers poised. "Trust me?"

Pico nods. I raise his hand up to the light, and there it is – a black grain of wood lodged into the skin. I slide the tweezers up to it, clamp down, and pull the splinter free. Pico bucks and yanks his hand away. But after a moment, he examines his finger and looks up at me in awe.

"Nothing to it," I tell him. But Pico has already turned his attention to my fish, the splinter apparently forgotten. He sits on my bed, regarding them with vague interest.

"Cool, huh?"

"Great," says Pico.

I struggle to think of some interesting fish fact, something remarkable and fascinating.

Pico beats me to it: "Did you know fish only have memories for five seconds?"

"Huh. I had no idea."

"Yeah," Pico says, brightening. "They forget their whole lives every five seconds – then it's like they're new fish again."

"Or they think they are."

Pico gives me a funny look. "How come you're the only Block Parent on this street?"

"I'm not – really?"

"Yep. I went around looking for signs, and you're the only one."

"It's because we're the nicest."

"Can I feed your fish?" Pico asks, standing up.

"Sure." We trade places, and I settle into the groove he's left in my bedcovers. "The food's just there. But don't give them too much –"

Pico glances at me over his shoulder, already sprinkling the coloured flakes into the aquarium. "I know what I'm doing, Les."

On my bedside table is a deck of playing cards. I pick them up and try making a house, but the cards keep slipping off one another. Pico comes over, shaking his head.

"You've got to make triangles." He sits down beside me, takes two cards, and leans them against one another. He succeeds in building a few levels before the whole thing collapses.

"Hey, want to see a trick?" I ask.

"A card trick?"

"Sure. Just pick a card and tell me what pile it's in."

This is the only card trick I know, and it's a simple one: after three times through the same routine, the person's card is always the eleventh out of the pile. But I choose it with a flourish, throwing the cards around the room, and then walking around as if confused, before pulling the right one up off the floor.

Pico claps. "Again," he commands. "Again!"

"Nope." I shake my head severely. "Magicians never do the same trick twice in a row."

"Oh, come on."

"Sorry. Maybe some other time, Pico."

Pico looks at me carefully. "The kids at school call me Pee-Pee-Co, sometimes."

"That doesn't even make sense," I say. Here I am, sitting with this boy on my bed, this odd little fellow with the face of a diabolical American president. "You want to stay for dinner?"

Pico considers, tilting his head toward some indefinite place on the ceiling. "I'll have to call my nana," he says, nodding. "But I think it might be a good idea."

Judy comes home to Pico sitting on the floor of the kitchen, talking to the dogs. I've got a veggie moussaka in the oven, tomato and tarragon soup simmering on the stove, and a spinach salad tossed and ready for dressing on the counter.

"More bird food?" says Judy. She stoops down to greet Pico and his canine companions. "You must be Pico."

Pico looks up and grins. "I'm staying for dinner."

"Oh, are you now." Judy turns to me. "Did you check with his mom?"

"His nana," I tell her. But then I realize I haven't. I had stayed in the kitchen while Pico made the call from Judy's bedroom. Pico and I exchange a quick look, and then I turn to Judy. "I'm sure it's fine."

"She knows you're Block Parents," says Pico.

Judy shrugs, steps over Pico, and opens the fridge. "Don't we have any beer?"

"Beer?" I squeeze a wedge of lemon into a glass jar, add some olive oil, salt, pepper.

She slams the fridge door shut and then leans up against it. "What a day. I spend half my week wrist-deep in vaginas – you'd think I've got the best job in the world."

I frown and nod my head in the direction of Pico, but he seems oblivious, totally absorbed with trying to get the already prostrate dogs to lie down.

"Oh, shoot," she says, snorting. "Hey, would you believe I've got another couple who are burying their placenta? At least these two aren't eating it. Still, you'd think people would just be happy if their kid comes out all right, it's not –"

She catches herself.

"Oh, fuck. Les – I'm sorry."

The room has changed. Even Pico is quiet. I shake up the jar of oil and lemon juice. I shake it, I keep shaking it, I stare out the window and I shake the jar, and all I can hear is the wet sound of the dressing sloshing around.

Judy is beside me. She has her hand on my arm. I stop.

"It's okay," I tell her.

"It's okay," she tells me.

We finish dinner by seven o'clock, so Judy and I ask Pico if he wants to come along while we take the dogs down for their evening walk. Before we ate, Judy decided Pico needed to know I had a lisp when I was a kid, and he kept my sister in hysterics, calling me "Leth" and "Lethy" for the better part of the meal.

Everyone helps clear the table, and then we collect the dogs and head down to the creek behind Judy's house. We call it the creek, but it's basically dried up, just a gentle dribble through the ravine. The dogs love it, though; we let them off their leads and they go bounding and snarling off into the woods.

The sun is just setting as the three of us make our way down along the path into the ravine. Judy's brought a flashlight, but she keeps it in her coat. "It's for when they poop," she tells Pico, and shows him the fistful of plastic bags in her pocket. Pico's eyes widen.

Under the canopy of trees overhead, the light down here is dim – almost as if the ravine is hours ahead of the sunset. We unleash the dogs, who bolt, disappearing into the gloom. Judy and Pico follow them, but I move the other way, climbing over a mound of roots and earth, arriving in the dried-up riverbed. I kneel down, put my hand out, and I'm startled to feel water, icy and streaming urgently over my fingertips. But then I realize I can hear it, I probably could have all along – the happy, burbling sound of it barely above a whisper. I close my eyes, listening, my hand dangling in the thread of river.

Rachel and I went to an art exhibit once, some gallery a friend of hers from college had just opened. There was this room that you went into, and it was dark, totally black. When you entered, a single light bulb turned on and lit up the room. And in this light you saw, written on one of the walls, text about guillotined criminals who were found able to communicate after their heads had been chopped off. Then, right when you read the last word, the light bulb turned off, leaving you in darkness.

As we were coming out of the room, Rachel took my hand and whispered, "Man, that was spooky."

"Yeah," I said, but later I realized she was only talking about being left in the dark.

Out of the woods, one of the dogs comes trotting up to me and nuzzles its nose into my hand, then starts lapping at the creek. I smack its muscled haunches and the tail starts pumping. Judy and Pico are close, moving through the trees, their voices muffled. Then Pico starts calling, "Leth-eee! Leth-eee!" and Judy gets into it too, their voices ringing out in chorus. Judy turns on her flashlight – it swings through the darkness, sweeping the forest in a fat, white band. I hunker down, my arm around the dog, and wait for them to find me.

Autumn has arrived, the smoky, dusty smell of it thick in the air. The leaves are starting to fall, and in the mornings my breath appears in clouds as I putter around the backyard. I figure I'll get a space heater for the cabin once it gets really cold, but the big problem is that I don't know how much longer I'll be able to work outside. I had an indoor workshop at the old house, back when carpentry was only a hobby. It was odd moving, clearing out that room – with all my tools missing, it became just an empty space in the basement, smelling vaguely of sawdust and leather. I'm sure Rachel's since turned it into the darkroom she used to talk about. When their parents would let us, we used to take pictures of the kids at Family Services – Rachel always thought it would have been nicer to develop them at home, rather than having them done by some stranger at a photomart.

I don't see Pico for over a week. Then one afternoon I'm out in the front yard doing the first rake of the season, and he wheels up on a bicycle.

"Les!" he yells. "Look at the bike my nana bought me."

He does a wobbly circle on the street. The bike is a throwback to a time well before Pico's birth – tassels dangle from the handlebars, and the seat curves up into a towering steel backrest. I give Pico the thumbs-up.

With some minor difficulties Pico dismounts, lowering the bike gingerly onto Judy's lawn. Today he is wearing a pink K-Way jacket about two sizes too big for him, blue sweatpants, and a pair of rubber boots. He runs up to me and we both stand there for a minute, silent, breathing in the crisp autumn air.

"I'm not scared of squirrels anymore," he says, finally.

"Yeah?"

"I'm doing my science project on them. They bury their nuts in the fall, and then they find them later because they rub their feet on them and make them smell."

"Is that how it works?"

"Yep. People think they remember where they put them, but they don't. It's just the smell of their stinky feet." Pico starts giggling.

"Isn't that something else."

"You never showed me that card trick again."

"Help me bag these leaves, then we'll go in and I'll do it. But this is the last time."

In a drawer in the kitchen I find a pack of cards, and I deal them out on the table. Pico, eyes narrowed to slits, scrupulously watches my hands. Then I do my big theatrical bit at the end where the cards get tossed all over the room. I walk around for a few seconds in feigned indecision, before snatching Pico's queen of spades off the floor.

"I saw you counting."

"No way! This is a magic trick, it's all –"

"You counted the cards, Les, and mine was number eleven."

Pico gets down off his chair and silently collects all the cards scattered around the kitchen. I follow his lead and start to clear the table. "Well, now you know the trick, at least."

Pico picks up the last card and hands me the deck, his face solemn. "Thanks, Les," he says. "But I have to go home now."

And that's it. Pico abandons me in the kitchen. The front door wheezes open and a cool breeze floods into the kitchen, briefly, before the door slams closed. The house is silent. I look out through the kitchen window at the dining table, sitting half-refinished in the backyard.

I head back there intending to do some work, but I can't figure out where to start. After hovering around the table for a while, I rearrange my tools, then head inside my cabin and, leaving the light off, lie down on the bed. I look over at the fish, their aquarium glowing blue in the darkened room. Five seconds of memory. A lifetime composed of these five-second instalments, just flashes of existence, only to have them vanish, recede mercifully from you like an accident you'd drive by at night on a highway.

Two weeks later, autumn is in full swing. Every morning I wake up to a backyard buried in leaves, which I dutifully clear away before starting my day's work. By the end of the afternoon, the grass is already disappearing again, the lawn just green scraps under a patchy brown cover. I've finished the kitchen table with one last coat of mahogany stain, and I'm keeping it under a tarp out back until I find a buyer. It looks about a hundred years older than it actually is.

Judy has convinced me to go to this thing with her this afternoon – that weird hippie couple intent on burying their baby's placenta. Judy, the deliverer of the baby, is guest of honour. Last weekend we were down at the creek with the dogs, and she told me all about it.

"I'd really like you to come," Judy said. She sat down on an old mossy log and looked up at me. Nearby the dogs were chasing one another through the trees, the patter of paws on fallen leaves fading as they ran farther and farther away.

"Who are these people?"

"Les, it'll be nice. Sort of weird, maybe, but . . . good."

"Jude, I don't know."

"Think about it," she said.

When we got home, I went right out into the backyard and sat down at the head of the dining table, the tarp ruffling in the wind. Judy stood at the kitchen window, watching me. For a moment we locked eyes, and then she pulled away.

I've decided to wear a suit, a starchy navy thing I used to pull out for meetings or home visits back in my days of social work. In the cabin, I struggle to knot my tie, then head out to the front of the house to wait for my sister. A chill in the air hints at winter; the street is quiet and still. The neighbours have their Halloween decorations up: front porches are framed with orange and black streamers, cardboard cut-outs of witches and ghosts perch on lawns. Daylight is just starting to drain from the sky.

Some kid is weaving down the street on a bicycle, tracing these slow, arching parabolas from one curb to the other. The kid comes closer, closer – and then I recognize the bike, that retro frame, those tasseled handlebars, the banana seat. The pink jacket. And a gorilla mask.

"Hey!" I yell.

The kid slams on the brakes and looks over at me. The mask comes off, and underneath is the face of a girl. She's probably twelve, and Asian – maybe Vietnamese, maybe Cambodian.

"Hi," she says.

I walk over to her. My tie is choking me.

"Cool bike."

"It's from the centre," says the girl. "It's old. It's only a one-speed."

"The *centre?*"

"It's the only bike they have."

"Oh."

"Yeah."

I point up to the sign in the window of Judy's house. "We're Block Parents, so if you ever get into any trouble . . ."

The girl is giving me a look that says, *Can I go now?*

I tell her to ride safe.

In Judy's car we listen to one of her French language tapes. She practises her verbs along with the voice on the tape while she drives.

"*J'ai eu, Tu as eu, Il a eu, Elle a eu,*" says Judy, and so forth. I sit staring out the window, playing absently with the power locks. "Try it, Les," Judy encourages me.

"*J'ai! Eu!*"

Judy grins. "*Bravo, monsieur.*"

The woman on the tape continues to chatter away, but Judy seems to have lost interest. We pull up to a red light and sit, idling, while cars stream by in front of us. Out of nowhere, Judy does one of her snort-laughs. She covers her mouth with her hand, her eyes twinkling.

"What's up?"

She turns to me, smiling. "I just remembered how when you were a kid, you used to tell Mom's friends that you could remember being born."

"What? Never."

"Yeah, always. You'd describe it to them and everything."

"Shut up." I'm laughing now too.

"Christ, Les. You were such an odd little fellow."

We drive for a while in silence, then pull up in front of a grand old house, the front yard full of people. Judy cuts the engine and pats my knee. "Ready to bury some placenta?"

"Yep," I say and we high-five.

Judy straightens her skirt. "Seriously, though – make me laugh and I'll kill you."

Not only am I the only guest wearing a suit, but there is a couple in matching muumuus, and a woman with an owl perched on her shoulder. Music starts up, and everyone shuffles around until they've formed a delta with an open space in the middle. Judy and I retreat behind a tree. I look up through branches scrawling black and empty into the grey October sky.

The mother and father appear from somewhere, the mother carrying her newborn, the father toting a platter with what looks like a lump of meat heaped onto it. The placenta.

"Jesus Christ," I whisper, nudging my sister. "That thing's enormous."

Judy, the corners of her mouth twitching, does her best to ignore me.

The parents move into the empty space in the middle of everyone, where a sort of grave has been dug from the garden. Dirt lies heaped up around the hole in brown piles.

The mother steps forward and begins talking. I don't hear what she says. I am thinking, suddenly, of Pico, and considering what the three of us – me, Judy, and Pico – would look like together in this context. Maybe people would mistake us for a family. Sure: a father and mother, friends of the happy couple, and little Pico, who we might have brought on the way to his soccer game. We'd drive him there afterwards in our minivan, go sit with the other happy, proud parents along the sideline. Later, everyone would go out for ice cream; plans would be made for sleepovers and birthday parties and summer camps.

I look over at my sister and her expression has changed. She seems focused, solemn. There is applause, and Judy steps forward. She waves, then reaches back and grabs my hand and drags me up with her. The parents take turns embracing us. When the mother wraps her free arm around me, the baby, resting its head on her shoulder, regards me across her back: it's like we're sharing a secret.

The father lowers the platter into the hollow and hands Judy a small shovel. She casts me a quick glance over her shoulder, then steps forward and stabs the blade into the earth with a crisp, dry sound. Everyone is silent. Judy lifts a shovelful of dirt and sprinkles it over the placenta, the pattering sound of it landing below like the footsteps of a hundred tiny feet.

When the ceremony is over, after the placenta is buried and the last spade of earth patted down, we are all invited inside for a reception. Judy seems to know everyone. She introduces me to countless midwives and clients and former teachers, all of them wanting to know what I do for a living. At one point, I corner my sister and tell her I've had enough.

"Christ, I can't leave now," she whispers. "Can you stick it our for another half-hour?"

"I'll walk – it's nice out."

She looks at me with this weird, sad smile. "Thanks for coming, Les."

"Sure."

With that I leave my sister, I leave the party, I leave them all behind and make my way outside. An earthy smell hangs in the air, and beyond it, something cold and sharp and distant. I pause for a moment on the front steps of the house, surveying the empty front yard. A squirrel sits in the branches of one of the trees, and just as I notice it, the animal springs to life. It scrabbles down the trunk, lunges, and lands silently in the yard. An acorn appears from its mouth. The tiny paws claw at the earth, then stuff the nut into the ground. The squirrel straightens up. It turns, staring in my direction from two black buttons in its face.

Something twitches inside me, and I have to grab the railing to steady myself. I inhale, closing my eyes, and count five seconds while my breath drains into the autumn dusk. When I open my eyes, the squirrel has disappeared. The neighbourhood is silent, washed in dusty twilight. I let go of the railing and step down, one stair, then the next, and begin the walk home.

JOSH BYER

Rats, Homosex, Saunas, and Simon

My friend Simon Simpson had decided not to be a homosexual. He was sixteen years old and lived in a jungle of duplexes located in Ottawa South. It was the Deborah Street area, a collection of badly cracked roads and mean kids who drank Malibu rum out of Coca-Cola bottles. Those mean kids were real bastards. This story is not about them.

Simon's neighbour, Stan, was a similarly impoverished young man. He was a big, fat, doughy kid who was not jolly.

Stan had introduced Simon to the casual, nobody-has-to-know, teenage blow job. So that was Simon's thing for a while, until he discovered that it was "gay." In the summer of 1994, Simon was in violent withdrawal from his participation in homosex.

A week after he decided not to be "gay," he set Stan's house on fire with a bottle of Zippo lighter fluid and a roll of toilet paper. The house did not burn down. All the toilet paper did was burn toilet-paper-shaped marks into the paint job.

His parents, staunch and strict career aggressives, grounded Simon for six months and would not allow him any social contact. In retaliation, he sold his mother's microwave at a pawnshop for sixty dollars. Then he came to live with my family.

We didn't have a spare room, so he set up an army cot in our broken sauna. By the end of the summer, Simon and I had jerry-rigged the sauna machine and got it sort of working again. Then we invited a bunch of girls over. Well, two girls, sisters, who lived down the block and were conservative agnostics. One of them suffered from chronic acne, and the other was pretty in a Candace Cameron kind of way.

We had a sauna party in Simon's bedroom. Everything was steamy and fine. All the posters slowly peeled off his walls. His sheets gradually became red-hot and soaked. Then the floor flooded.

It cost seven hundred dollars to fix all the water damage. Simon gave my folks the sixty microwave bucks at dinner that night. I acted like a complete ass and revelled in the irony. "You're taking stolen money, you bastards!" I yelled at my parents. I wasn't in my right mind.

I had just discovered water-drunkenness, which is caused by an overconsumption of H_2O. A four-litre bottle of Evian, which my mother loved to buy, would get you right and royal zipped-out if you could drink it in ten minutes.

The only drawback was the constant peeing, but Simon and I had secret plans to buy Depends adult diapers and walk around town listening to the satisfied crinkling noise while we pissed ourselves to utopia.

"LAY OFF THAT GODDAMNED WATER," my father yelled. I told him water was necessary for human survival. He took Simon's sixty bucks and left the table.

The next morning, my mother told us that for the rest of the summer, we couldn't spend time in the house during the day. 8 a.m. to 5 p.m. were to become the vagrancy hours. My folks figured if they restricted our time in the house, they could limit the liability for the amount of damage caused to their property.

So myself and Simon wandered the streets of suburbia, past pool parties and yups washing their Honda CRXs, past the park where they handed out limeade beverages to poor people, through the random placement of plywood fences, finally finding privacy in a large grassy field on the edge of a triplex housing development.

The field was thirty acres wide. It had been zoned for housing twenty years prior. The city came in and laid storm sewers down, but then ran out of funds and abandoned the housing project altogether.

So what you had was a big field, with endless kilometres of sewers underneath, and a bunch of trees and bulrushes up top. We stole a crowbar and some flares from a parked caboose in a CN rail yard, pried open an overgrown manhole cover, and descended into our own personal labyrinth. I felt just like David Bowie.

The tunnels stretched on forever. Eventually, if you followed them east, they'd lead to the street sewers, and you could go anywhere in the city with street sewers.

There were rats. Simon the not-gay attacked rats with two lit train flares once and got bit. We were too scared to go to a doctor, in fear that he would narc us out to my water-damaged parents. Simon coasted the rest of August out, wondering if he would fall victim to rabies or herpes or whatever disease that you catch from rats.

We found all kinds of things in those sewers. Someone had set up a home in a cubbyhole where water couldn't flow. There was a cot and a poster of Jane Fonda on the wall. It was old, maybe from the 1970s.

I told Simon if we got kicked out of my house, then we'd have to come live here. He nodded and tore the Jane Fonda poster off the wall. He still has it, even today, framed and in the kitchen of his half-a-million-dollar condo. But I digress.

We found a dead dog, still wearing his collar. Simon wanted to find the owner and take them their dog corpse, so they could have closure. I strongly argued against it, because the dog was very, very deceased and slowly falling apart.

Simon was intense and offended, so I told him he was acting rat-bite crazy. He told me I was being homophobic. I told him that he had told me that he wasn't homosexual, so I couldn't be homophobic. He told me to shut up.

One day in August, before it was all done and Simon went home and I went back to school, we decided to take one last venture – to go as far as we possibly could through the tunnels. Our previous record had been three kilometres, coming up in

Ottawa East, near Jojo's, a pub that served minors if you knocked on the back door and drank in the storage room.

So this time we went past Jojo's. Past the abandoned cot. Past the dead dog. And we found a small tree, alive and green, not a ray of light or sunshine in sight. It was growing in a pile of dirt-mud in the middle of the sewer. It was impossible.

We climbed up and out and never went back.

RANDY BOYAGODA

Rice and Curry Yacht Club

It was the salad fork; he could tell by the number of tines that jabbed into his leg when his sister showed him she knew what he was doing. Just as they'd sat down, when his mother marvelled to Paul's mother how beautiful the table settings were. While his father tried to impress Paul's father by telling him how there had been a Royal Yacht Club in Sri Lanka too, back when it was Ceylon, though their dining room was of course nothing compared to this one. Because Chandra had a plan, he'd started with the humming. A song known to all at the table, but embarrassing, humiliating to his sister alone, though hopefully worrying his parents too.

"What's that song, um, Chandra?" Paul's mother asked warmly, a look of self-congratulation on her face for pronouncing his name correctly. He didn't answer at first, mesmerized as she pulled the fan-tailed napkin from her plate and onto her lap in a single motion that he knew would have awed and shamed his mother. If she had been watching. She was still examining her own napkin as it stood starchily on her plate, her lacquered fingernails running along its crest as if it were a delicate and rare flower. Probably trying to figure out how it was folded, he thought, so she could do the same the next time they had relatives over. She'd place those napkins on the plates so that she could casually tell his aunties in the kitchen that "it was how they did it at the RCYC in Toronto" as they moved the curry and rice pots into the dining room and called the men from their darts and carom, the children from their videos and Sega. His

117

mother smugly knowing that the acronym would be greeted with silence, utter ignorance. Smugness, the family trait; the coat of arms would have a smear of it across the bottom.

"Chandra." His father's voice a perfect measure of anger and politeness. They were with company, after all, the first official dinner between the families after Paul had proposed to Krisanthi on a Victoria Day jaunt to his family's Haliburton cottage. "Mrs. Sunderland asked you a question. Not polite not to answer."

"Sorry, Dad, I was thinking of something else."

"But that song, Chandra, on the tip of my tongue, what was it?" she asked, and now they were all watching him.

He started humming again, his hands tapping on the cutlery on each side of his plate. "Do you mean that song?"

"It's 'Pretty Woman,' right, Chan?" Paul chimed in, with his annoying habit of cutting their names in half. Kris. Chan. Mr. and Mrs. Rut. Thankfully for his parents, pronounced Root. Because they would never correct him, he thought. Spend the rest of their lives as the Ruts if it meant Paul would keep coming around, if it meant Paul would carve the turkey at Christmas dinner and smoke in the garage with the uncles afterwards. If it meant, he thought acidly, as he admitted, "Yes it was 'Pretty Woman' by Roy Orbison, also the title of a movie," if it meant the real live Canadian would marry the daughter, make them all Canadians.

It was then that his sister had jabbed him. His parents glared at him, but then conversation took off, a back-and-forth comparison of old singers between the fathers, his clumsily trying to start a singalong of "Going to the Chapel" with the soon-to-be newlyweds. Krisanthi, having smoothly replaced her fork, immediately and happily acted embarrassed by the singing, his mother slapped her husband on the shoulder and announced she was fed up with his madness, and all was well at the table. His humming had been forgotten by all save his sister, who he could almost hear next to him, asking, pleading, "Why, Chandra? Why are you going to ruin this? This night means so much to all of us. But don't think of what it means to *Aummi* and *Thathi*, but for me, please, don't do it. Don't tell them about us."

His father had brought them into the recently fully finished basement with wet bar and full entertainment system just before they'd left for dinner. Krisanthi and his mother were already nervous they'd be late, had no idea what *Thathi* was planning. But Chandra knew, he'd been told to cue up the video while the others got ready. So he found the spot where the hotel manager sits Julia Roberts down and shows her the various forks, tells her about counting the tines.

"First off, we won't be late. I just checked CFRB and the DVP's clear all the way to Bloor. Second, I know you all are going to laugh at me and say I'm gone crazy and a stupido, but we are going to sit down and watch this and memorize it. These people are expecting us to show up and act like real Scarborough curry-shop *hunas*, and we must show them we can eat in their places just like they do. Chandra."

He started the tape while his sister pleaded to *Aummi* to make *Thathi* stop, but then his father threatened that he wouldn't go unless they studied it together and knew the right forks. So the four sat on the sectional couch counting tines with Julia, four times through the scene before he was satisfied. And in the car, with Krisanthi and his mother in the back seat, the one taking turns consoling the other, his father quizzed them on the tines as they drove down the 401, the women ignoring him, and Chandra happily answering each question. "You see that, you bloody stupidos? Only my son will know how to eat properly with these Canadians. My son and I, we shall show them, and when you use a bloody butter knife to drink your soup, don't blame me!" He'd laughed with his father then, laughed at him, planning his attack.

He was unsure of how much work it would take him to show Paul's family how they really were, to send them back to Pickering, where he knew they belonged. Comfortably suburban wealthy among high-school principals, Italian pavement contractors, Korean video-store owners. Hopefully the other side would help.

He wasn't disappointed.

"Oh, Sheri!" Paul's mother began, taking up a menu and addressing the entire table, though focusing on the professional name his mother had taken on and now used with Canadians. She had changed her name, learning quickly that Sheri's Styles attracted more customers to the strip-mall fabric store she ran in Ajax than Shiroma's Modern Fashion Boutique.

Paul's mother beamed across the table. "You know what you absolutely must have? They do a *wonderful* shrimp and chicken curry here, very spicy and as good as anything we've had on Gerrard Street!"

Four brown backs arched in their chairs. Chandra's slid down quickly, and he gleefully glanced at the horror and shock on his family's faces.

"Jeez, Mum, do you have any idea how insulting a suggestion that was?" Paul asked sourly, but with unmistakable self-righteousness that, judging from the breathy sigh Chandra heard from his sister, hit the mark. Chandra had more reason than ever to hate him now that he had short-circuited the moment into immediate apologies and demurrals. Eventually, his father spoke up, giving Paul's mother a chance at redemption.

"So then, Mrs. Sunderland," his father said in a forced, jovial tone. "Since you are the expert on what not to eat here at RCYC, what does the chef know how to cook?"

"I'll tell you, Mr. Rutnayake, he makes a wonderful roast beef with a nicely crisp Yorkshire pudding, and invariably, that's my other choice when we dine here."

"Ah, a chef and a patron after my own heart!" his father exclaimed theatrically, again too loud so that, as Chandra and his sister imagined it, ears at other tables cocked at the accent. "There is nothing in this world I enjoy more than a good piece of roast beef." There was a pause, as if he was waiting for a challenge. "Go ahead! Ask them," he nearly scoffed at Paul's parents, pointing at the rest of the family aggressively. "Ask! I eat roast beef every meal if I could."

Paul's parents were a little confused about the response they were expected to give, but when the mothers made eye contact, Chandra's gave a beaming nod to her husband's statement and elicited polite if confused smiles from across the table.

When the waiter returned, the orders were a set of funhouse mirrors. Chandra's parents each ordered the roast beef in a self-consciously casual manner. Paul's parents, out of a strange mix of guilt and refracted desire, both asked for the curry. The young couple, caught between generations and cultures and absolutely in love with the sense of crisis that was attached to the orders they were to make, decided they were above the task and rejected both burdens. They ordered the fish.

"And you, sir?" the waiter asked Chandra.

"He'll have the roast beef too," his father said shortly, snatching the menu away from him and passing it to the waiter. Chandra looked across the table and knew then his course.

"Actually, I think I'll try the curry, too."

"You, curry?" his father asked, astounded.

"Yeah, Dad, curry. I haven't had any since Mount Lavinia, and I have this sudden craving for it."

"Good for you!" Paul's father exclaimed with validation and relief.

There were no fork jabs, no worried glances from his mother. Only his father sensed the tragedy that was coming.

With the exception of three five-day funeral trips for two grandfathers and a grandmother, the entire family had never been back home since his parents had come over in the early seventies. Having quietly checked around the GTA to ensure that no other semi-prominent Sinhalese family was going that summer, Upali Rutnayake announced to one and all at a niece's First Communion in Brampton that the family was going back home. It was as much a surprise to Chandra, his sister, and his mother as to the rest of the family, many of whom later expressed disgust with his father for upstaging a First Communion party for which the proud parents had secured a clown, ice cream cake, and the attendance of the teacher's blonde educational assistant.

Two months, four passport photos, and a six-hour Bangkok airport delay later, they arrived. And he didn't mind the aunties and uncles and cousins and drivers and servants competitively drenching his face with kisses and tears. He didn't mind the thick heat, the stench from the fish stands, the mosquitoes that burrowed into his ears in the middle of the night. He even didn't mind the constant comparisons to his father, being told he was the living image, a snapshot come alive, first-rate carbon copy. He had expected and therefore accepted all.

It was after the dinner where Upali Rutnayake had made his son a Canadian that everything changed for him and he wanted to go home.

Chandra's father had arranged for a long banquet table at the country's most prestigious Sunday dinner location, the dining room of the Mount Lavinia hotel. He invited every important relative and friend on the island. Minimum entry requirements: a board of director position, a white-collar business ownership, or a child in medical school.

At the dinner, Chandra was seated near the head of the table, on his father's right side, facing the ocean and surrounded by half of the 1960 Royal College all-school cricket team.

The waiter slunk up to his father for his order, and Chandra felt a sudden pride at how everyone at the table, everyone on the island seemed to regard his *Thathi* – who had come over to Canada but lived in a house in the suburbs, not an apartment by the 401; who owned his own store but made money on real Canadian eyeglasses and contact lenses, not Bollywood videos and rice.

"Is your *ambul thiyal* as good as it was twenty years ago?" his father asked imperiously.

"Pleasesirdontknowsiryeseverythingverygoodsirplease."

He made a majestic show of ordering and then, loud enough for the entire table, turned to Chandra.

"And you, my *Putha*? What will you have, eh? Big Mac?" He laughed louder than his cricket friends and then quickly, vehemently explained to all that neither Chandra nor the girl ate rice and curry in Canada, only Canadian food.

Chandra had been quiet then, unsure of himself at the head of the table among the red-rim-eyed men who smoked cigarettes and smiled at him, who bobbled their heads and mock-consoled him. "No Big Macs, only rice and curry, *Putha*, no Big Macs."

When the food was served, the entire table looked again to his father, the waiters surrounding them anxiously, everyone waiting. His father motioned for them to start, and as Chandra gripped his knife and fork, he noticed a thin, ugly smile on his father's face. "What has happened to my countrymen since I left?" Upali Rutnayake boomed, peering down the table.

It was loud enough for everyone in the dining room to hear.

"What has happened? Are we no longer Sri Lankans? Look at all of you, with beautiful *sambols* and *mallungs* and dhal made with real coconut milk, and what are you doing? Eating with knife and fork!"

It was the ultimate reversal, his father's moment of triumph. The diners had awkwardly picked up the heavy, colonial-leaden silverware so as to avoid embarrassing themselves in front of their guest from Canada, and now the guest from Canada was requesting a finger bowl from his waiter.

"I don't care how many years I live in Canada, I will never disgrace a good plate of curry with fork and knife!" They responded with laughter, even applause, and because the table thudded with abandoned cutlery, no one heard a dhal-soaked hand grab Chandra's wrist just as the boy excitedly tried to scoop a handful of rice. No one heard an urgent whisper.

"No, not you, Chandra. Son, you must eat with a knife and fork."

They merged back onto the DVP alongside the tail end of baseball traffic. The radio was off and the air conditioning low enough so Chandra could hear his sister crying in the back seat. She'd started the moment they entered the car, pausing only when his father had warned through clenched teeth that the parking attendant might see her and tell Paul's family. Because over dinner, they'd done an incredibly good job of hiding their horror as Chandra instructed Paul's parents on how to eat rice and curry the proper way. His father had tried to stop them just as Chandra ordered three finger bowls, but was silenced by Chandra informing the table that it was wrong "to disgrace good plate of rice and curry with fork and knife."

Chandra avoided his father's stare the rest of the dinner but could feel it. He instead coached the Sunderlands on how to mash the chicken into the rice, how to hold their wrists over their plates so the droppings would mix right in and not be wasted. His mother, still scandalized by the idea of mixing chicken and shrimp in the same curry, picked at her plate and chimed in half-heartedly with his father in response to the Canadians' praise of eating with their fingers.

Paul and Krisanthi were again caught in the middle, though Krisanthi was genuinely miserable this time, unable to answer her future mother-in-law's questions directly because she was too embarrassed to point out the grains of rice stuck to strands of her silver-blonde hair. Together, the couple made the best of a difficult situation by piercing salmon steaks with forks and eating the watercress garnish with fingers.

Chandra would apologize to his sister. He did feel badly that her night had been ruined. He still hated Paul for being the Canadian son and still thought they didn't belong there, but he could accept all if it meant *that* world knew that Upali Rutnayake had a Sri Lankan son. Only that much would balance the Mount Lavinia account.

They were waiting for his father to say something, his sister and mother wanting to hear the punishment they knew he deserved, Chandra curious to see how his father dealt with irony.

"Chandra, what you did tonight –," cut off by a stream of high-pitched, tearful complaint from the back seat, English mixed with Sinhalese. Chandra's father held up a hand and commanded silence. Chandra waited again, smiling to himself, eager for the entire family to hear why he'd done it.

"Chandra, what you did tonight was prove to your father, your mother, your sister, and those people only one thing about you."

"What's that?" he asked.

"Shiroma, Krisanthi, do you remember the Mount Lavinia Hotel dinner? Then, just as now, Chandra ate," suddenly he saw that terrible smile return to his father's face, "like he should have. Just like me. Proud to show others where he comes from."

They were silent in the back seat from confusion and his father hummed a song that now sounded terrible to his ears. Chandra played numbly with the door lock, staring out his window at the approaching highway sign. Welcome to Pickering.

NEIL SMITH

Scrapbook

A Diagram of a Building

Robertson Hall has lost its roof. It's as if a twister has blown the top off the building to reveal the mouse maze of classrooms and corridors on its fifth floor.

The diagram appears in *Maclean's* magazine. Lucy wonders who drew it. A man, she assumes. A man with the clinical fortitude of a coroner. He's peopled his diagram with stick figures. They walk the hallways, bend over drinking fountains, raise their hands in class. Perhaps they're thinking what a fine institution Scott University is. And Petertown, what a peaceful community.

The stick figures, Lucy notes, are shadowy grey. Except in room 523. The eight women huddled together on one side of the German class are pale pink. The five men lined up on the other side are deep purple. Like good boys, these purple men filed out of the room when Buddy MacDonald told them to.

Where's Buddy? The question is like Where's Waldo? But Lucy doesn't need to search long. She knows where Buddy is: the women's washroom down the hall from the German class. Buddy is the red stick figure. He's lying in a toilet stall, a chunk of his head floating in the toilet bowl. Brain, scalp, skin, skull. Buddy got down on his knees, leaned over that bowl. In one hand he held a gun, a silencer attached to its barrel. He put the gun to his temple and squeezed the trigger.

The Label from a Prescription Bottle

"In the pink" is the expression her parents use for sound health. Lucy has always been in the pink. If she has taken prescription medication in her twenty-three years, she doesn't remember. Consequently, although the pills are intended for her boyfriend, Thomas, her name typed on the label seems portentous.

This afternoon, she went to the campus clinic and feigned insomnia. She could have told the truth: her boyfriend had been in room 523. But she lied. "I knew one of the girls who were killed," she told the doctor, who then scribbled on a prescription pad.

The prescription was for sleeping pills, and she's now sitting at the kitchen table crushing a tablet with the back of a spoon. She mixes the powder with some applesauce because Thomas has trouble swallowing pills whole.

Thomas's face is flushed with blood. He's in the living room doing the downward dog on a yoga mat, his hands and feet flat on the floor, his rear end pointing up, his head dangling between his extended arms. He looks like no dog Lucy has ever seen, certainly not like Bugaboo, their female Dalmatian.

His German parents nicknamed Thomas "*der Gepard*" – the cheetah – a tribute to his gracefulness and speed. But despite his streamlined body, wide-set hazel eyes, and mane of tawny dreadlocks, Lucy doesn't see a big cat either. She sees simply a man. A man down on all fours. She recalls the first time she lay naked in bed with Thomas, how she inspected the meat of his calves, his flat, bluish nipples, the walnut folds of his testicles. She thought, So this is a man.

Thomas puffs out a last gusty exhale as the brooks on their relaxation tape stop babbling. "How many pills did you mix in?" he asks when Lucy brings over his mug of applesauce.

"Just one."

"I need two."

"The label says one tablet at bedtime. You've never taken these before. You could have an allergic reaction or be extra sensitive."

"Spare me the lecture, Lucy." He rubs his eyes. "I haven't slept in days. Just give me another fucking pill."

Later, as they lie in bed, Lucy wonders whether in the night Thomas will again whisper, "Do you still love me?" Will he curl himself around her again? God, she hopes not. She can't stand his touch. Yet she can't bear to push him away.

She turns to him now. He has dozed off. He's so quiet and still that she's struck with the irrational fear that two pills might constitute an overdose. She holds her breath. When he makes a soft smacking sound with his lips, she breathes out. She whispers, "Yes, I do." She says it not to him but to herself and to her witnesses: the spill of moonlight across the ceiling, the glowing digits of her clock radio, the bottle of pills atop her nightstand.

The Cover of a Grammar Book
The book's cover is the German flag: three horizontal stripes, black, red, and yellow. In the red stripe are the words *Sprechen Sie Deutsch?* The colours are glossy. The book looks new despite a gouge hacked into the red stripe. Grey-brown pulp pokes out. As Lucy fingers the pulp, she pictures Thomas deflecting a bullet with his grammar book. My hero, she thinks, the sad irony pinching her face and gunning her heart.

Before the shootings, Lucy hadn't even known Thomas was enrolled in a German class. After all, German was his mother tongue. He took the class on the sly to boost his grade point average, even flubbing answers so the professor wouldn't twig to his fluency.

By the time the shootings started, Thomas's grammar book was no longer in room 523. It was tucked under his arm as he hurried along the hallway, down the stairs and out of Robertson Hall. One guy from the class pulled a fire alarm. Another called 911. As for Thomas, he stepped around students as they sat on the lawn, sunning themselves on an Indian summer day. When he reached the edge of campus, he ran. He ran all the way home to Lucy.

Lucy didn't hear him come in. She was in her workshop sketching designs for the dog boots she sells to pet shops. A thud from the living room jolted her. "Bugaboo," she called out. She peeked down the hall. There was Thomas sitting on the futon couch in front of the steamer trunk they used as a coffee table.

"Was yoga class cancelled?" she asked, since that was where he supposedly spent Wednesday mornings. No answer. On the steamer trunk, beside some of her boot-making tools, lay a textbook. He was staring at this book.

"What's wrong, love?"

His Bob Marley T-shirt was speckled with sweat. His forehead too. He looked up, face contorted, lips quivering. He exhaled hard. Then he grabbed an awl, raised it above the book, and drove it straight down.

Lucy's heart beat in her ears.

Days later, her heart is still in her ears. *Sprechen Sie Deutsch?* is splayed out on her drafting table. She has just amputated its cover with an X-acto knife. As she picks at the gouge in the cover, she thinks of bullet holes, of having one in her chest as she thrashes on the floor of room 523. She could have been one of the eight. She damn well could have been. All those times she promised Thomas's mother she'd learn more German than just *Gesundheit.*

She takes her awl and pokes it all the way through the gouge in the grammar book. Then she holds the book's cover to one eye and peers through the hole. She homes in on Thomas's back as he stumbles in a sleeping-pill stupor down the hall to the bathroom.

"Freeze," she says, "or I'll shoot."

Thomas is too far away to hear.

The Back of an Envelope

Thomas sits on a stool in the middle of the kitchen. He's wearing cut-off jeans and, over his bare shoulders, two green garbage bags taped together like a flimsy sandwich board. With her fabric scissors, Lucy has snipped off his dreadlocks, which now lie at her feet like sections of rope. As she finishes clipping around his ears, he says, "I wonder who's on that envelope."

Every day, she spoon-feeds him a few details from the newspaper articles he can't bring himself to read. Today the *Petertown Examiner* reported that Buddy MacDonald (or "the Silencer," his posthumous nickname) left no suicide note. While searching his apartment, though, the police did come across a list of names on an envelope. A hit list. These names are of local women, all fairly prominent. "Leading lights" is how the police chief put it, although he wouldn't divulge exactly which leading lights Buddy wanted extinguished.

Lucy goes to the sink, snaps on a pair of plastic gloves, and shakes a bottle of hair dye. Thomas, meanwhile, picks up a pen and begins writing on the back of their unopened phone bill. She watches him. With short hair, his eyes look smaller, more wizened, and his forehead looks as square and white as a slice of sandwich bread. Lucy seems to be the only person who knows he was in that German class. The police haven't called. When their friends phone, she feeds them a story about Thomas visiting his sick mother in Montreal.

He hasn't ventured outdoors since the shootings, but there will be a memorial march this weekend and she wants them both to go. At first, he vetoed the idea: he's afraid of running into "the others," meaning his classmates from room 523 – the two women who survived, the four guys who fled. She suggested he go incognito: sunglasses, no dreadlocks, brown hair. A new man.

When the dye is ready, she lathers the soapy mix into his hair. "Let's play a game," he says, tapping the phone bill against his knee. "I give you clues and you tell me which famous Petertown woman is on the back of my envelope."

"I don't want to play games."

She yanks off the plastic gloves and chucks them into the sink.

He grabs a grapefruit from a fruit bowl and shot-puts it into the living room. "She really throws her weight around," he says.

She stares at this boy with his garbage-bag apron and foamy ammonia head. She wants to hug him close, she wants to slap him hard. Finally, she says, "Olympic bronze medalist Becky Pepper."

"Bingo." A devious smirk cocks up one side of his mouth.

She plays along because they both have a warped sense of humour and this game feels restorative, although a bit painful, like blood flowing back into frostbitten toes. She plays along because she wants to hear him talking again after a week of his mumbling little more than "yep" and "nope."

For his next clue, he holds out his arm and pretends to saw it with a long breadknife.

"Violinist Margaret O'Reilly."

Other names on his envelope belong to a police officer, a novelist, an abortionist, an alderwoman, and a country singer. After she guesses, he strikes the name off his list.

In search of his final clue, he heads into the workshop, Bugaboo at his heels. She settles down on the couch, thankful for this momentary let-up in their storm, till he returns with colourful dog booties, her DogPoz, stuck on the ends of his fingers. He straddles her lap and taps her head and face with the boots. She closes her eyes, endures the tiny kicks. Finally she hisses, "Quit it!"

He lowers his hands.

"I'm no leading light," she says.

A treacherous look in his eye, he flicks off the booties and snatches a framed newspaper article hanging on the wall above the couch. "Lucy Hamilton," he reads, "an up-and-coming businesswoman with a go-getter attitude." She shoves him backwards into the steamer trunk and wrests the frame away. How unhinged he looks, the dye dribbling down his forehead, his garbage bags askew.

She goes into her workshop and slams the door, locks it.

The day the *Petertown Examiner* ran "A Cobbler for Canines" on the front page, she felt such a balloon of elation. Thomas was so proud he yelled, he hooted, he went right out and had the article and its photograph matted and framed.

Now she stares into the face of the girl in the photograph. There she is, beaming behind Bugaboo, who offers a booted paw to the camera. She sees her blithe smile and imagines Buddy MacDonald, highlighter in hand, ringing her face in yellow.

"Bud MacDonald had a list, ee-eye ee-eye-oh," Thomas yells from the living room, "and on his list he had some gals, ee-eye ee-eye-oh. With a pow pow here and a pow pow there, here a pow, there a pow, everywhere a pow pow!"

The air sweeps from her lungs. Sweeps back in.

"Shut up!" she screams.

"Ee-eye ee-eye-oh . . ."

"Shut up!"

He's at the door, shaking the knob.

"A pow pow here and a pow pow there . . ."

Her anger is an awl through her chest.

"Piss off, you fucking coward!"

She has said it. What she knows he's wanted her to say all along. What she has felt. A sick, wavering, guilty feeling.

He stops shaking the knob.

Silence.

Eight women shot and all the papers talk about is Buddy. Was he beaten with a yardstick as a child whenever he wet the bed? Was he a model employee at the paint shop where he worked? As a man, was he an aberration or the Hyde hidden in every Jekyll?

Her own man is on the floor now, his shadow edging under the door. The sounds he's making – short, sharp coughs – she recognizes as sobs. She shuffles to the door, opens it, kneels. He's on his side, his face planted in the crook of his arm. His front garbage bag is gone, but the back bag remains taped to his shoulders, a superhero's cape. Bugaboo licks his hand while Lucy strokes his chest and plucks away stray snips of hair. So this is a man, she thinks numbly. When there's a lull in his crying, she whispers, "We've got to rinse your head, love, or your scalp will stain." She helps him up. The envelope drops from his back pocket. She sees her name. The only one without a strike through it.

Excerpts from Newspaper Profiles

Heidi mastered French's pluperfect, Spanish's imperfect, and German's future perfect, but her favourite mood was the subjunctive. "It conjures up our wishes and desires," she would tell her students, "our fears and possibilities."

Her friends say that Louise often tried signing them up as volunteers for the Meals on Wheels program she helped run.

Tamara planned to become an accountant, but was also toying with the idea of writing detective novels featuring a female private eye.

Mimi acted as a kind of resident therapist at her dorm. If a girl had a problem, she'd stop by Mimi's room. Her dorm-mates made her a sign to hang on the door when she wanted peace and quiet. She rarely used that sign, but it hangs there now. It reads, THE DOCTOR IS OUT.

Susan handled publicity for the local punk band Wuzzy and was often found in the mosh pit during the group's concerts.

A fan of Frida Kahlo, Vera painted self-portraits. Her younger brother has hung a dozen of these works on a wall in the family den.

Cynthia plans to return to the Magdalen Islands when she has recovered. What she misses most about her tiny island home is the endless horizon. "Everywhere you look, there it is – infinity."

Despite her ordeal, Myuko has decided against returning to Tokyo. "Most people here are good people," she says. "Very, very good."

A Double Loop of Ribbon

Everywhere Lucy looks, there it is – infinity.

A ribbon looped twice into a figure eight is being pinned to Thomas's sweatshirt. The ribbon is deep purple, the university's official colour. "You wear it on its side," says a girl with a pierced eyebrow as she adjusts Thomas's ribbon. "Like the infinity symbol."

"Doesn't she get one?" Thomas asks, nodding toward Lucy.

"Only the guys," says the girl, who then drifts off through the crowd with her canvas purse full of pins and ribbons, on the lookout for other ribbonless men.

"Infinity is the theme of the march," explains Lucy.

"Why?"

"Something to do with remembering the dead for eternity."

She leaves out how men are also meant to reflect on the infinite number of women whose lives they've snuffed out.

It's mid-October. The sun is shining, but the ground is muddy from an overnight rainfall – hence the boots, the lighter fall model, that Bugaboo is wearing. Lucy and Thomas are in Davies Park with two thousand other students, a good chunk of Scott University's student body. Despite the crowd, people are subdued. Lucy sees a few girls weeping quietly and guys hugging the way guys do, two quick slaps on the back.

Under his mirrored sunglasses, Thomas's eyes are bloodshot, not from crying, but from the pot he smoked to muster the nerve to go outside. Lately, Lucy has barely been out either, other than to scoot to the store or to walk Bugaboo in the woods behind their apartment. She tugs on the dog's leash now to draw the animal closer, but Thomas, she feels, is the one who needs leashing: he keeps wandering off, craning his neck in search of her and then scurrying back.

"You okay, love?"

He nods absently.

The march is to begin in fifteen minutes. It will be a silent march attended only by students from Scott University. They'll walk out of the park and, accompanied by a police escort, follow George Street past the downtown core, with its small shops tidily arranged like canisters of coffee, sugar, flour, and tea. They'll then head north, past the library and petting zoo, and on to the subdivision where Lucy and Thomas live, and finally up the road to the university campus. People from Lucy's town, her parents and little brother among them, will line the sidewalks all the way, as will journalists from across the country and beyond.

A volunteer with a reddish goatee approaches Lucy. "Would you like to carry a sign?" The young man is clutching a half-dozen placards, each bearing a blown-up photograph of one of the women killed.

Lucy holds up Bugaboo's leash. "I've got my hands full." The dog sniffs the volunteer's muddy shoes.

"I'll take one," Thomas says.

"No can do," the volunteer replies. "The guys get the ribbons, the girls get the signs."

"Just give me a sign, man." Thomas grabs the sign displaying the Meals on Wheels girl. The volunteer pulls the sign back.

"I said you can't have one."

"Fuck you, asshole!"

"Take a pill, bud," the volunteer says, hurrying off.

"I already did," Thomas yells. "And don't call me Bud!"

People stare.

"Real cool," Lucy snaps.

"Well, what's with the boy-gets-this, girl-gets-that crap? What's with rules when this whole fucking horror is, like, so . . . *unruly*?"

In his sunglasses, Lucy sees herself, her fatigue warped into a jolly clown face by the funhouse mirrors of the lenses. She glances away and scans the crowd, recognizing a bald, furrowed head, the reporter who interviewed her about DogPoz. He's speaking to three girls. She turns away. She doesn't want to talk to him. He'd ask, "What are you feeling?" and she'd stare at the faces of the dead women bobbing over the heads of the crowd and say, "Relief." Relief as potent as guilt. Relief that no one is waving a sign with her face on it. Or with Thomas's.

The march begins. On the long walk to the university, Lucy endures the silence by counting the number of fallen purple ribbons, muddied and trampled, that litter the way.

Excerpts from an Encyclopedia Entry

The first commercially successful gun silencer was designed by Hiram Percy Maxim, the son of Sir Hiram S. Maxim, the inventor of the automatic machine gun.

To cancel out sound, Maxim used a turbine chamber to churn the gases produced by an exploding charge. The idea came to him after he flushed a toilet and watched the water swirl away.

The term *silencer* is somewhat of a misnomer as gunshots cannot be truly silenced, but merely suppressed.

A Japanese Character

A Japanese girl is sitting under a pine tree. She wears a fuzzy cardigan sweater, a crisp white shirt, and capri pants. A leatherbound notebook is on her lap, and her felt pen hovers over the page as she gathers her thoughts.

Despite his sunglasses, Lucy can tell Thomas is staring.

The girl looks past them to the crowd on the football field, where students are filling the bleachers in preparation for the upcoming speeches. The silent march has ended here, just around the corner from Robertson Hall.

"I have to talk to her," he says.

"You can't. You're incognito, remember."

He slips off his sunglasses. "Don't do it," she says. "Chrissakes, Tom, you don't need to." He'll make things worse. Their friends might see him and think he's comforting a survivor. "That's just like Thomas," they'll say, and, though her face will burn, she won't blurt out the truth.

He walks away and she watches him interrupt the girl, whose name, she recalls from the newspaper, is Myuko. Myuko looks up, puzzled, and then smiles and with two fingers pantomimes scissors across her bangs. Thomas sits on the grass. Lucy watches them talk. He has his demons to grapple with, she tells herself. They don't involve her. She is a bystander. A grey stick figure on a diagram. Yet when Bugaboo pulls on the leash, draws her toward that pine tree, she doesn't resist.

Bugaboo scampers to Thomas and noses him in the ear. "A dog in go-go boots," Myuko says. She has a fleshy mole on her upper lip and faint eyebrows like a pair of smudged thumbprints. Thomas introduces Lucy and the dog. Lucy sits on the damp yellowing grass, and the three of them pretend to be absorbed by Bugaboo gnawing a pine cone, until Myuko mentions Cynthia, their classmate who's still in the hospital. "Have you been to see her?" Myuko asks Thomas. Lucy begins to say Thomas was out of town all week, but he cuts her off.

"I'll go tomorrow."

The newspaper said Myuko escaped with a flesh wound, and Lucy wonders where underneath the girl's clothing that wound is. She stares. When Myuko catches her eye, she quickly looks away. She glances at the columns of Japanese characters filling the pages of Myuko's notebook.

"Are you keeping a diary?" Lucy asks.

"Very healing." Myuko pats the pages. "You keep one?"

"Lucy keeps scrapbooks," Thomas says.

"Mementoes, keepsakes, that kind of thing," Lucy says. She attempted a diary in high school, but found her entries never captured the intricacy of her feelings. Her words simply toddled across the page like a string of daycare tots, infantile and un-coordinated. In contrast, the objects in her scrapbooks conjure up a spectrum of emotions and memories.

Thomas peers at Myuko's notebook. "I wish I could write like that."

"Maybe you can study Japanese," Lucy says, "after you've learned German." Thomas blinks fast, won't look at her, and she regrets her jab.

Myuko turns to a blank page in her diary and draws a large Japanese character, a blend of sabrelike dashes and strokes in black ink. She rips the page out and lays it on the grass between them.

"What does it mean?" Thomas asks.

"*Hyo*," Myuko says. "That means 'big cat.' The closest kanji to 'cheetah.'"

"You know Thomas's nickname?" Lucy says.

"*Der Gepard*," Myuko says. "And he knows mine."

"*Die Sonnenblume*," Thomas says. "The sunflower." He explains that Heidi, their professor, had them choose German nicknames.

"Heidi was crazy lady," Myuko adds. "She said language is a virus from outer space." Myuko and Thomas look at each other and their eyes well up. "Poor Heidi," Myuko whispers. She presses her palms into her eyes. "Poor *Glocke* and *Taube* and . . . and . . ."

"*Hündin und Giraffe und Apfelsine*," Thomas finishes.

He leans into Myuko till the two of them are hugging, faces tucked into shoulders. Silent. Lucy puts one hand on Thomas's back, the other gingerly on Myuko's back. She feels the heaving of their breath. She feels the heaving of her own. She glances down. On the grass, between the three of them, lies the big cat. Lucy tries to make out a cheetah in the random lines and dashes, but the character could be anything. An elephant, a tulip. Or something less easy to define. Rage, love, shame, forgiveness. Any of these things.

Or all of them at once.

BARBARA ROMANIK

Seven Ways into Chandigarh

V2: two major roads intersecting at the city centre

P.L. Varma and P.N. Thapar sit quietly looking at Le Corbusier. They tell him they would be honoured if he'd become the chief architect of the new capital in the province of Punjab. He thinks, "Shit." Sequestered and Swiss, Le Corbusier whispers, "*Merde.*" The English say "Bloody shit." The Indian officials speak better English than most of the English he's met. If it wasn't for their skin colour, he'd expect them to invite him up to London for tea. The Punjabi city is to be named Chandigarh after an existing village and the Hindu goddess of power, Chandi. *Garh* means fortress. Yvonne is who he thinks of next. When they tell him about their lack of resources and the pitiful budget, he swears under his breath. But he likes the idea: a new capital of Punjab with its Caesarean birth, rising between the river valleys of Sukhana Cho and Patiali Rao, and him as its chief architect. They have an American company's plans, but it wouldn't take too long to augment those. They are persistent, but he says no. He will not live in India. If they want him, they'll let him work from his office, here at 35 rue de Sèvres.

Pierre, his cousin, is involved. "Listen, Corbu," Pierre says. "Take it on – you won't regret it." Even though Pierre Jeanneret has been his shadow for the last thirty years, Le Corbusier doesn't understand his quiet cousin. At a dinner party, Yvonne says,

"Tell us about this Indian project, Pierre." Pierre is excited; old fools shouldn't get excited like this, and Le Corbusier's not an old fool. He watches Pierre; Pierre is fifty-four, and nine years younger than himself. Corbu hates dinner parties. It is one of Yvonne's artist friends who says, "I still don't understand. Why would a woman like yourself marry someone like Le Corbusier?"

"Temporary lack of judgment, a fit of madness," Le Corbusier answers for her.

Yvonne laughs; that's enough for him. The woman is persistent though, like a terrier. He must have insulted her work at some point. Finally he says, "Wait a minute, how is your mannequin exhibit doing? It was installed in that tasteless little gallery off rue Marie, wasn't it?" Yvonne shakes her head. Small people require smallness; it is not his fault that he is a severe judge of character, of art.

"You've been out of sorts," Yvonne tells him before she turns off the lamp. "Pierre is right: you will need a little probing, but you will take that project."

"I will not."

"Yes, you will."

"*Merde.*"

He wishes she would not snore so. He wishes she'd not take in air with such greediness. Such singleness of mind, perhaps the way he slices the city in half, like an apple, cutting again to get at the perfect centre. He thinks about solving the traffic problem of Chandigarh. Seven Vs, *voies*, or levels of transportation. The pedestrians must be isolated from the street traffic. He hates cars, he hates their evil little uncomplicated engines. "Stop snoring, Yvonne." It's the backhanded way her breath comes out through her mouth instead of her nose, unnatural, almost wheezing. "You're going to take that job, *oui, oui, oui.*"

"*Merde.*" He turns over in bed. But the buildings are already lining up on a grid, eight hundred by twelve hundred metres. They are popping into his head with her every breath; a facade and its balconies take shape and the goddamn hallway leading to the stairway. Up into the roof. The stairs curve the way her breath . . . "SHUT UP!" He jumps out of bed, puts a coat over his pyjamas, and walks out.

Yvonne turns over in bed, smiling.

He hates people who satisfy him completely. There are only two and one of them is himself. He forces his thoughts into a line; he will speak to Pierre again.

Pierre telephoned after he left the dinner party. "Corbu, I have a letter to you from Nehru himself."

"So?" Le Corbusier had answered. But he was flattered.

Since the failure of the United Nations project, his role in it, he's felt a little useless. And whatever kind of man he is, he is not a useless one. But the Indians have warned him about tall buildings; they can't afford the technology to build them. Le Corbusier feels the lining of his coat, just like Nehru must have felt the lining of his new suit *Made in India* when he spoke wistfully of the clean, open spaces of Chandigarh. On one hand Indians in Chandigarh will be free from the tyranny of the filth-ridden, overcrowded cities, and on the other, they'll be free from the dirty toil of farming. Independent India must have the best, even if the best isn't quite Indian. Nehru hired Albert Mayor as the city planner and Matthew Nowicki as its architect. Then Nowicki's plane crashed in August of 1950, *merde* indeed. Via Jane Drew and Maxwell Fry, in London, a delegation made its way to Paris and Le Corbusier's door. The politics of this do not interest him; Le Corbusier merely notes the circumstances that have led here.

V7: pedestrian paths through strips of parkland in various city sectors

Yvonne and Le Corbusier sit in the park. A little girl stands near them staring at the pond, at the swans in it. Le Corbusier cannot help but say, "Take your finger out of your nose. Look at you, you don't look like a girl, but like a little piggy. Only little pigs in a pigsty act like that. You don't want to act like a pig now, do you?"

The girl takes her finger out of her nose and looks at him grumpily, near tears. "I'm not a pig, you are a big pig, you are . . ." The child is lost for words.

"Swine," Yvonne suggests.

"Swine!" the girl yells. "You're a really big swine."

Yvonne laughs, patting the child's head. "Listen," she says, "if you get me one of those twirls, you can get one for yourself." She points to a boy with a long Popsicle on a stick. And as she's trying to win over the child, Yvonne's head moves like a tulip in the breeze, pendular, swaying left and right. "I'll give you the money. What do you think?" She opens up her purse, takes her wallet, and hands the money to the little girl.

The child nods and Yvonne lightly touches her on the shoulder, sending the little girl toward the ice cream cart. She waves and nods reassuringly to the mother of the child, who watches them, concerned.

"You'll never see that money again," Le Corbusier adds.

"Swine, priceless," Yvonne says, ignoring him.

"Chandigarh can be the city I've always wanted to build. My city."

"*Ville radieuse?*"

"No. Not exactly."

"Not another Algiers." She touches his sore spot. He fidgets as if stung but ignores her.

"In India man is face to face with nature, with her violence too. I will need to search for solutions that surpass ordinary architecture. Innovation and imagination, the conquest of fundamental problems of town planning. Economy, sociology, and ethics – imagine mastering all these."

"Mastering – *tu es fou!*"

The girl comes back with the twisting Popsicles and hands one to Yvonne. "*Merci, j'aime les glaces,*" Yvonne says, satisfied just like that.

Le Corbusier looks at the child, annoyed.

"Listen. If I give you the rest of this money, do you promise to put it in your piggy bank and save it up?" Yvonne asks the girl.

"*Oui, oui.*" The girl jumps up. Le Corbusier watches. The ice cream will surely capsize and topple to the ground.

"*Oui, oui,* you sound like a piggy in a sty, tail in the air and her snout in the mud. You keep squealing like that and you'll drop your ice."

The little girl gives him a dirty look and then sticks her tongue out at him.

Yvonne laughs and turns the child away from him. "Put out your hand, *chérie*."

She hands the child her change.

"Greedy little piggy," he says so the child can hear him.

"Edouard!" Yvonne sends the girl on her way and licks her ice.

"Well, greed should not be encouraged in children." Yvonne ignores him and inserts the Popsicle in her mouth and pulls it out. "Aren't you too old to be eating a Popsicle?"

She shakes her head and hands him the tall, red-, blue-, and white-swirled Popsicle. "Well, go ahead, eat it. I know you want to."

"No." He makes a face and pushes his glasses up on his nose, holding the Popsicle at a distance like an article of dirty clothing.

"Come on, Le Corbusier, are you afraid of a Popsicle?" Yvonne raises her eyebrows and frowns. Then she gets up from the bench and looks around the park.

Tasting the tip of the Popsicle, he indulges in the treat. He watches his shadow, its head in the pond. He must look into this issue of Indian parks.

"Not bad," he says.

"See."

Yvonne leans in and affectionately kisses him on the cheek. She upsets his balance and he drops the Popsicle right between his legs.

"*Merde!*" He takes out his handkerchief and starts wiping it off. "There should only be white ice cream. Blue and red, this will never come off. Well, what are you laughing at me for?"

Yvonne holds her stomach with one hand and her mouth with the other, the laughter bubbling over.

"Stop laughing, for God's sake. Old fool." He throws the last of the broken Popsicle into the garbage can. "Well, what?" he says to her.

"I do like ices but if you think I'm going to lick it off your pants, you . . ." She bursts out laughing again.

"Ahh . . ." He throws the handkerchief at her. "You are disgusting." But he smiles.

V3: roads surrounding residential sectors intended for fast motor traffic

In the spring of 1951, a magician came to a sandy rest house on the road to Simla. He was riding the tail of a thirty-kilometres-per-hour wind. He brushed his coat and took off his black hat. To the people around him, he seemed unnecessarily pale on top of being white, like a chimney on top of a house. His wire spectacles made his eyes look beady. He drew India, and then the city, with such speed that his crayon bled into the pages of his sketchbook. He was conjuring up and selling a city: Le Corbusier believed he carried innovation and imagination in his breast pocket and that it was something worthwhile to give to the dream-hungry. He spent four weeks in the rest house on the road to Simla with his team of architects, but he itched to be gone sooner, and the city's guiding principles were ironed out in only four days.

Mayer's curved roads were straightened, and the order of the grid reigned supreme. In his bag of tricks, Le Corbusier had a famously presentable repertoire: file folders for strict separation of living, working, circulation, and leisure; pocketed seeds for trees and parks; a geometrical scalpel to cut grand vistas and processional axes; a mild claustrophobia, or affinity for open spaces rather than enclosures; belief that with his monocular eyesight he could see the future coming, like the Japanese bullet train, and Jeanneret and Fry, with his feeble French, made minor suggestions, but no one proved a match for the man in the black hat. The Indians more than anyone seemed converted because the magician was also a prophet; oh, the velocity and determination with which he could speak! What the magician glimpsed was that Indians have no shortage of land and like to make their beds under the stars. There's no need for skyscrapers to bring them closer to the plummeting fate, night and day. Caste and custom forced reimagining of the uniform, communal, medium-rise apartments into a variety of houses (small as that variety was). Le Corbusier could not sit still on the roof of the rest house at night. Even though he hadn't left yet, he kept noting that his team would do well to encourage loggias and sleeping terraces, ·

already composing long lists and letters of instructions for his underlings. While it was decided the magician would focus his energy on designing the buildings of the Capital Complex, the governing seat of Punjab, it would be up to Jeanneret, Fry, and his wife, Jane Drew, and their Indian assistants to design and build the rest of the city.

Before he left, the magician put his hand in his pocket and handed his cousin a yellow handkerchief. As he turned, the yellow handkerchief, which was still partly in Le Corbusier's pocket, slipped out farther and turned out to be tied to a brilliant red handkerchief. And as Le Corbusier continued to walk, and Pierre Jeanneret held on, the red turned out to be tied to a sky-blue one and that one to a burgundy one, burgundy to green, orange, pink, etc. This continued long after the magician stepped into the car, into the train, and then onto the plane. The magic stretched thin all the way from Chandigarh to Paris.

Le Corbusier stopped making his brief visits, and Drew and Fry moved on after five years, but Pierre Jeanneret remained in India for fourteen years. Tongue gymnastics didn't interest him. Pierre carried on with the project, worked on-site. "Control, continuity, and professionalism" was his motto; he liked his job. Often he'd draw the first sketches for the plans he and Le Corbusier would later refine. He was clear-headed, soft-spoken, and polite. A realist, he made do. But no one who sees the Gandhi Bhavan at Punjab University can doubt Pierre Jeanneret was a talented architect in his own right. He said to himself, sooner or later, I'll get what I want. And he did. He saw others' and his own buildings rise, monumental and non-monumental, impractical and practical, perfect.

As the Indian workers (thousands of women and children included) used half a dozen concrete mixers and one crane, rickety scaffolding, and donkeys to pull the concrete slabs into place, Pierre Jeanneret watched them build Chandigarh by hand. While supervising the construction, Jeanneret became available to a group of young Indian architects. They were looking not only for someone to learn from, but also for someone to teach. He seemed malleable yet form-giving.

"Bansi Lal," Le Corbusier once exclaimed when he stayed with Pierre in Chandigarh and Pierre's multi-purpose cook, bearer, and valet served him mussels in white wine and garlic. "You're not only an immaculate chef, but I'm told your floral and animal dhurrie and carpet designs are extraordinary. I must see them sometime."

"Yes, Sahib," Bansi said to Le Corbusier, but looked at Pierre Jeanneret. Pierre winked at him. Whether self-interested or altruistic, Jeanneret had a knack for seeing potential and helping it along. Every project needs a man who takes the time, and Chandigarh needed Pierre Jeanneret.

Pierre died only two years after he left India, in Geneva, the city where he was born. But he asked that his ashes be scattered on Sukhna Lake in Chandigarh. By the end of his life, Pierre Jeanneret felt more at home there than anywhere else.

V4: bazaar streets following a slightly irregular path and permitting slow-moving traffic

Haat, Chandigarh 1964 (day market). Park your bicycle and do your groceries. Easier said than done. What do I need, what can I have, what will make do? Keep pace, weaving between the traffic among the *rehri* and *pattriwallas*. Having little certainly makes your choices easier. Buy directly from the farmers. Keep track of Apni Mandi market, opened for business just once a week but cheaper. I want a mango, I want a pear, I want a comb for my hair. Is the English and American money metal or paper? Does it dirty one's hands? Does a sari get in the way? Are there book carts? A *rehri* cart full of western books? Architecture books? In English? Doubt even the English can afford these books with pictures. How quickly one forgets the foreignness of somebody else's tongue, permeating, peppering your own. How much for this? How much for that? Can I supplement it with vegetables from our garden? "Is this fish good? Oh delicious –" You smile at the pretty woman bargaining with the hawker, and not getting her way. Will the rice go around? Then the smell from the *dhaba* hits you, warm food is irresistible, so is the temptation of sitting down on one of the charpoys, to rest your feet. You turn away. You can't really afford that, so instead you approach a man selling roasted peanuts and chickpeas and, pointing, you buy some.

You had a dream last night that a man from the Kumhar squat housing was following and harassing you as you were walking your bicycle toward the university. Your chain had fallen off its spikes yet again, and this made getting away on your bicycle impossible. You shouted for him to leave you alone and, eventually, he did. Then you were on the roof of one of the university buildings with Jeet and Sarbjit, the taller building on the left providing limited shade. You tripped in your sari over the various platforms you had to cross, stairs you had to climb. Jeet helped you up. You were in love with either him or Sarbjit, but you couldn't remember which one. It was some kind of restaurant on the roof. On your white table stood ice creams in tall glass dishes, the kind Europeans and Americans own in the architecture magazines at the university's library. Across the table you looked at Sarbjit and he was polite but disinterested, the way people who care about you but don't love you are. He pointed out to you the Swiss architect Pierre Jeanneret, who looked no bigger than a white ant on the ground below you. It was all a horrible dream because buildings came together brick by brick in your head, but you would never have the skill to build them. If you got lucky, you might end up some wealthy man's over-educated wife.

In the middle of the night, you woke. Your fears, like the breeze through the wet, *khuss-khuss tattie*, filtered, hovering, whispering – right now you are young, but you might as well be dead. You might as well be for sale with the rest of the cheap handwoven cloth of any of the *thariwallas*.

V5: loop road intersecting and distributing traffic within the sector

Closing letter from Le Corbusier's 1965 edition of *The Radiant City*:

March 9, 1964

I have just corrected the proofs of the reprint of this book: The Radiant City, written between 1931 and 1933 and first published in 1935.

Well, Mr. le Corbu, congratulations! You posed the problems of forty years in the future twenty years ago! And you received your full and copious share of kicks in the backside for your pains!

This book contains an impressive mass of meticulous and complete plans for new cities — plans that go from the detail to the whole, from the whole to the detail.

You were told: No! You were treated as a madman! Thank you very much!

Have you ever thought, all you "Mister NOs!" that these plans were filled with the total and disinterested passion of a man who has spent his whole life concerning himself with his "fellow man," concerning himself fraternally. And for this very reason, the more he was in the right the more he upset the arrangements or schemes of others. He upset things. Etc. etc . . .

[Le Corbusier's signature]

L-C

PS On pages 270 to 287 you will find the plan for Antwerp, an amazing total project put before the authorities during the Urban-Planning Competition. Read it: you will find yourself in an Homeric world.

This PS is also a coda.

V6: roads giving additional access to houses

Le Corbusier has been blind in his right eye since 1918. Yvonne puts her hand over his good eye. "Don't look at me. I'm old, I'm ugly, I'm dying."

"I want to see you."

"Liar. You never look. Nothing's as good as what's in that head." Ungently, Yvonne taps him on his head with her other hand. In the dark, he leans over her. Her hand covers his left eye; he is blind.

"Not true."

"Don't lie to me. Only a blind man would think that a city can belong to him, and only an egomaniac believes he knows what's best for millions of people. Your city, such a thing cannot be. Your city is a dream, it has mastered you. I have mastered you." Her hand falls away from him, quivering. She is exhausted from the effort. He seeks her eyes out in the dark.

"You have."

Yvonne laughs at that and begins to cough. She turns to the side so the cough can escape her body more easily. He pretends he is drawing the Modulor on her back with his nose. She breathes out. From her breathing, he can tell she is smiling. He leans into her back, his face seeking the shape of shoulder, mitre of muscle. Her strength. He kisses her neck, pulls her to him.

"You're only tender when I am sick."

"You always laugh me off when I'm tender. When you're sick, you're less mean."

"You need mean." She turns to him. Everything about her twists like a staircase that fails to lead anywhere. "Why are you always dressed for my funeral?"

"Yvonne."

"You are." She cries into his pyjama shirt. "The dark suits and that awful bow tie." She holds onto the pockets as if she were going to rip them off.

"*Mon couturier*, you know clothes mean little to me." He tries to calm but instead enrages her.

"I hate you," she says, turns away. He smiles into her hair. Embraces her more tightly.

On October 1, 1957, at 19:00, Le Corbusier draws Yvonne's hand in his portable atelier, his notebook. The fingers of her right hand curl around the thumb of his left hand. He draws while she is holding onto him and slowly dying. One can assume he adds later, *M le 5 octobre 57 a l'ambe*, and farther down, *en souvenir d'Yvonne Le Corbusier merci! L-C.* Someone dies, within the pages of Le Corbusier's notebook. You would think he'd stop drawing, but he cannot. The city has got him in its hand.

The Open Hand Monument Le Corbusier designs for Chandigarh's Capital Complex is not built until 1986. This giant hand, a metal sheet rising twenty-six metres from a sunken trench, rotates freely in the wind. Placed on a high concrete pedestal, it conveys the city's emblem: *Open to give, Open to receive.*

VI: regional roads leading into the city from the outside

Norma Evenson, you told me that Le Corbusier may have sensed that his talents were primarily those of a monumental architect, and thus chose to dedicate himself to the sphere in which he excelled. You're always compassionate in your criticism, even to Le Corbusier.

Chandigarh and now Delhi, Madras, and Calcutta, dear Norma, no one has written these cities into being quite like you have. You have brought me here. I want to show you the picture I've found of Le Corbusier and Yvonne Gallis. You might think it irrelevant, Norma, but this one's my favourite. Look, Le Corbusier and Yvonne are sitting on the beach in their bathing clothes. Leaning into each other, both are looking right into the distance, both are laughing. A caryatid, she is heavier and steadier in her one-piece suit, leaning back on extended arms. There's a handkerchief encircling her 1920s-like bob. Half lying, he leans his head on her shoulder. His body bevelled, his shoulder meets her left elbow. They are not young and I suspect better for it.

Norma, imagine Chandigarh's Capital Complex at our breakfast table, the morning after. Our world is plate flat but for the square grates, the cinnamon waffles stacked into the secretariat. Its texture: reinforced concrete. The spout of the assembly's roof awaits monsoons and orange juice. Intermittently sun and water fall into the yellow pools, the soft-boiled eggs.

We'll watch each other, you reading the paper and me staring at you through opera binoculars I bought at the market of Madhya Marg. You'll take away my binoculars. "The half-circles below my eyes are not the arches of the High Court. Shouldn't you be doing something . . . constructive?" you'll say.

"Ah, Norma, justice is a building with a beehive lattice, *brise-soleil*, and three columns. We'll gather up our sins until en masse they'll turn amber and pour like honey on your pancakes. How many architects does it take to screw in a light bulb?" Screw over a city?

Norma, you'll shake your head and go back to your paper. Perhaps I am a pest. "I began with wooden blocks someone always kept knocking over, then I moved onto Lego and three-thousand-piece picture puzzles. What did you do when you were a kid?"

"I carried umbrellas like bridges over my head," you'll tell me, Norma.

"Umbrellas? Like Le Corbusier's parasols? Upturned? Over-hanging roofs supported by arches, piers, or *pilotis*. Not a down-ward movement, but opening up-out." I imagine you carrying an upturned umbrella just waiting for rain.

"The Governor's Palace, or the Museum of Knowledge, when will it get built, Norma?"

"The last of Le Corbusier's Chandigarh dreams . . . maybe never." You'll brush your greying hair out of your eyes.

"Norma, think of us intrepid at the complex with the dust storm sanding our skin and the sun scorching it to blackened toast. You could invite death just by lying down."

You'll disapprove of my morbid turn and improve upon my childish ignorance by informing me about sliding objects and subtle axial shifts of a Mogul palace or gardens that inspired the plan of Chandigarh. "Norma." I'll get up and put my arm around your neck. "I don't mind the flat tracts of concrete, scrubby grass, and the cracked cement. Like dust, it gives me heart that things have been and always will be."

"Perhaps," you'll say, always weighing your words like buildings, leaning back. "But this city was not built for you."

EMILY WHITE

Various Metals

"**M**y son could use a girl like you," said Mrs. Greer.

"Oh?" Elena asked, looking up briefly. It wasn't unusual for her clients to proposition her this way, assuming the efficiency she brought to wills could be detached from the law and resettled upon some gay or dissolute son with the same orderly results. None of her clients knew about Robert: most looked at her bare hands and assumed she'd never been married. Their mistake was frustrating but professionally convenient: Elena doubted that many of her clients would want their estates handled by someone unlucky enough to lose a husband at thirty-one.

"I'm assuming you're not married," Mrs. Greer added. She leaned back in her chair and glanced at the windows that lined the far wall of Elena's office. At sixty storeys up, the light seemed pale and unfinished, as though in need of more time to collect itself.

"No. I'm not."

"I forget sometimes how much things have changed," Mrs. Greer said, stretching a hand out into the light. "Girls want different things now, don't they?"

"No," Elena replied, watching the shadow of Mrs. Greer's hand against the carpet. "I think we still all want the same things."

Robert had been a set-up. "A *scientist*," a friend had whispered, scratching Robert's email address onto Elena's notepad. From his stilted responses, she'd been expecting someone short or in some other way compressed – neat or pale or dogmatic.

Instead she had walked into the Hart House cafeteria and seen a tall man fidgeting with a pair of muffin tongs. The January light had been falling in a diamond pattern across the back of his coat and trousers, and when he turned to look at her it ran like water across his hair. She'd stopped in the doorway, letting the cold air and other students press past her, and when he mouthed her name and pointed toward her chest, all she could do was nod.

He was an analytical chemist. On the top floor of the Walberg building on College Street, he had a high-windowed lab with sprinklers in the ceiling and drains in the floor. In the middle of the room sat a man-sized, plexi-glassed bed of dirt. Sometimes he planted cabbages, sometimes carrots or sweet potatoes. Once, Elena had come in and found the whole bed covered with a soft curtain of chives.

"Don't touch," Robert warned, as she reached to pluck for a strand. The soil was contaminated. She knew this but he had to keep reminding her. His explanations were gentle, almost apologetic. The soil was filled with whatever he was studying at the time – lead, nickel, cadmium, arsenic. It was his job, Robert explained, tracing a big-knuckled finger against the side of the glass, to measure the speed and ease with which the different metals moved into the food source.

Elena worried it wasn't safe, but when she asked Toshi, one of the other chemists, about whether Robert might be breathing in contaminants, he'd just shrugged and pulled his mug out of the test-tube sterilizer.

"You're breathing in metals all the time. Lead, some arsine. You've got them all in you right now."

"But he's working with them directly. Isn't that different?"

"Not really."

Just then Robert came out of his lab, his beetle-eyed goggles hanging loosely from his wrist and his lab coat covered with a fine film of dust. He saw Elena biting her lip and asked what was wrong.

"We're in a panic about your safety," Toshi said, looking around for a spoon.

"Toxicity, you mean?"

Elena nodded.

"Don't worry," Robert said, leaning to kiss the top of her head. He'd smelt of dirt and starch and of something sharp and comforting, like cloves.

After Robert's death, Elena had kept their apartment but emptied it out. She gave his books to the lab and his clothes to Goodwill, traded their king-sized bed in for a double, and dismantled the desk he'd made out of bricks and a door. She kept one photograph of him – standing tall and lean on the edge of a beach in North Carolina – and put the rest of her pictures in boxes in the closet.

Within a year, the apartment gave little indication of having ever housed anyone but herself. Her body was so noisy with grief that the empty space provided some relief, but her parents objected to it. Divorced for nearly thirty years, they held remarkably similar views of how Elena should respond to her loss. For them, the answer lay in accumulation. Her mother and father had been young when they divorced, and they'd seemed to dedicate the rest of their lives to buffering against future losses. Elena's mother had remarried and started a new family; her father had moved to Vancouver and begun speculating in land. He'd used the proceeds of sales to buy an enormous house, carvings, and abstract art. He had also, at some point Elena barely noticed, acquired Sophie, a woman so small and self-effacing that Elena had once spent twenty minutes on the phone in her father's overstuffed living room before noticing her stepmother curled like a scarf between cushions on the sofa.

"It's like a Dali painting in here," Robert had remarked during a visit they'd made after their engagement. He'd been leaning against her father's marble kitchen counter, eating carrot sticks. Copper-potted plants hung from the ceiling, a parakeet was flying loose through the house, and Sophie's two young children were at the table, eating bologna sandwiches in matching leopard-skin bathing suits.

"He likes it like this. It lets him pretend he's still ethnic."

"That's one word for it. What do we do with the kids?"

Cosmo and Celeste looked up expectantly. They wanted the PlayStation Palace downtown. "Or maybe the zoo," Celeste said, pronouncing her words carefully and settling her small hands on the table like a negotiator.

"How about the turtle pool?" Robert responded. Without waiting for a reply, he'd headed to the yard to look for the hose, Cosmo trailing behind him, chanting "bor-ing," and Celeste staying next to Elena at the table, looking sadly at her half-eaten sandwich.

Children and the possibility of having them were not subjects she and Robert had ever discussed. It wasn't a conversation they needed to have. It seemed to Elena that children required some space to claim as their own, some territory they could assemble from what their parents didn't need, and she and Robert didn't have any such room between them. Even in the period immediately after the accident, when her waking life was more hallucinatory than real, she'd never wished for a child. When her mother, at Robert's funeral, said the real tragedy was that there had been no children, Elena had fallen hard against a friend's arm. With mourners averting their eyes, Elena had explained that a baby wouldn't make any difference, that Robert would still be dead.

"You should go, El," her stepfather said. "I'll go with you. It could be fun." David was a film critic who wrote at home in the afternoons. He could usually be counted on to take her side in the face of her parents' demands, so Elena was surprised to find him supporting her father's quest to redecorate her apartment.

Her father had come to visit two weeks earlier, and had walked from room to room with his hands pressed to his head as though the lack of furniture caused him physical pain. He'd ordered Elena into the car and stopped at the first boutique he'd seen – a store called Au Naturel that sold nothing but bathroom accessories. Elena had nodded as he handed her a pewter soap dish and a rhinestone-encrusted toothbrush holder, but she drew the line at a bath mat as fat and white as a pillow.

"It's too much," she said. "It's like it's designed for someone else's house."

"Maybe now," her father said. "But once we're finished, your whole place is going to look like this."

Elena hadn't been sure what this meant, but a week later a card arrived from Vancouver. Inside was her stepmother's child-like script, advising that "with sheets really the most important thing is threadcount," and a cheque for eight hundred dollars.

She told David she planned to put it in the bank.

"You've got enough money," he said.

Elena paused. "I wouldn't know what to spend it on," she said evasively.

"Well, one idea would be sheets."

"I don't know where you buy them."

"I can find out," David said. "I have friends with sheets. We might have to go through some pretty murky channels, but I bet we can get some."

The bedding department at Sears was in the basement, with the ceilings so low the beds looked like they were cowering against some sort of attack. Elena had brought the card her stepmother had sent, and consulted it against the labels on packages of sheets.

"Sophie says three hundred or higher. These are in the hundreds."

"I think she just meant it as a suggestion."

"No. Sophie knows about these things. That's all she does, is run her house." Like her own mother, Elena realized, but it was too late to retract the comment. David ignored it and walked toward the designer section. A white cardboard "Sale" sign sat inelegantly on a four-poster bed. David pulled at the top sheet.

"This is nice."

"Check the label."

David reached for the plastic display sheet looped to one of the pillows.

"Bingo. 350. You could stop a truck with one of these."

The duvet had a harsh gold sheen, but the sheets underneath were plum coloured, with copper piping along the edges. "They're all right," Elena said. There were matching pillowcases and gold-threaded cushions embroidered with small round mirrors.

David collapsed onto the bed.

"You going to take them? I'll find us a clerk."

"I don't know. It's a bit much, don't you think?"

"How so?"

Elena blushed. "I mean, it's just me, isn't it?"

David sat up and reached out a hand, pulling her to the bed. "Get the sheets, El. And the pillows. Buy the whole goddamn bed."

"It's too much for one person."

"You're only thirty-five, El. You don't have to be *one person* for the rest of your life."

"You make it sound like it's some sort of a choice."

"It is," he said.

She didn't respond, and he watched her as though counting off the seconds before he would make the decision himself. This was just what Robert used to do, propping his elbows on the table and tapping his fingers together like a metronome, waiting for her to either speak or surrender the decision to him.

"Right," David said, after about a minute. "I'll get us a clerk."

Elena's status as *one person* was not something her parents or step-parents ever discussed, except in the most indirect of terms. Her mother encouraged her to have children, and her stepmother sent jewellery and camisoles on birthdays, but the subjects of sex and dating were avoided. Elena had been on dates, but the loss of Robert had led to a corresponding loss of whatever energy or enthusiasm it was that men responded to. The word that came to mind most frequently on these dispirited occasions was *ruined*. "I am a ruined woman," she'd muttered to her reflection in a restaurant washroom two years after the accident. And it was true. People could be ruined, like fruit left too long in the sun, or wood left standing in water. A rot – unnoticeable from the outside – could creep in and ruin the whole.

And it was this – her fundamental sense of herself as beyond repair – that had made her reluctant to acquire expensive sheets and soft cushions. These were things a woman expecting a lover

would buy. Her first night in the bed, tossing against the unnaturally smooth, almost cool feel of the bedding, she'd felt like
a corpse in a winding sheet. She'd gotten up that first night and
slept on the couch.

"Anything else?" David asked. He was phoning from home.
Elena noted the time on her billing pad and nudged the binder in
front of her shut. She was trying to help a man leave nothing to
his wife. She'd encouraged him against this – not only was it
illegal, it was unethical – but Mr. Briscoe, thin and faded in a suit
that looked too large for him, had removed his glasses and said
that the golden retrievers he'd raised during his lifetime had
brought him more joy than the woman he'd married. When
Elena explained that his assets had to pass to his wife but that
he could place restrictions on how she disposed of his property,
he'd nodded and said that that was a good solution but not the
best one.

"What would the best solution be?" she asked.

He'd looked genuinely surprised that the answer wasn't
obvious. "Her dying first," he said. "That would solve everything."

Elena pulled her office chair into a pool of cool January light
and fished her father's envelope out of her purse.

"There was another card," she said, examining the handmade paper.

"What did he tell you to get?"

"Nothing this time. Or nothing specific. He mentioned
plants and lamps."

"Not plants, that's getting ahead of yourself."

"How so?"

"It's like a building project," David said. "You start from the
ground up. I'm thinking carpets."

Elena was surprised to hear that he was thinking about her
furniture at all. "I don't really need any," Elena said.

"No," David replied, as though he hadn't heard her. "I have
a place in mind. On King. It's Persian. Or Moroccan. Whatever
you call the place now."

David had appeared in the tired months that followed her parents' divorce. He'd had long hair then, and wore tasseled vests, and he used to lie on his back in the attic and blow smoke rings into the grainy winter light. He had seemed at ease in the house in a way that Elena and her mother had never been able to master. With her father gone, whole rooms had begun to ring with a sort of mocking emptiness, as though Elena and Susan weren't substantial enough to fill them. They'd retreated into the more manageable corners of the house: Elena to the attic, where she hoarded blankets and thermoses of milk; and her mother to the kitchen, where she sometimes fell asleep on the warm tile floor.

David's appearance stripped the house of its smug air of victory and provided a focus for their scattered attention. David asked Elena if she minded sharing the attic, and he swiftly assembled a small office in the stripped-down room, hauling up a desk, a manual typewriter, and a 1920s projector nailed to a workbench. His goal, then, was to be a film reviewer, and he had progressed from filing free reviews with the *Willowdale Mirror* to having his own byline in the *Toronto Star*.

He'd wanted to do more than that, though. He had a letter of encouragement from Pauline Kael framed on the wall above his desk, and he sometimes sat with Elena on the attic floor and read *New Yorker* reviews aloud as though he were reading out parts of a play.

During Elena's engagement, David had settled on the idea of a book. It was not something he'd ever attempted before, and his editors at the *Star* offered only tempered support. The book – *Rethinking Our Relationship: Canadian Creators and American Audiences* – had been meant to demonstrate that Canadian participation in the U.S. film industry had resulted in the interweaving of Canadian mores into American cultural products; it had also been meant to establish David as a cultural critic. He hadn't succeeded: a kindly worded review in the *Star* suggested that David had perhaps failed to account for the ways in which the American media influenced his titular creators from their earliest years; a harsher critique in *Cineforum* said that real influence was measured in dollars, not lines of script, and that by this standard Canada's contribution to American film probably ranked somewhere just south of Peru's.

David had asked Elena what she thought of the book, but it had appeared just nine months after Robert's death, and she'd been too tired to read it. She told him that his next book would do better.

"There aren't going to be any more books, El," he replied.

They had been sitting in her kitchen, waiting for the kettle to boil, and David had looked at her with eyes rung round with circles. She knew what he wanted to hear – that he should write again, that his ideas were valuable and that it was only a matter of time before he found his audience. She could hear the platitudes rattle around in the back of her skull, but she was too drained to voice them. All she had the energy to do was to raise her hand to her head and block the light from her eyes. David had waited a moment, and then he had patted her on the shoulder and risen to make the tea.

When they arrived at the carpet store – with its concrete floors and peach-coloured walls, its delicate men in tasseled shoes and their proffered glasses of apple tea – David seemed immediately at ease. He knotted his fingers into a bed of tassel ends and nodded mutely when Elena said she was going to remain seated atop a stack of carpets in the corner.

The manager, who had introduced himself as Abbas, quickly settled his attention upon David. Elena watched as the two men haggled about quality, with Abbas at one point holding up a stretch of rug until David dutifully removed his glasses and examined the stitching along a seam. They discussed colour schemes, patterns, cleansers, warranties, and what to do in the event of spilled wine.

"We've got it," David announced. He and Abbas stood like new parents on either side of a long red carpet hanging from hooks in the ceiling.

"It's handmade," they said, almost in unison. As Elena came closer she saw that the background – which had looked mostly solid from her perch across the room – was composed of fine, nail-sized points that gathered force as they left the centre of the rug, exploding into a colourful pattern of elephants, fish, and peacocks that looked lively enough to march right off the edge.

"It's beautiful," Elena said.

"It will be lovely in your home," the salesman said, not to Elena but to David, and David simply agreed, asking if they could bring it with them that afternoon. With the assistance of three young men who slid quietly out of the back room, the rug was dropped from the ceiling, expertly rolled, and stuffed into plastic wrapping.

"It'll fit on top," David called, as the clerks tried to cram the rug into the back of his minivan. He rushed out to help them, leaving Elena and Abbas alone in the shop.

"Your husband has a good eye," Abbas said appreciatively, making no move to help as David and the clerks tried to keep the carpet from sliding into a snowbank.

"He's not my husband."

"Your boyfriend, then."

David was now on the hood of the minivan, trying to pull the carpet forward. He was laughing and flushed with exertion. Elena was holding his gloves and hat, and she looked at them as though she had just been asked who owned them.

"He's my stepfather," she replied. But Abbas had already turned his attention away and had not asked for any such explanation.

At her apartment, David hauled the carpet into the living room, and with a bustling, distracted air told her to move the sofa aside. He began pulling books out of her bookcase and stacking them in neat, foot-high piles along the wall.

"You don't have much in here, do you?" he asked, dragging the bookcase into the hallway.

"I gave it away," Elena reminded him, but David was already in the kitchen, going through her drawers in search of a steak knife. He returned to the living room with knife in hand and stood like a butcher above the rug, considering it from side to side before cutting a quick jagged line from top to bottom. The plastic wrap fell away in even halves, flooding the room with the acrid smell of new wool.

Elena was about to open the window when David reminded her that the rug still had to be positioned. She hadn't heard him so bossy and satisfied since the years following his move into the house on Roselawn, when he used to stand in the middle of the attic in a T-shirt and jeans, smoking and looking serious while Elena, balanced on a chair, held movie posters against the wall so that he could decide on their placement.

The carpet – perhaps the whole day, the idle errands and the bright exoticism of the store, the lavish purchase and the gasping efforts to get the rug up the stairs – had brought out something youthful in him. The clean lines of the door frame made him look leaner, more angular, and he brushed his hair from his eyes with the quick energy of a younger man.

"It has to go more toward you," David said, and Elena obligingly dropped to her knees and tried to pull the carpet in as best she could. The wool itched her fingers, and the rug was difficult to manoeuvre. David kicked his shoes off and crossed the room purposefully, dropping down beside her like a man taking position in a trench, and on the count of three they both pulled, hauling the rug in quickly until they had their backs to the wall and the rug up to their chins.

"Is this far enough?" Elena asked.

David laughed, and leaned over to kiss her. The kiss was so light that for a moment she thought a tassel from the carpet had fallen across her lips. It was only when she turned her head and saw David beside her, very close, looking at her with confused affection, that she realized what had happened. The air around her suddenly felt very thick, as though she were trying to breathe through water. The red rug in her hands seemed too vivid, like a wound, and she wanted to get away from the carpet and into fresh air as quickly as she could.

She heard David say her name, but all her attention was focused on trying to get out from under the rug. It was pressed like a blanket over her legs and waist and she had to slither out from under it like a cat. David said her name again, and once she had reached the doorway – with its mercifully bare floors and its promise of the kitchen window – she turned to look at him.

He was still on the floor, with his back to the wall. The rug was pulled up to his chest, so that all she could see were his thin shoulders and the dark mat of his hair. Grey light from the window behind him turned the lenses of his glasses into opaque discs.

"I'm sorry," he said, in a voice she didn't immediately recognize. It was as though someone had taken his vocal cords and cut them in half, leaving him with less than his normal range. The radiator began its hourly series of knocks and wheezes, and David dropped his chin to his chest. With his head lowered, she could see the smooth curve of his eyelids, as well as the small layer of fat pressed in under his jaw. In that moment he looked not fifty-five but much older. And it was this posture, the pathetic droop of the rug over his lap and his downcast eyes, that made Elena do what she did next. Which was to cross back across the rug toward him, and touch his head lightly with the flat of her hand.

"I'm sorry. I didn't mean it," David muttered.

"I know," she said quietly. "I know how hard things can be."

Robert had died at thirty-one. The last time Elena had seen him, he'd been rushing out the door in a crewneck sweater and corduroys, his peacoat flopping around him, and his scarf trailing off to the side. When she saw him next, he was in a blue hospital gown, open at the neck, with a thick blanket pulled over the lower half of his body. His trousers had been cut away and his sweater sat in a white paper bag on a shelf beside his body.

The police had collected witness accounts of the accident and she'd read them all. Everyone talked about a tall man leaving the Chemistry building, seeing the streetcar at the stop and running toward it, covering the yard between the doorway and the stop with easy, even strides. There was a grey van trying to overtake the streetcar, and as the light turned green, it muscled forward, catching Robert by the side and throwing the top half of his body forward.

"It went really quiet," the streetcar driver told her. A heavy-set Korean with watery eyes, he'd sat with her at the police station with his hand pressed to his mouth, as though trying to muffle what he was saying. Robert's skull had broken. A girl waiting at the lights had been sprayed with blood and Robert's bookbag had exploded, releasing a snowfall of papers and pens.

In the first few years following the accident, Elena had tried to age Robert, attempting daily reconstructions of his face and body so that he would be maturing along with her. She'd tried to do the same with his tastes and expressions and his laughter; tried to imagine how his breath might smell differently now; how he might have developed a scar on his hand from an accident in the lab; how his understanding of chemistry might have deepened in the same manner as her understanding of the law.

It was difficult and lonely work, keeping him alive. And as she lay on her back in her bedroom that night she felt not dismay or embarrassment but a strange sense of relief. David's kiss had been unexpected and inappropriate but it had been meant for her alone. In all the time she'd been responding to it – pulling David out from under the rug and blocking the door until he sat with her in the kitchen and had a cup of tea and a shot of gin – she'd thought of no one but herself.

Right before David left, Elena had told him that she wouldn't tell anyone what had happened. David thought she'd meant Susan, of course, and it was true that she had no intention of telling her mother. But the person Elena had really meant was Robert – she meant she wasn't going to share what had happened with him, wasn't going to try to judge his reaction or summon him up to assist her with her thinking.

She had a secret to keep from him, the first one she'd had in years. And as she pulled her knees up to her chest and felt the floorboards below her spine, she was surprised to find that it made her happy.

About the Authors and Their Work

Randy Boyagoda on "Rice and Curry Yacht Club"
The primary focus of my writing is the chutney-rich landscape of contemporary Canadian life, with its sweet and sour mixtures of colonial experiences from near and far, its immigrant designs on native affirmation and native desires for exotic blandishment, and its suburban reinventions of civilization and urban provisions for smug sophistication. With the present story, these elements first came into constellation when I was thinking about that showy Old Toronto acronym RCYC, which, from my vantage, held within it the possibility of both "Royal Canadian Yacht Club" *and* "Rice and Curry Yacht Club." To bring out the deeper tensions and ironies of what struck me as a deliciously ambiguous arrangement of letters, I structured the story around dinner parties at one of Sri Lanka's finest hotels and at one of Toronto's most exclusive clubs. I was especially interested in exploring the internal ructions that the main character, Chandra, feels in both settings, and then in bringing these into play during two already nerve-wracking events: a successful immigrant family's momentous return to their homeland, and the first meeting of a newly engaged couple's respective families. At the core of Chandra's mischief is the bitterness that he feels over his inability to sit and eat with confidence at either table, a bitterness compounded by the self-aggrandizing ways of his bumptious father. Seeking adolescent, table-turning revenge, Chandra receives instead a boy's worst punishment: his best efforts to fight the inevitable only serve to confirm him as his father's son.

Randy Boyagoda is a Postdoctoral Fellow with the Erasmus Institute at the University of Notre Dame, and currently resides in South Bend, Indiana. Originally from Oshawa, he moved from Toronto to the United States in 1999, and completed his

Ph.D. in English at Boston University earlier this year. He regularly contributes fiction, reviews, articles, and literary essays to Canadian and American publications. His story "Water Spider," excerpted from a novella-in-progress, will appear in an autumn issue of *The Walrus*.

Krista Bridge on "A Matter of Firsts"

I remember that when I wrote this story, I was thinking about reversals – a married parent introducing a child to a lover, a crush on a person not typically crushworthy, fatness as sensual, a resplendent and wonderful thing. I was also thinking about an experience that is probably familiar to many young girls: a crush on an older girl or woman. Although these crushes aren't strictly sexual, they're deeply romantic and full of longing. I remember wanting to be adopted, in a sense, by these older girls, rescued and mothered and comforted by them.

The first draft of this story is quite different from the version that appears in this anthology. In the earlier version, the mistress turns on the girl toward the end; she is almost predatory in one scene. This felt so forced and predictable and wrong. I left the story for a year. The following summer, I was swimming alone in a lake, looking up a cliff at the cottage my entire family was staying in, and I was thinking about how I could only feel any kind of peace with the world when I was alone. The week after that, I rewrote the story, a version twice as long as this one that deals with the girl as a married woman. Then I cut it for publication until it was just this, the girl and the mistress.

Krista Bridge's fiction has been published in *Toronto Life's* Summer Fiction issue, *PRISM international*, and *Prairie Fire*, and has been nominated for a National Magazine Award. Her collection of short stories, entitled *The Virgin Spy*, will be published by Douglas & McIntyre in spring 2006. "A Matter of Firsts" also appears in *05: Best Canadian Stories*.

Josh Byer on "Rats, Homosex, Saunas, and Simon"

My teenaged mind was a sticky and caustic thing, drenched in anger and passion. For too long, I clung to the grotesque presumption that I should never abandon my youthful rage, or I'd instantly transform into an assembly-line automaton destined to die of a sledge-hammer heart attack weeks before retirement. I hid behind a cynicism-powered force field until my mid-twenties, plodding through the hallways of life with an attitude still half-formed.

As the emotional footprint of steel-toed-boot stomps and roving bully gangs gradually faded, the icy angst of trauma slowly loosened its grip on my brain. A head full of memories tainted by intoxicating, narcotic agony suddenly unglued – and the past became a glowing mosaic of meteor showers on mountaintops with my father, all-night ghost hunts in haunted farm fields, and tiny, amused glances from the electric blue eyes of my raven-haired first love.

"Rats, Homosex, Saunas, and Simon" was written during a cigarette-laden, microwaveable-burrito-fuelled rage caused by too much coffee and not enough common sense. I had flooded my mind with the pain of teenaged oppression, and it had drowned all the joy of those days from remembrance. I wanted to re-examine some of these seemingly horrifying events and pull out the small, beautiful moments of humour and light from their soupy depths. The result was the piece of fiction that appears in this anthology.

Josh Byer is an author, screenwriter, and journalist living in Burnaby, British Columbia. His prose has been featured in *Terminal City*, the *Ottawa Citizen*, the Canadian University Press, *Broken Pencil*, *Crank*, the *Surface*, the *Harrow*, *Forget*, and *Trip*. He has also written scripts for Keystone Entertainment, Ocean Productions, Mighty Pharaoh Films, and the *Tom Green Show*.

Craig Davidson on "Failure to Thrive"

Where did the inspiration for this story come from – geez, do we really want to open that particular can of worms? I honestly can't recall – could be I've purged the whole creative process from my brain, though perhaps, years from now, it will all come back to me in one of those horrible "repressed-memory" scenarios. Shudder! But that's not to say I consider myself a spectacularly depraved person for writing it – and should readers happen to enjoy it, they should not feel awful for whatever guilty pleasure it may provide. Enjoy it, I tell you!

Craig Davidson lives in Iowa City, where he is attending the Iowa Writers' Workshop. His first story collection, *Rust and Bone*, will be published by Viking Canada in October 2005. He's at work on a boxing novel.

McKinley M. Hellenes on "Brighter Thread"

Writing "Brighter Thread" took place sometime in 2004, somewhere between my sheets and my comforter. I like to write in bed. Looking for my stories where I sleep helps me to catch hold of them. I wanted to write about people who are baffled by love. I think we are all baffled by love, the way it can be like a freight train passing by another freight train in the night, and the passengers are never sure if those headlights were for real, or if they were merely an echo of a ghost of a freight train that passed by long ago. I think love is like that. I think it boggles the brain, and we are never quite sure whether to believe in it, but we do anyway, just in case. Like we do dragons, or God. I write because everything else I do feels like a dream, and writing is the part where I wake up and try to remember what I've dreamed before it all goes away again. This little-bitty story makes me think I managed to remember something relevant and got it down in time. It never occurred to me that such a small story would kick up such a fuss. It just goes to show you that you never can tell about stories anyhow. They are very contrary creatures – rather like dragons, I imagine.

McKinley M. Hellenes lives and writes in the Lower East Side of Vancouver, British Columbia. Her work has appeared in *Hot & Bothered 4*, *Quills, terminus1525* (both in an online exhibit and in the printed magazine), *Kiss Machine, The Liar*, and in *Red Light: Superheroes, Saints, and Sluts*, an anthology about the resurgence of the female icon edited by Anna Camilleri. She has work upcoming in *Broken Pencil*, among other places. She is currently working on a novel (isn't everyone?) and sometimes edits for *Quills* magazine.

Catherine Kidd on "Green-Eyed Beans"
These characters are suspended between what their expectations have taught them to hope for and their own brave ignorance of disappointment. From the first line I tried to set up expectations very different from what the reality turns out to be: riding stables and red roses suggest that the scene will be refined, aristocratic, materially "stable," when this is far from the truth.

Agnes is not sure she is ready to be a mother, even questioning what a mother is supposed to be in the first place. She questions the sanctity surrounding motherhood, which she herself feels out of synch with. Her surroundings express a hope for stability and structure that turns out to be false: her mother is obsessed with seeking lasting attachment but only finds temporary distraction. Dr. Spector appears an upright member of society, but his personal life is filled with deception.

Agnes becomes preoccupied with boundaries, with looking beneath the surfaces of things, with hidden fault lines. She questions the nature of structures – whether they represent anything real and absolute, or only provisional props.

Certain qualities of light and colour are meant to reflect Agnes's essential enquiry: the too-sunny lawn, where everything seems to be in plain view, but is not. The primary colours of the swing set, like a child's building blocks, suggest some original or elemental state of things that must at some point be fallen from, or left behind. Is there some primary structure that supports everything else, and is it family, or something else?

Catherine Kidd is the author/performer of *Sea Peach*, a CD/book of stories as well as a critically acclaimed show. Described as "an adult blend of Dr. Seuss and Aesop's Fables, *Sea Peach* won the 2003 Montreal English Critics Circle Award for Best New Text. The show toured to the Yukon International Storytelling Festival, the Edinburgh Fringe, and Toronto's World Stage 2005, as well as to festivals in Oslo and Bristol. Kidd looks forward to performing in Shanghai this summer, and to the release of her DVD/book *Bipolar Bear*.

Pasha Malla on "The Past Composed"
I wrote "The Past Composed" almost three years ago, and my memories of it are sort of foggy. I do remember writing the first draft in one eight-hour sitting, which is strange for me, as I usually take months getting from the beginning to the end of a story. The kid, Pico, is a hybrid of kids I've known over the years – although his outfits belong exclusively to one funny little guy who was a regular at an after-school program where I used to work. The art installation that Les mentions is real, by a great artist named Douglas Gordon. That was a big inspiration, the dialogue between death, time, and memory, which I also borrowed from a movie called *I'm Going Home* and from Annie Dillard's fantastic essay/story "Aces and Eights." I guess, ultimately, I like stuff that's a little bit funny and a little bit sad, so I hope I achieved something of that with my story.

Pasha Malla wrote "The Past Composed" while living in Montreal. These days, he could be anywhere. Hopefully, wherever he is, the collection of stories he's been working on is finally finished.

Edward O'Connor on "Heard Melodies Are Sweet"
The first line of this story floated into my head over a cup of coffee at the breakfast table. A Saturday morning, if I remember correctly, nobody else around. From there the rest was easy.

Edward O'Connor is the author of *Astral Projection*, a novel, and recipient of the 2005 K.M. Hunter Artist Award for Literature. He works as a freelance writer and editor in Toronto.

Barbara Romanik on "Seven Ways into Chandigarh"
The modernity and severity of Le Corbusier's buildings first attracted me to him six years ago, when I picked up a stray architecture book. His personality, his unfaltering vision, and his ideas about the city and the world solidified the attraction. Le Corbusier wasn't content to just build buildings; he wanted to transform the way people lived and thought, and he wasn't shy about telling them how they should go about it. I wanted to engage with some of his ideas.

Unlike most critics who outright condemned Le Corbusier for his "impractical" functionalism, Norma Evanson wrote insightfully about him in the context of his buildings in Chandigarh, India. I was taking a course in Indian literature and became obsessed with Indian cities and wanted to write about them. In a way, I came to understand how Le Corbusier could create something extraordinary and impractical, Indian and modern, without fully understanding the context he was working in. Evanson's writing about architecture in India was inspiring because it was so engaging – downright sexy! Try writing about architecture and you'll realize how hard it is to put buildings to paper.

Finally there is Yvonne Gallis, Le Corbusier's wife, about whom so little is known. She must have been an extraordinary person to put up with, and fascinate, Le Corbusier. I hope I haven't failed her in writing "Seven Ways into Chandigarh." But if I have learned anything from Le Corbusier, it is that if you must fail, you must do so ambitiously.

Barbara Romanik lives in Edmonton. She graduated with an M.A. from the University of New Brunswick in 2004. Her fiction has most recently appeared in *The Malahat Review*, *Descant*, and *The Fiddlehead*. Three of her stories will be published in *Coming Attractions 05*.

Sandra Sabatini on "The Dolphins at Sainte-Marie"

My friend Cathy and I have children and we talk about them. We are interested in the details of their lives, whether they passed their science tests or are riding their bikes with their helmets on. We encourage and rejoice and console each other, but on the day that Cathy mentioned her daughter Bronwyn's grade six trip to Midland, Ontario, my whole body groaned with the visceral memory of my dreary day there, though it was decades ago. When I combined my recollection of that feeble experience with what I had been hearing most often on television, and what seemed a terrible opposite – Marineland's aggressively cheerful advertising campaign, full of colour and music and splashing – the result was a character who was waiting for the dolphins at Sainte-Marie.

Sandra Sabatini's first collection of stories, *The One with the News*, was published by The Porcupine's Quill and was short-listed for the Upper Canada Writers' Craft Award. Her new collection, *Balance of Probability*, will be published by Penguin Canada in spring 2006. She has also published a critical work, *Making Babies* (WLU Press), on the figure of the infant in Canadian fiction. Sabatini works in Guelph, where she lives with her husband and five children.

Matt Shaw on "Matchbook for a Mother's Hair"

"Matchbook for a Mother's Hair" was a single afternoon's mistake.

The prompting idea was to write a story in a focused stream of details using a character with limited capacities. But I remembered a writer who pointedly said that I would be a fool to follow a theory and should take up surgery or brickwork if I was interested in technique. Following a formula proved to be too restrictive; I had a handful of paragraphs and nothing to lead me. I felt alone.

However, I had discovered Gordon, who existed then only in a paragraph about his age. I tried to talk to him, to get him to relax and open up. Once prompted, he eagerly told me everything within a few hours. Correcting my errors gave Gordon a story and a personality, and I tried to let him show me whatever he wanted. I realized that my theory had been too simplistic and didn't give Gordon any credit as a character or storyteller.

I think it is fallibility – both the writer's and the characters' – that makes fiction compelling or sympathetic, worthy of an ear. Gordon, my first-born in published fiction, shares my own inexperience. I am very proud of him and grateful for his companionship. His misinformed choices have been his good fortune, and I'm lucky enough to live vicariously through him, although I suspect this aligns me more with his matrons than himself – a fact I refuse to acknowledge.

Matt Shaw is a young writer who lives in Sarnia and Toronto. He graduated from York University with an Honours B.A. in 2005 and is working on a novel, *An Everyday Unhappiness*, and a collection of poetry/short fiction. "Matchbook for a Mother's Hair," which appeared in *Exile*, is his first published short story.

Richard Simas on "Anthropologies"
I attempted to write this piece a number of years ago. After multiple rewrites and revisions, I finally accepted that the story still didn't work, and let it go, tucking the manuscript away for years at the bottom of a box. In the fall of 2003 I was sorting through a different box of letters, notes, and photos. This sorting led me to consider, yet once again, how fiction writing for me is an attempt to interpret daily reality, both past and present. As in the case of "Anthropologies," this interpretation becomes a dialogue between fragments crossed in a box of memorabilia and a piece of fiction. My impulse to write the story again emerged as an imperative that I didn't question, nor did I reread the earlier versions of the story. Rather, I sat down and wrote a new story from the same source. I didn't stop until I was absolutely pleased with each detail.

Some of the roots of the piece come from the questions about whether it's ever possible to start all over again: your life, relationships, a journey. It's about moving from one side of the country to another, about a chance meeting. It's about trying, yet again, to understand someone else. Perhaps all said, it's about making risky leaps and figuring out how to land on your feet.

Richard Simas lives and works in Montreal, Quebec. He is the founder and artistic director of an interdisciplinary performing centre in Montreal, Théâtre La Chapelle. In addition to working on translation, dramatic texts, and essays, his short fiction has been published in Canada, the United States, and Switzerland.

Neil Smith on "Scrapbook"

In a newsmagazine some years ago, I came across a diagram of Columbine High School, the Colorado school where two students shot dozens of their classmates. The diagram was so neat, so sterile. The dead, the wounded, the bystanders, the killers were all depicted as stick figures, each drawn in a different colour. The diagram looked like the floor map of a shopping centre. To get your bearings, all you needed was a helpful X and a YOU ARE HERE.

I was there on December 6, 1989, when a man murdered fourteen women at the Université de Montréal. I wasn't in the engineering building, thankfully, but in the nearby sports complex. That night, when I got home, sickened and shaken, the women I lived with said, "We were so worried about you."

But we men should be the ones worrying about them.

The man I now live with attended the École Polytechnique. He wasn't there that night but had known one of the women who had been shot. Shortly after the killings, he had classes in the room where many of the women died. That room had been scrubbed down and repainted. It was creepy at first, he says, but eventually you forgot what had gone on before.

When we're faced with such horror, what ultimately sticks in our minds? What mementoes do we place in our own scrapbooks? What do these keepsakes reveal about us? These are questions my story explores.

Neil Smith has had his work anthologized in two previous volumes of *The Journey Prize Stories* and in *Coming Attractions*

04 (Oberon Press). A new story will soon appear in the anthology *Lust for Life: Tales of Sex and Love* (Véhicule Press). In early 2007, Knopf Canada will put out his first book of stories, *Bang Crunch*, as part of its New Face of Fiction program.

Emily White on "Various Metals"
The idea for this story arose when I was living in a nearly empty apartment in Toronto's north end. I'd rented the third floor of an old house, and the staircase leading to my apartment was so narrow that I'd had to abandon my sofa and armchair on the street. I told myself that I'd buy new models and assemble them in the apartment, but I never got around to doing so.

The result was that I was living with almost no furniture. I had a mattress on the floor, a futon couch, a desk made out of a door, and a kitchen table. And that was it, in a fairly large flat. The emptiness struck me as strange – especially since I was working and could have afforded more – but I also found it comforting. I liked the way the sunlight hit the wooden floors, and I liked the echoing feel the place had with so little in it.

My complete lack of furniture seemed *right* somehow; it seemed to complement an emotional emptiness I was feeling around that time. Yet I couldn't quite let go of the fantasy of someone sweeping into my life and furnishing the whole place for me, top to bottom. And these feelings of loss and ambivalence came together when I found myself writing about Elena and her empty flat. I was curious to see how things would turn out for her.

Emily White is a former lawyer working on a non-fiction project in Toronto. "Various Metals" is her first published story.

About the Contributing Journals

For more information about all the journals that submitted stories to this year's anthology, please consult *The Journey Prize Stories* website: www.mcclelland.com/jps

Broken Pencil is the magazine of zine culture and the independent arts. We review underground publications, including zines, indie-published books, videos, artworks, e-zines, and music. We run groundbreaking features on art, culture, and society from an independent perspective. We reprint from the best of the underground press. In each issue, the new fiction section of the magazine celebrates the edgy and the unpredictable. For a sample copy please send a $5 cheque or concealed cash to *Broken Pencil*. Submissions and correspondence: *Broken Pencil*, attention Fiction Editor, P.O. Box 203, Station P, Toronto, Ontario, M5S 2S7. Website: www.brokenpencil.com

Descant is a quarterly journal, now in its third decade, publishing poetry, prose, fiction, interviews, travel pieces, letters, literary criticism, and visual art by new and established contemporary writers and artists from Canada and around the world. Editor: Karen Mulhallen. Managing Editor: Mary Newberry. Submissions and correspondence: *Descant*, P.O. Box 314, Station P, Toronto, Ontario, M5S 2S8. Email: descant@web.net Website: www.descant.on.ca

Exile: The Literary Quarterly is a distinctive journal that has published over one hundred issues during the thirty-plus years since it began in 1972. In those three decades, it has become recognized, and respected, as a forum that always presents an impressive selection of new and established authors and artists – soon to reach one thousand contributors. We draw our material (literature, poetry, drama, work in translation, and the fine arts) from French and English Canada, as well as from Britain,

Europe, Latin America, the Middle East, and Asia. And, because *Exile*'s history of publishing is so uniquely appreciated, it now acts like an antenna, locating and attracting many diverse voices, searching out and encouraging the most distinctive new writing at home and abroad. Publisher: Michael Callaghan. Editor: Barry Callaghan. Submissions and correspondence: Exile/Excelsior Publishing Inc., 134 Eastbourne Avenue, Toronto, Ontario, M5P 2G6. Email (queries only): exq@exilequarterly.com Website: www.ExileQuarterly.com

The Fiddlehead, Canada's longest-running literary journal, publishes poetry and short fiction as well as book reviews. It appears four times a year, sponsors a contest for poetry and fiction with two $1,000 prizes, including the Ralph Gustafson Poetry Prize, and welcomes all good writing in English, from anywhere, looking always for that element of freshness and surprise. Editor: Ross Leckie. Managing Editor: Sabine Campbell. Submissions and correspondence: *The Fiddlehead*, Campus House, 11 Garland Court, P.O. Box 4400, Fredericton, New Brunswick, E3B 5A3. Email (queries only): fiddlehd@unb.ca Website: www.lib.unb.ca/Texts/Fiddlehead

Grain Magazine provides readers with fine, fresh writing by new and established writers of poetry and prose four times a year. Published by the Saskatchewan Writers Guild, *Grain* has earned national and international recognition for its distinctive literary content. Editor: Kent Bruyneel. Fiction Editor: Joanne Gerber. Poetry Editor: Gerald Hill. Submissions and correspondence: *Grain Magazine*, P.O. Box 67, Saskatoon, Saskatchewan, S7K 3K1. Email: grainmag@sasktel.net Website: www.grainmagazine.ca

Kiss Machine is a rebellious little arts and culture magazine that highlights the surrealism inherent in day-to-day life. It's a "community on paper" (*Toronto Star*) and a foray into independently produced culture in Canada. Our fifth anniversary, in March 2005, provided a milestone for launching our new line of *Kiss Machine Presents* comic books, which are published twice a year in between regular issues of the magazine. Past responses to our calls for submissions have included: fiction, non-fiction, poetry, art, photography, limited-edition inserts, online exhibits, songs, animations, public interventions, and performances. A journalist writing for *Quill & Quire* commented that "reading *Kiss Machine* leads you to wonder if [a more traditional magazine's] editorial board is sipping a bit too much embalming fluid." Submissions and correspondence: *Kiss Machine*, P.O. Box 108, Station P, Toronto, Ontario, M5S 2S8. Website: www.kissmachine.org

Maisonneuve Magazine is a bimonthly magazine based in Montreal and published in English, which aims to keep its readers informed, alert, and entertained. *Maisonneuve* was recently awarded the prestigious President's Medal at the twenty-eighth annual National Magazine Awards for best overall editorial achievement of the year. *Maisonneuve* has been described as "the magazine for people who give a damn." Editor-in-Chief: Derek Webster. Managing Editor: Poppy Wilkinson. Submissions and correspondence: *Maisonneuve Magazine*, 400 de Maisonneuve Boulevard West, Suite 655, Montreal, Quebec, H3A 1L4. Email: submissions@maisonneuve.org Website: www.maisonneuve.org

The Malahat Review is a quarterly journal of contemporary poetry and fiction by both new and celebrated writers. Summer issues feature the winners of *Malahat*'s Novella and Long Poem prizes, held in alternate years; all issues feature covers by noted Canadian visual artists and include reviews of Canadian books. Editor: John Barton. Assistant Editor: Rhonda Batchelor. Submissions and correspondence: *The Malahat Review*, University of Victoria, P.O. Box 1700, Station CSC, Victoria, British Columbia, V8W 2Y2. Website: www.malahatreview.ca

Based in Montreal, **Matrix Magazine** is in its thirtieth year of publishing innovative literature and art. *Matrix* is widely regarded as one of the most irreverent and experimental literary magazines in North America. Editor: R.E.N. Allen. Managing

Editor: Jon Paul Fiorentino. Submissions and correspon-
dence: *Matrix*, LB 502, 1400 de Maisonneuve Boulevard,
Montreal, Quebec, H3G 1M8. Email: matrixzine@yahoo.ca
Website: www.alcor.concordia.ca/~matrix

The New Quarterly publishes fiction, poetry, interviews, and
essays on writing. A three-time winner of the gold medal for
fiction at the National Magazine Awards and a two-time winner
for poetry, the magazine prides itself on its independent take on
the Canadian literary scene. Recent features include "The
Writers of the Burning Rock," "Weddings and Other Disasters,"
"The Writer Abroad," "Hockey Write in Canada," "Painting,
Plays, and Poetry," plus our ongoing series on the seductions of
verse. Editor: Kim Jernigan. Submissions and correspondence:
The New Quarterly, c/o St. Jerome's University, 290 Westmount
Road North, Waterloo, Ontario, N2L 3G3. Email: editor@
newquarterly.net Website: www.newquarterly.net

subTerrain Magazine publishes contemporary and sometimes
controversial Canadian fiction, poetry, non-fiction, and visual
art. Every issue features interviews, timely commentary, and
small-press book reviews. Praised by both writers and readers
for featuring work that might not find a home in more conservative periodicals, *subTerrain* seeks to expand the definition of
Canadian literary and artistic culture by showcasing the best in
progressive writing and ideas. Please visit our website for more
information on upcoming theme issues, our annual Lush
Triumphant contest, general submission guidelines, and sub-
scription information. Submissions and correspondence: P.O.
Box 3008, MPO, Vancouver, British Columbia, V6B 3X5.
Website: www.subterrain.ca

Submissions were also received from the following journals:

The Antigonish Review   *The Claremont Review*
(Antigonish, N.S.)   (Victoria, B.C.)

dANDdelion Magazine
(Calgary, Alta.)

Event
(New Westminster, B.C.)

filling Station
(Calgary, Alta.)

Green's Magazine
(Regina, Sask.)

lichen
(Whitby, Ont.)

The New Orphic Review
(Nelson, B.C.)

NFG Magazine
(Toronto, Ont.)

Pagitica in Toronto
(Toronto, Ont.)

Prairie Fire
(Winnipeg, Man.)

Prairie Journal
(Calgary, Alta.)

PRISM international
(Vancouver, B.C.)

Queen's Quarterly
(Kingston, Ont.)

Room of One's Own
(Vancouver, B.C.)

Storyteller
(Ottawa, Ont.)

Taddle Creek
(Toronto, Ont.)

This Magazine
(Toronto, Ont.)

The Journey Prize Stories
List of Previous Contributing Authors

* Winners of the $10,000 Journey Prize
** Co-winners of the $10,000 Journey Prize

I

1989

SELECTED WITH ALISTAIR MacLEOD

Ven Begamudré, "Word Games"
David Bergen, "Where You're From"
Lois Braun, "The Pumpkin-Eaters"
Constance Buchanan, "Man with Flying Genitals"
Ann Copeland, "Obedience"
Marion Douglas, "Flags"
Frances Itani, "An Evening in the Café"
Diane Keating, "The Crying Out"
Thomas King, "One Good Story, That One"
Holley Rubinsky, "Rapid Transits"*
Jean Rysstad, "Winter Baby"
Kevin Van Tighem, "Whoopers"
M.G. Vassanji, "In the Quiet of a Sunday Afternoon"
Bronwen Wallace, "Chicken 'N' Ribs"
Armin Wiebe, "Mouse Lake"
Budge Wilson, "Waiting"

2

1990

SELECTED WITH LEON ROOKE; GUY VANDERHAEGHE

André Alexis, "Despair: Five Stories of Ottawa"
Glen Allen, "The Hua Guofeng Memorial Warehouse"
Marusia Bociurkiw, "Mama, Donya"
Virgil Burnett, "Billfrith the Dreamer"
Margaret Dyment, "Sacred Trust"

Cynthia Flood, "My Father Took a Cake to France" *
Douglas Glover, "Story Carved in Stone"
Terry Griggs, "Man with the Axe"
Rick Hillis, "Limbo River"
Thomas King, "The Dog I Wish I Had, I Would Call It Helen"
K.D. Miller, "Sunrise Till Dark"
Jennifer Mitton, "Let Them Say"
Lawrence O'Toole, "Goin' to Town with Katie Ann"
Kenneth Radu, "A Change of Heart"
Jenifer Sutherland, "Table Talk"
Wayne Tefs, "Red Rock and After"

3
1991
SELECTED WITH JANE URQUHART

Donald Aker, "The Invitation"
Anton Baer, "Yukon"
Allan Barr, "A Visit from Lloyd"
David Bergen, "The Fall"
Rai Berzins, "Common Sense"
Diana Hartog, "Theories of Grief"
Diane Keating, "The Salem Letters"
Yann Martel, "The Facts Behind the Helsinki Roccamatios" *
Jennifer Mitton, "Polaroid"
Sheldon Oberman, "This Business with Elijah"
Lynn Podgurny, "Till Tomorrow, Maple Leaf Mills"
James Riseborough, "She Is Not His Mother"
Patricia Stone, "Living on the Lake"

4
1992
SELECTED WITH SANDRA BIRDSELL

David Bergen, "The Bottom of the Glass"
Maria A. Billion, "No Miracles Sweet Jesus"
Judith Cowan, "By the Big River"
Steven Heighton, "A Man Away from Home Has No Neighbours"
Steven Heighton, "How Beautiful upon the Mountains"
L. Rex Kay, "Travelling"

Rozena Maart, "No Rosa, No District Six" *
Guy Malet De Carteret, "Rainy Day"
Carmelita McGrath, "Silence"
Michael Mirolla, "A Theory of Discontinuous Existence"
Diane Juttner Perreault, "Bella's Story"
Eden Robinson, "Traplines"

5
1993
SELECTED WITH GUY VANDERHAEGHE

Caroline Adderson, "Oil and Dread"
David Bergen, "La Rue Prevette"
Marina Endicott, "With the Band"
Dayv James-French, "Cervine"
Michael Kenyon, "Durable Tumblers"
K.D. Miller, "A Litany in Time of Plague"
Robert Mullen, "Flotsam"
Gayla Reid, "Sister Doyle's Men" *
Oakland Ross, "Bang-bang"
Robert Sherrin, "Technical Battle for Trial Machine"
Carol Windley, "The Etruscans"

6
1994
SELECTED WITH DOUGLAS GLOVER;
JUDITH CHANT (CHAPTERS)

Anne Carson, "Water Margins: An Essay on Swimming by
   My Brother"
Richard Cumyn, "The Sound He Made"
Genni Gunn, "Versions"
Melissa Hardy, "Long Man the River" *
Robert Mullen, "Anomie"
Vivian Payne, "Free Falls"
Jim Reil, "Dry"
Robyn Sarah, "Accept My Story"
Joan Skogan, "Landfall"
Dorothy Speak, "Relatives in Florida"
Alison Wearing, "Notes from Under Water"

7

1995

SELECTED WITH M.G. VASSANJI;
RICHARD BACHMANN (A DIFFERENT DRUMMER BOOKS)
Michelle Alfano, "Opera"
Mary Borsky, "Maps of the Known World"
Gabriella Goliger, "Song of Ascent"
Elizabeth Hay, "Hand Games"
Shaena Lambert, "The Falling Woman"
Elise Levine, "Boy"
Roger Burford Mason, "The Rat-Catcher's Kiss"
Antanas Sileika, "Going Native"
Kathryn Woodward, "Of Marranos and Gilded Angels" *

8

1996

SELECTED WITH OLIVE SENIOR;
BEN McNALLY (NICHOLAS HOARE LTD.)
Rick Bowers, "Dental Bytes"
David Elias, "How I Crossed Over"
Elyse Gasco, "Can You Wave Bye Bye, Baby?" *
Danuta Gleed, "Bones"
Elizabeth Hay, "The Friend"
Linda Holeman, "Turning the Worm"
Elaine Littman, "The Winner's Circle"
Murray Logan, "Steam"
Rick Maddocks, "Lessons from the Sputnik Diner"
K.D. Miller, "Egypt Land"
Gregor Robinson, "Monster Gaps"
Alma Subasic, "Dust"

9

1997

SELECTED WITH NINO RICCI;
NICHOLAS PASHLEY (UNIVERSITY OF TORONTO BOOKSTORE)
Brian Bartlett, "Thomas, Naked"
Dennis Bock, "Olympia"

Kristen den Hartog, "Wave"
Gabriella Goliger, "Maladies of the Inner Ear"**
Terry Griggs, "Momma Had a Baby"
Mark Anthony Jarman, "Righteous Speedboat"
Judith Kalman, "Not for Me a Crown of Thorns"
Andrew Mullins, "The World of Science"
Sasenarine Persaud, "Canada Geese and Apple Chatney"
Anne Simpson, "Dreaming Snow"**
Sarah Withrow, "Ollie"
Terence Young, "The Berlin Wall"

10
1998
SELECTED BY PETER BUITENHUIS; HOLLEY RUBINSKY;
CELIA DUTHIE (DUTHIE BOOKS LTD.)
John Brooke, "The Finer Points of Apples"*
Ian Colford, "The Reason for the Dream"
Libby Creelman, "Cruelty"
Michael Crummey, "Serendipity"
Stephen Guppy, "Downwind"
Jane Eaton Hamilton, "Graduation"
Elise Levine, "You Are You Because Your Little Dog Loves You"
Jean McNeil, "Bethlehem"
Liz Moore, "Eight-Day Clock"
Edward O'Connor, "The Beatrice of Victoria College"
Tim Rogers, "Scars and Other Presents"
Denise Ryan, "Marginals, Vivisections, and Dreams"
Madeleine Thien, "Simple Recipes"
Cheryl Tibbetts, "Flowers of Africville"

11
1999
SELECTED BY LESLEY CHOYCE; SHELDON CURRIE;
MARY-JO ANDERSON (FROG HOLLOW BOOKS)
Mike Barnes, "In Florida"
Libby Creelman, "Sunken Island"
Mike Finigan, "Passion Sunday"

Jane Eaton Hamilton, "Territory"
Mark Anthony Jarman, "Travels into Several Remote Nations of
    the World"
Barbara Lambert, "Where the Bodies Are Kept"
Linda Little, "The Still"
Larry Lynch, "The Sitter"
Sandra Sabatini, "The One With the News"
Sharon Steams, "Brothers"
Mary Walters, "Show Jumping"
Alissa York, "The Back of the Bear's Mouth"*

12
2000
SELECTED BY CATHERINE BUSH; HAL NIEDZVIECKI;
MARC GLASSMAN (PAGES BOOKS AND MAGAZINES)

Andrew Gray, "The Heart of the Land"
Lee Henderson, "Sheep Dub"
Jessica Johnson, "We Move Slowly"
John Lavery, "The Premier's New Pyjamas"
J.A. McCormack, "Hearsay"
Nancy Richler, "Your Mouth Is Lovely"
Andrew Smith, "Sightseeing"
Karen Solie, "Onion Calendar"
Timothy Taylor, "Doves of Townsend"*
Timothy Taylor, "Pope's Own"
Timothy Taylor, "Silent Cruise"
R.M. Vaughan, "Swan Street"

13
2001
SELECTED BY ELYSE GASCO; MICHAEL HELM;
MICHAEL NICHOLSON (INDIGO BOOKS & MUSIC INC.)

Kevin Armstrong, "The Cane Field"*
Mike Barnes, "Karaoke Mon Amour"
Heather Birrell, "Machaya"
Heather Birrell, "The Present Perfect"
Craig Boyko, "The Gun"
Vivette J. Kady, "Anything That Wiggles"

Billie Livingston, "You're Taking All the Fun Out of It"
Annabel Lyon, "Fishes"
Lisa Moore, "The Way the Light Is"
Heather O'Neill, "Little Suitcase"
Susan Rendell, "In the Chambers of the Sea"
Tim Rogers, "Watch"
Margrith Schraner, "Dream Dig"

14
2002
SELECTED BY ANDRÉ ALEXIS;
DEREK MCCORMACK; DIANE SCHOEMPERLEN

Mike Barnes, "Cogagwee"
Geoffrey Brown, "Listen"
Jocelyn Brown, "Miss Canada"*
Emma Donoghue, "What Remains"
Jonathan Goldstein, "You Are a Spaceman With Your Head Under the Bathroom Stall Door"
Robert McGill, "Confidence Men"
Robert McGill, "The Stars Are Falling"
Nick Melling, "Philemon"
Robert Mullen, "Alex the God"
Karen Munro, "The Pool"
Leah Postman, "Being Famous"
Neil Smith, "Green Fluorescent Protein"

15
2003
SELECTED BY MICHELLE BERRY;
TIMOTHY TAYLOR; MICHAEL WINTER

Rosaria Campbell, "Reaching"
Hilary Dean, "The Lemon Stories"
Dawn Rae Downton, "Hansel and Gretel"
Anne Fleming, "Gay Dwarves of America"
Elyse Friedman, "Truth"
Charlotte Gill, "Hush"
Jessica Grant, "My Husband's Jump"*
Jacqueline Honnet, "Conversion Classes"

S.K. Johannesen, "Resurrection"
Avner Mandelman, "Cuckoo"
Tim Mitchell, "Night Finds Us"
Heather O'Neill, "The Difference Between Me and Goldstein"

16

2004

SELECTED BY ELIZABETH HAY;
LISA MOORE; MICHAEL REDHILL

Anar Ali, "Baby Khaki's Wings"
Kenneth Bonert, "Packers and Movers"
Jennifer Clouter, "Benny and the Jets"
Daniel Griffin, "Mercedes Buyer's Guide"
Michael Kissinger, "Invest in the North"
Devin Krukoff, "The Last Spark"*
Elaine McCluskey, "The Watermelon Social"
William Metcalfe, "Nice Big Car, Rap Music Coming Out the
    Window"
Lesley Millard, "The Uses of the Neckerchief"
Adam Lewis Schroeder, "Burning the Cattle at Both Ends"
Michael V. Smith, "What We Wanted"
Neil Smith, "Isolettes"
Patricia Rose Young, "Up the Clyde on a Bike"